MAKE ME YOURS

Bayshore #3

Ember Leigh

Published by Ember Leigh, 2020 | EmberLeighAuthor@gmail.com

Cover art: Covers by Combs

Editing: Elisabeth R. Nelson

Proofreading: Leona Bushman

ABOUT 'MAKE ME YOURS'

As one of the best matchmakers in the industry, I could find a rotting stump its Prince Charming.

After a bad break-up forces me to uproot and start over, I'm feeling a lot like a rotting stump in need of a spa day. So when I find my dream gig in a new city, this is a chance for me to wipe the slate sparkling clean—professionally and romantically.

But this new gig has a few problems. The biggest one being that the man I have to match off is someone I went to high school with. Not only that, he's less Prince Charming and more King Asshole.

Varsity baseball star turned rock star cardiologist. One of the hottest guys you've ever seen in the flesh. But also one of the most untouchable men ever, because five minutes around this man shows me he stops for nobody.

The holier-than-thou eldest Daly brother, who is only looking for a wife-of-convenience, even though his ice-blue gaze and chiseled jaw could send a woman to the ER.

Worse yet? There's more to King Asshole than I thought. I know his perfect love match...and it looks a lot like me.

Except I'm not falling for the 'dating in the professional pool' trick again. So this thing between us? Just once—er, twice...nope, thrice—and done.

Even though the longer this goes on, the more I think Dom is trying to make me his.

Sign up for Ember Leigh's newsletter to receive updates on all things sexy, funny, heartwarming, and occasionally angsty! As a thank-you for signing up, I'll send you a FREE story set in the angsty and emotional world of my newest series, *The Bad Boys of Wall Street*. Click here to receive *The Price of a Promise* (https://BookHip.com/ZBGRSRB).

contents

CHAPTER ONE

"London, London, London."

Her name is Nancy, and the way she's saying my name suggests that she's either about to make a joke—and I promise you, I've probably heard it already—or she's very pleased with our first in-person meeting.

Since I've only been in this office with her for about ten minutes, I can't exactly tell. I barely know the woman, much less her tones. But I do know she loves purple, based on the infinite shades of lavender she has on her spiral-designed scrub top.

This is the final meeting in what I am absolutely, positively, persistently hopeful will be the last interview before I can stamp *NO LONGER UNEMPLOYED* on this chapter of my life.

She and I have been emailing back and forth in informal interviews for weeks while I packed up my apartment and left my life behind in Columbus, Ohio. This job opportunity appeared after I updated my profile on HireMe and waited with bated breath for an entire two weeks with absolutely no solid job leads here in Cleveland. Wait, scratch that. I've had plenty of job leads. But no job follow-through.

And I'm pretty sure I know why. It has everything to do with the fact that I'm the new girl in town. The new girl with an enormous, unsavory stain following her around. Like, you spilled wine on white carpet *and then* the dog shit on top of it. And then someone took a picture and put it on the internet, just to make sure everyone remembered *forever*.

"Nancy, Nancy, Nancy." I offer a smile, though I'm not sure what comes next. Nancy and I are technically pen pals, if that was still a thing in this day and age, based on all the emailing. I feel like she's my relatable aunt whom I've never spoken to my entire life until this one time I needed a favor. And she's going to hire me because *obviously*.

Or maybe this is just my wild positive self-talk trying to con the universe into giving me a steady paycheck again. *Please, Nancy and God, let me be hired by this doctor so that I can continue paying my bills and being a successful adult.*

"I have to say, if it were up to me, I'd hire you on the spot." Nancy grins, setting aside my resume, which I suspect she caresses each night before bed.

"I'd hire you right back," I tease, adding a playful wink. Dimples flash as she sends me a warm smile. Yes, we are definitely on our way to wine-buddies level. *Please, Nancy and God, let us be wine-buddies level.*

"But you know, there's one important last step." She folds her hands over the desk carefully. The smile droops a little. A cold breeze rolls in from somewhere, reminding me that we might not be wine-buddies level after all.

"Yes," I say, clutching my laptop-sized briefcase in my lap. This final step is the entire reason I'm here today. The final barrier between me and a potential big-ticket client that will pay my way through the next six months.

"You need to meet the doc," Nancy says simply, pushing back from the desk as if to suggest *it's out of my hands*. Her cinnamon-brown hair glints in the sunshine streaming into the office in the late-September morning. I can tell she's a looker when she's not scrubbed out and waiting for lunchtime to finally get here. The thin wisp of her eyebrow tells me all I need to know. This woman and I are more alike than she realizes.

And really? This is all part of my job. The job that Nancy knows I'd be great at.

The job that "Doc" has yet to hire me for.

"Let's go into his office," she says, standing.

I push onto wobbly legs, waiting for her to come around her desk and lead me to the plain black door nearby that says "DOCTOR DALY."

I'm hesitant to think this job is in the bag, even though Nancy and I are probably long-lost friends in-waiting. Even though Nancy contacted me herself because she was so impressed by my HireMe profile.

I'm hesitant because I've been smeared by my ex-boss, though that wasn't the only ex he qualifies as in my life. Nobody wants to touch me with a ten-foot pole, because that asshole knows everybody in the brand image industry. That's why I thought the medical field might be a surer bet. I've never worked with doctors before. Only politicians, tech start-ups, football players, and bumbling data geniuses. But people who could look at the pinky toe I stubbed three weeks ago and tell me whether or not I actually broke it?

Yes. Sign me up.

I can only pray that my ex-everything hasn't drained this playing field for me already.

Nancy leads me into the spacious and immaculate office of Dr. Daly. It smells faintly of cologne and latex, like a musky vetiver had sex with a doctor's glove. Nancy encourages me to sit in one of the two spartan chairs facing the expansive desk. She promises that the doctor will be in soon, and as soon as the door clicks shut behind her I snap into analysis mode.

Dr. Daly. I still don't know his full name, because this entire job offer is so hush-hush that she didn't even admit that she was in the medical industry until interview email number four. A lot of people don't like being associated with me, and I get it. It's sometimes uncool to admit that you work with a brand manager, much less a matchmaker. And I am proudly both. Sometimes one more than the other.

But God help me, I will manage your image, whether it's for the entire world or just one special lover.

I lean over Dr. Daly's desk, searching out some clues for who he might be. The building we're in is used by a hodge-podge of medical professionals, but I am most certainly in the cardiac unit. His desk yields no clues. A metallic cup of pens sits nearby, as well as a laptop cord waiting for the unit to return from wherever the doctor has carried it. The desk features no mementos. No heartwarming family pictures. No mess of folders or half-scribbled notes reminding him to *thaw turkey* or *buy more underwear—URGENT.*

This man has left no clues as to his brand *or* his potential match-ability. I frown, sitting back in my seat and tapping my finger against the armrest as I scan the rest of the office for more. The place is so pristine that I wouldn't be surprised if a carpet cleaning crew came in each night.

So the man values cleanliness. Probably he's a neatnik—which makes sense, given germs and his general involvement with health. Maybe even bordering on germaphobe? I'll have to make sure not to swipe at my nose or visibly pick a wedgie. Not that I'd ever do those things in front of a client; it's just better to know the hard *nos* prior to meeting someone. Definitely don't cough all over his face. *Check.*

But what else? I spot a few framed images on the far wall of the office, next to a tall, wooden wardrobe set off from another door that I can only assume is a closet or a secret, celebrity-doctor-only entrance to the operating room. I head over to the frames. Some showcase certifications. The largest one contains his degree.

THE UNIVERSITY OF WASHINGTON has conferred upon DOMINIC DAMON DALY the degree of MEDICAL DOCTOR.

Dominic Daly. I blink a few times, my gaze washing over the fancy script again as the words settle into me. The name is familiar. Too familiar.

Voices beyond the office door snag my attention, and I scurry back into the chair facing the desk. The door cracks open and I hear the rumble of bass, "Hang on." Practically a bark. It has to be Dr. Daly. Nancy comes into the room a moment later, her smile straining at the edges.

"Dr. Daly is almost ready to see you," she says. "He's still finishing up with a surgical consult, and it takes him a few moments to switch gears."

I understand what she's saying, but I can also see through her words to the real meaning. *He's a prima-donna who I need to handle with white gloves.* I've worked with everyone, on all rungs of the ladder. And this situation already smacks of white gloves and eggshells.

The door opens all the way behind her, and Dr. Daly strolls in. I'm not sure if it's a full three seconds or only a half second for me to drink him in and recognize who I'm dealing with. At any rate, it happens quick. This is what I'm trained to do. And my computer input is telling me the following:

This man is a fox.

This man is a dick.

And this man is too busy.

His neck is bent as he studies some files in his hands, barely watching where he's going, a laptop tucked under his other arm. He damn near barrels into Nancy, who leaps out of his way because that's probably what she has to do every day, like ballet rehearsal.

Nearly pitch-black hair is swept away from his face in soft waves, framing black eyebrows drawn together in doctor-grade focus as he brushes past me and behind the desk. I'm not sure that he knows I'm here. I'm not sure he *cares.*

But once the breeze of his wake settles, I catch the vetiver tang of his cologne, and something inside me clenches. It might be paired with the squareness of his shoulders or the fact that he stands six foot sexy in a white coat and a frown.

When he comes to a stop behind his desk, he sets the laptop down with a sigh. Icy blue eyes sweep up over me, igniting parts of my body that I didn't know existed. He could make my spleen feel erotically charged with that blue gaze shivering over it, and I wonder if his patients are getting turned on while under anesthesia.

But when his gaze settles on my face, something else courses through me. It's the thick sludge of recognition. Not just the veiled horror of seeing someone you know in the grocery store after ten years apart, but the dim recognition that you're suddenly in a very sticky situation.

I know this man. His presence connects with the name on the diploma in a final, thundering crack.

Dominic Daly. *Of course.*

This is a blast from my Bayshore past if I've ever seen one. An incredibly sexy, well-aged, super-hot-doc blast from the past. One that is currently scowling at me, his eyes doubling as daggers.

"You have to be kidding me," he spits, that whip gaze flinging past me, landing on Nancy. *I pray for you, my gal pal Nance.* "Is this a fucking joke?"

Nancy comes to the edge of the desk, much more confidently than I'd have imagined. This guy has probably been less than peachy to work with. "What are you talking about?"

"Her." Dom gestures toward me like I'm nothing. No, like I'm worse than nothing. Like unceremonious trash left on the curbside for six weeks. Like I'm the forgotten Tupperware in the way back of the *third* drawer, the place that people have been purposefully ignoring. "She won't work. Interview over."

I grit my teeth as I watch him press his fingertips against his desktop, leaning forward as though establishing dominance over my meek and seated frame. I straighten my back as I weigh my options. I wasn't expecting Dominic Daly to be the other side of the interview today, but I *definitely* wasn't expecting him to react like this.

He and I never had issues in high school. I can't imagine why he'd be treating me like this.

Unless my ex-everything got to him somehow. But that seems impossible. Like something from an exaggerated fever dream.

I don't have time to be treated like this. Not anymore. Not after what happened in Columbus. Not even if it means foregoing a five-figure payout for six short weeks of work.

"Great. Interview done." I hold Dominic's gaze as I come to my feet, making sure he can feel the razor edges of my gaze.

My only twinge of regret comes from seeing Nancy's devastated expression as I march past her.

CHAPTER TWO

DOM

This whole week has been a shit show. No, worse. It's been a traveling circus with scary clowns and underfed elephants and a ride operator promising me that the Ring of Fire hasn't killed anyone *recently.*

And right now, the headline act to this second-rate circus is the way my trusted assistant is scampering out of my office to follow the one woman I could never hire.

"London!" Nancy calls out as she disappears through my office door. "Please wait!"

"Let her go," I bark, but Nancy doesn't listen to me. Of course she doesn't. I tasked her with this stupid project, and she's been coddling it like a newborn kitten struggling to drink milk. Which means that suddenly my opinion doesn't matter. Nancy knows best, apparently—and exactly how many CC's of milk to siphon into my mouth.

Silence fills my office, which amplifies the raucous thoughts in my head. I've had a hell of a morning in the ER, visiting cardiology intakes per my usual Monday morning rounds. Except every patient I visited today showed a clear lack of follow-up care from their primary doctors. I added about six new patients to my already packed schedule for reasons that could have been managed with even the slightest bit of primary care.

Story of my fucking life. Cleaning up after everyone else's mistakes. Being the last fool to give a damn.

Hushed voices fill the hallway outside my office. I can't tell if Nancy has convinced London to stay, but I hope she hasn't. Because London is a non-option. And it has *nothing* to do with the way her glossy blonde hair made my gut shrink on sight, or the way her business-casual blouse damn near sent this cardiologist to the ER for his own heart problems.

No, London is a non-option for enough reasons that I could fill an entire legal pad. I could even alphabetize it, but realistically, I'd ask Nancy to do that. First and foremost: she's a Bayshore native.

We went to high school together, which means she *knew me when*, including my awkward-as-hell hairdo senior year which looked like I'd been caught in a windstorm that left my hair permanently vertical.

But more than that, she's Hazel Matheson's best friend. Hazel is my younger brother Grayson's current girlfriend. I've been seeing London splash across Grayson's social media the last few weeks as he posts happily-in-love photos of him integrating with Hazel's life back in Bayshore. Of course that's included outings with Hazel's best friend and partner-in-crime, that platinum babe who was just feet away from me moments ago.

If there's anyone I do not want finding out that I have to army crawl my way into a matchmaker's planner because I'm too busy to find a wife, it's my siblings. But *especially* Grayson.

London knows my family. Which means she knows too much. There's no way in hell I can hire her for the job at hand.

Nancy pokes her head into the office a moment later, her eyes narrowed to slits. I can tell she's pissed, but probably London is out there, keeping her PG.

"Dr. Daly," she says through gritted teeth.

"Yes, Nancy?" I open my laptop, clicking through log-in screens.

"You need to meet with her." Her voice is low, threatening. A tone I've never heard her use with me before. I look her up and down, trying to figure out where on the scale of *I'm Fucking Serious* this falls.

"Why?"

"Because I've been searching for the perfect candidate for *weeks*, and she's the only one who comes close."

Her words cut a little bit too close to the bone. Nancy's rationale reminds me of why there's any urgency at all. I've tasked her with an unsavory assignment—*find me a matchmaker so I can find myself a wife*. It's awkward, at best. Unprofessional, at worst. But the clock is ticking, and I don't have time for propriety anymore.

I need a wife three weeks ago.

"You don't understand," I say, pushing to my feet, annoyance surging through my veins. "She. Won't. Work."

"Actually, *you* don't understand," Nancy says, taking a few solid steps into my office. Her fists are balled, and suddenly I realize exactly where this falls on the *I'm Fucking Serious* scale. I've pushed her too far. "There's *nobody else*. So you need to suck it up, buttercup."

I work my jaw back and forth, holding her gaze in a weird version of a showdown. If this were the Wild West, we'd have guns in our hands. If we were in the OR, we'd have scalpels. But here, in my office, we just have clenched teeth and repressed insults.

"Fine." I'm hot suddenly, and pull off my white coat to hang by the bathroom door. She's never called me "buttercup" before, and that's the clinching piece of evidence that I need to yield a bit. I don't want to meet with London, but I can at least humor Nancy. I'll meet with London until I can find some other outrageous reason to nix her.

Still, this is fucking embarrassing. Because London is the type of babe who can get anyone, and the situation I'm in reeks of the opposite. This is the least sexy, least masculine position I may have ever been in. Sure, I know how to wield a scalpel, which scores some sexy points. But this bona fide babe hunting me a betrothed?

I just don't know if I can go through with it.

Nancy disappears from the office and returns a few moments later, a suspicious London in her wake. Nancy stands by the door once London is seated in front of my desk again.

"Should I stay?" Nancy asks.

"You might need to watch him," London says with a sniff. "In case he throws me out again."

"It's up to you, Nance," I say, shoving my hands in my pockets. I'm not ready to sit down and face her yet, so I pause by the windows overlooking the clinic parking lot. I try to focus on mundane details: there are a lot of cars out there today. The leaves are just beginning to turn colors. Some asshole has parked too close to my BMW again.

But all I can see as I look out over the downtown Cleveland landscape is the unfinished chart waiting for me on the computer, and the last words from my patient—"I'm ready for this pain to be over."

And behind it all? The acidic anxiety bubbling just below the surface. A tightness that has been brewing inside me for almost a year.

London—or rather, the job that she represents—is supposedly the key to settling this feeling. But I'm still not sure it can be *her*.

"I'll leave the door cracked," Nancy finally says, holding her hands up like a dejected mom who has broken up one too many fights. "That way, London, you can call me if he pounces."

Not good. They're already banding against me. London laughs dryly, examining her nails, which is somehow more threatening than anything else she could have done. The unspoken retort simmering on her lips is practically a plea for me to learn more. And god, I'm more curious than I want to admit.

About *everything* this bombshell blonde has to offer.

I clench and unclench my jaw, heading for my desk. I can do this. I can politely investigate her qualifications, become fake outraged over an aspect of her services, and force Nancy to fast-track an emergency replacement. Well, an emergency-emergency replacement. Because the real emergency began two weeks ago. Now, we're in *holy shit* territory. Nancy will have to forgive me. I pay her to forgive me.

Her gaze is waiting for mine as I ease into the desk chair. I make the mistake of looking directly at her, and that same thing happens in my chest again. I'm not familiar with the symptoms as a cardiologist, but I did experience this sensation once before, a long time ago. Ancient history, in fact. Back when I fell for the fallacy of romance.

Her eyes are green, but not regular green. They're sea foam, but something matte and swirling at the same time. It's a color found in the fringes of fine art and in deep caves exclusively. I can't look away.

"What?" she finally asks, probably after the silence has become awkward.

"Is he giving you the silent treatment?" Nancy asks from her desk right outside my office. "He does that to me, too."

I wilt internally. "Nance. That's enough."

"Sorry, Dr. Dom," she says sweetly, the smile on her face shining through her tone.

"Listen. I don't know what my assistant has told you," I begin, using the all-business tone I reserve for pharmaceutical reps and especially unruly patients, "but the fact that we know each other is going to be a problem."

"I don't understand why," London says, her voice like delicate harp notes wafting over the breeze. I meet her gaze again and immediately regret it. All I can think of is the picture that Grayson posted three weeks ago of the three of them fishing out on Lake Erie. London's gray and black swimsuit—and the sun kissed curves it hugged—has been burned into my memory ever since.

I'd like to pretend that it's just because I haven't been with a woman in over a year, but something about London's smile snagged me through my phone screen. None of that matters. I'll be done with her shortly.

"This is a very delicate matter," I explain, leaning back in my chair and idly clicking the top of a pen. "It has a lot to do with my reputation, and if it ever leaked that I was...doing this, it might be the end of my career."

"But the fact that we know each other doesn't speak to my professional standards," London says, straightening her back. "It doesn't have any bearing on whether or not I'll keep our work together confidential."

She's right. Which means I need to lay it out more plainly.

"You're friends with Hazel." Again, my mind's eye flashes to the afternoon they spent on Lake Erie. Grayson must have uploaded thirty pictures. I couldn't say if they caught any fish, but I know all about London's dimples when she laughs. "And she is with my brother Grayson."

London's face falls slightly.

"My family, as you may or may not know, are the last people on Earth who can find out about this arrangement. So, I'm sorry, but the risk is too great."

She doesn't understand the competition pumping through the Daly veins. How our family thrives on beating each other and proving our worth. She doesn't understand how that same competition is the whole reason I need her services in the first place.

Grayson has found love. Connor has found love. And me?

I don't have time for love. But I need to look like I found it. Because looking like I've found it will get me one of the most prestigious, most coveted, most holier-than-thou positions I could ever hope to snag: a seat on the board of directors for the Physicians Guild, a well-respected—and famous—foundation with an elite roster of doctors as members. My dad will shit a brick once I snag this spot, and I'm almost in the final round of consideration.

And that's not all. If they accept me, I'll be the youngest physician *in the history of the nation* to join their ranks. I'm ready to make history. There's just one tiny thing missing from my stellar resume.

And that's a wife.

"We can sign an NDA," London says, her eyes narrowing with what I can only assume is a subtext of *duh*. "It's standard practice for all of my high-profile clients. I'll draw one up for you to look over. But I promise"—she leans forward, offering me a smidgeon of a glimpse of the cleavage lurking beneath that cream blouse—"you do not have to worry about my personal relationships interfering with the integrity of my work. Hazel will not know about this professional relationship, and neither will Grayson."

From beyond my office door, Nancy lets a satisfied *hm* slip out. I work my jaw back and forth, tossing the pen I've been abusing for the past five minutes back into the cup.

"I'm serious about this," I say again, running my thumb down the line of my jaw. "If it leaks somehow, you won't just be fired. I'll get a full refund. And I'll make sure you don't get any work like this in Cleveland ever again."

Something flashes in her gaze, and I can tell my threat is working. Her chin tips down, that sea-foam galaxy slicing through me.

Her hand shoots out a moment later. Looking for the handshake.

"You have a deal, Dr. Daly," she says.

I'm gripping her cool, dainty hand before I can think better of it. We stare each other down—equal parts challenge and suspicion—and the reality settles in.

I want there to be a lot more than a deal between us.

But there's nobody better than me at keeping the professional line drawn thick and dark.

London will be nothing more than an inconvenient solution.

A gorgeous, fantasy-inspiring, angel-voiced inconvenience.

CHAPTER THREE

LONDON

It's nine a.m. Wednesday, marking the first full week in my new office/apartment combo in Cleveland. I found the perfect space in a little neighborhood called Larchmere, which appeals to my funky-artisan, community-driven nature. I knew within the first thirty minutes of looking at this space that I could easily spend the next decade here.

Which, provided Dr. Dom doesn't make good on his threat to run me out of town like some sort of cardiologist mafioso, I might actually have a shot at making a good life in Cleveland.

My mug of coffee is still steaming on my freshly organized desk, which I keep spartan and tastefully decorated. Kind of like Dr. Dom, that spartan and tastefully decorated assho—I mean, possible new client.

I frown. It's been two days since that tense-as-hell interview with the lovechild of McSteamy and Henry Cavill, and I still haven't gotten a response to the proposed NDA I sent over the same day.

In fact, I'm thinking about him too much altogether, and not just in relation to, "Does he plan to hire me so that I can afford food for the next six months?" No, I'm thinking about Dom in all the ways a woman shouldn't think about her potential client.

Like his hairline, for starters. It is at once impossible and infuriating. Like the artistically shellacked hair of a Ken doll was transplanted onto his scalp but made somehow wavy and soft-looking. In fact, he *is* a Ken doll, scalpel included with the limited time Operating Room edition.

I don't really want to be thinking about anything beyond his hairline though, because it's dangerous. Like, my panties might spontaneously combust if I think back on the thick knobs of his knuckles as he dragged a thumb down his square jaw. Or those shoulders, wide and strong beneath the white coat, like he was just some model they cherry-picked from Hollywood to play a doctor. And Jesus, those eyes. Blue ice personified.

I definitely shouldn't be wondering about what he's like in his private time. Imagining him tossing popcorn in his mouth at a movie. Or shouting as he rides a bicycle down a steep hill on a sultry summer evening. Even though he probably never goes to the movies or rides bikes, it's somehow erotic to imagine him *enjoying himself.*

No, I can't think about any of that. Even though—oops, too late. My panties might already be smoldering.

Nancy assured me that the deal would happen, but personally, I won't believe it until I see it. I might even need the signature notarized, just to be extra sure that *Dr. Dom* plans to go through with the contract without ruining my career just for fun.

Because for me, this situation is double-edged. A man recently ruined my career, though he gave me no warning beforehand. So, kudos to Dr. Daly for that, I guess—advance warning of ruining a life should be standard practice. But my Columbus-based options being nil has forced me to restart in Cleveland, so it's not like he could ruin me much further. I have nothing built up here—yet.

Though knowing me, I'll have a head start on my Lake Erie empire by first quarter next year.

What can I say? I'm one efficient bitch.

A new email tinkle sounds from my computer, which sends a thrill of excitement through me. Much like any incoming mail does. Is it the signed NDA I've been waiting for? Is it a response from one of the *many other* leads I've been following while starting over in Cleveland these last few weeks? Or is it just another newsletter from that yoga studio in Austin that I went to *once* and I keep forgetting to unsubscribe from, even though two years have passed?

I glide into my new sleek office chair, which complements the spartan chic theme I've got going on. I hijacked most of the pieces from my old office in Columbus and picked up a few new-to-me pieces at the vintage shop around the corner. The entire front wall of my office is windows, allowing golden, autumnal sunlight to spill over everything. I love this place already. It's the best fresh start I never asked for. Never wanted. But absolutely needed, after the shit storm I went through.

NEW EMAIL: Dominic Daly.

My stomach pitches to my feet as I click the preview. His email fills the screen. The first thing I see is "Dear Ms. Hayes," followed by a one-liner: "Please see attached."

The attachment opens up to the NDA. And what do you know? It's filled out and signed.

A whoop of excitement escapes me, and I pump my fists in the air. *Thank the lord!* My career relaunch is officially underway. And sure, it might riding on one of the sexiest clients I've ever signed on, much less looked at from within a three-foot radius. And yes, he poses a high risk of being the most disagreeable person I'll deal with, possibly in my entire life.

But I'm making it on my own here in Cleveland, after the professional falling-out of the century. This is a promising turn after a slow start. But I have faith it will get better, due in part to the clause I added to the NDA that allows me to utilize Dr. Dominic Daly on my 'previous clients' page, listed strictly as brand management, of course. No mention of a wife hunt anywhere.

I take a few moments to sigh and whoop and scroll through the contract again, which I will possibly frame in a password-protected corner of my computer. Because it's official: I have my first heavyweight client. Which means the workload is *on*.

Once I'm composed and caffeinated, I dial Dominic's number. Nancy picks up on the second ring.

"I thought that might be you," Nancy gushes. "Boy, isn't this exciting?"

She's talking about this as if it were *her* scoring the network connection. Dr. Daly must pay her *really well* for her to be this invested in his personal life.

"I'm glad he came around," I say, which is professional code for *about fucking time.*

"He will be too," Nancy promises me. "Now what's the next step?"

"I'll need to speak with Dr. Daly," I tell her. "We'll need to meet a few times before the real matchmaking can begin. I need to get a better feel for what he's looking for and why."

"Well you're in luck," Nancy says, her voice turning into a whisper. "He's coming this way right now."

I can see him in my mind's eye: glowering at papers in his hand, advancing with the intolerable swagger of a man who knows he's the only one in the room who has ever held a beating human heart in his hand.

The sound over the phone muffles as she greets the doctor, and then I'm put on hold. It feels like an eternity before the line picks up again. A throat is cleared, and my forearms prickle, which means it's Dominic on the other end.

"All right," he says in lieu of a greeting.

"Yeah," I respond, already losing my tether with this man. "Hi. It's London."

"I know."

I swallow hard, my cheeks flushing even though there is no reason to be responding physically to this grump when he is five aerial miles from me right now. "I got your email. I trust we're good to proceed?"

"Sure."

He doesn't sound enthused, but then again, did I expect that? In the background, I can hear the clacking of a keyboard. Either he's drowning me out with work or sending an internal message to Nancy that says *I will seek revenge on you for convincing me to hire London.*

"I promise, this process will be painless. I'm a professional." I'm suddenly aware of how many p sounds I've made in the last ten seconds, and I pause, flushing again. I don't normally notice stuff like this. But with Dom, I'm constantly on edge. Waiting for him to strike like a viper with either his attitude or his impossible good looks. "What we need to do from here is a simple little question-naire. It helps me get to know you better. And I *do* need to know something about you in order for my methods to work."

He grunts. And that's it. I frown, wondering if I missed some-thing.

"Did you get all that?" I ask.

"Yeah." The keyboard clacking continues.

"Okay, so I'll make a note in my file that gorilla grunts also stand for 'yes.'" When my joke is met with silence, I barrel on. "So let's meet up." I click over to my computer planner, looking at the empty spread of dates stretching out before me. Once upon a time, back in

Columbus, my days were booked solid. And I have faith they will be again soon.

If I can snag the sexy demon from cardiology hell, then I can do anything.

"I'm a busy man," he says on the tail of a sigh. "Can't we do this through email?"

"We *could*, but then I wouldn't be providing you with the top-notch service you—I mean, *Nancy*—hired me for." If he can be brusque, rude, and short, then I can deliver the snark. This is an understood reciprocity in client-service relationships. And honestly, I have just enough pride to not roll over and choke to death on my own people-pleasing passiveness like some others in this industry. "There's a reason I don't conduct my initial interviews through email. It's too easy to lie. And I'm here to find someone that works *with you*. Not against you."

"Honestly, I don't even need to like her."

I blink a few times. It's not the first time I've handled a client looking for the trappings of love without any of the affection. But it always surprises me. What's better than finding someone who actually makes your heart flutter? Even if I'm on a temporary hiatus from all things warm and fuzzy while the cracks of my heart rejoin like an imperfect fracture after falling off a jungle gym, I still believe that there's someone out there for people. For me. Even for *him*.

But let's be real—Dr. Dom probably doesn't condone anything that interrupts the regular rhythm of his stony heart.

"It doesn't matter. You hired me to do a job, and I'm going to do it in the only way I know how. Which means I'm going to find you someone who appreciates your grunting and your five-word answers. Now let's set a date. I'll need one full hour at minimum, an hour and a half max. It can be wherever you want, whatever time of day. I'll accommodate your schedule because I know what a busy man you are." I want to roll my eyes, because I'm still a snarky teen on the inside. "I usually meet up at a cafe, the client's house, or my office."

There's an unnerving pause, and after so much speaking on my end, the absence of it on his end rings harsh.

"Figure it out with Nancy," he says a moment later, and then I'm back on hold again.

I sigh, leaning back in my chair. The view outside distracts me from my frustration. A cute hipster couple strolls by, hand in hand, matching septum piercings on full display. My gaze wanders to the stone pot by the door, which reminds me that I need to figure out what to plant there. I like to try my hand at gardening every once in a while. Just to remind myself that I can keep something alive. Not like it's my priority, just seems like a good skillset to have. In case I get gifted an unexpected aloe, or the Apocalypse happens.

"London?" Nancy asks a moment later.

"Yes?"

"Oh, good, he didn't hang up on you." Nancy lets out a terse sigh, the same sound I've heard from her after almost every interaction with Dr. Dom. "Now, let's see here."

"Be real with me. Is he *always* like this?"

Nancy is clacking on her keyboard in the background. "Like what?"

"You know what I'm talking about." When Nancy doesn't fill in for me, I summon my bravery to speak the truth. "Like he took off the wrong leg in an operation and now everyone else is going to pay for it."

"Dr. Daly doesn't perform amputations," Nancy says.

My points still stands...though not on two legs. While I'm imagining the *buh-dum-tss* at my imaginary stand up show, Nancy swears under her breath. "Hang on, London. His date book won't open."

"Are you scheduling this for him?"

"Yes, he's on his way to the OR right now, so it'll be best if I just tell him where to go and when."

"Sounds like a man who likes being told what to do."

A wheezing, staccato laugh tumbles out of her. She laughs—for a *long* time. When she finally composes herself, she says, "Oh, my *god* that was funny."

"Well, thanks. So it's true?" This is research, after all. If Dom is secretly submissive, I need to know this when matching him off.

"No. Not at all. I mean, yes, it seems like, well..." She pauses, then in the background, I hear her say, "Yes, Dr. Daly. It'll be on your desk when you get back."

Nancy returns to the line but doesn't say anything right away. When she speaks, it's in a lower tone. "Okay, he's gone. All I'm saying is that Dom wears the pants but likes for someone else to tighten the belt. If you know what I mean?"

That is 200% more risqué than what I expected Nancy to ever say, especially in relation to her boss. This inspires so many questions. Like: *Why do you know about how he wears his belt?* And: *What color underwear does this man prefer?*

"Are you and Dom...?" I begin.

"No, not 'wear the pants' like that! Oh, please. *Never*. I'm married."

"I didn't mean to imply that," I say, fighting a laugh. Nancy sounds genuinely mortified. "He *is* an attractive man." Attractive is the understatement of the century. He's attractive in the same way one might call Mount Everest a hill. "I'm sure he has plenty of...you know. Girlfriends. Dinner dates. One-night stands. Whatever you want to call them."

Nancy snorts in a way that I understand to mean *yeah, right*. "Dr. Dom *would* have plenty of dinner dates if he ever paid attention to anything other than his computer screen and his patients. And that, my dear, is where you come in. I want this man to be happy. He claims to be happy saving people's lives, but you and I both know he needs more than that."

This is fascinating. Nancy *actually* cares about him. Even when he grunts like a hog and tries to kick strangers out of his office. "Is he paying you to say all this?" I ask it like a joke, but I mean it.

Nancy laughs again, the wheezing kind that comes from the depths of her soul, on the heels of "paying me to say this!" When the laugh clears, she says, "Are you always this funny?"

No. I am only this funny when I don't try, or when I'm confused about a new client's true character. Both of which rarely happen. Instead, I say, "You bet your ass I am."

When she calms down, Nancy says, "Dr. Daly is rough on the outside to those who don't know him, but he's got the best bedside manner of any doctor I've seen in my life. That's really saying something. Even though he's covered in barbs, in the center he's allll gooey chocolate."

I blink a few times, trying to refrain from desiring the gooey chocolate of Dom's innards. But damn, I love chocolate. Especially the melty kind. "I'll take your word for it."

We figure out the earliest possible time for me to insert myself into Dominic's schedule. By a stroke of luck, it's the following day at lunch. He always takes an hour, which he usually spends in his office, Nancy explains. But his one o'clock surgical consult for tomorrow canceled, which means he'll have no excuse not to meet me for my questionnaire interview. She suggests someplace with light lunch fare, based on his preference for heart-healthy options, like fish and sparkling water.

"Typical cardiologist, right? He's probably legally required to eat that for lunch," I murmur offhandedly, which sends Nancy into another giggling fit. "It was part of the Hippocratic Oath—Cardiology edition," I add, which only sets her off more.

She's in tears by the time we hang up, and I'm feeling equal parts rock star and incompetent newbie. If only Nancy were my client. Not only would I hit it out of the park, I'm sure she'd sing a five-star review from the top of her lungs for the rest of our combined lives.

But Dom? I might be lucky to get a three-star rating from him—probably on Bing only—and that's provided I can find even one person to warm his deep-frozen heart.

This questionnaire interview will be the perfect litmus test to assess just how difficult the next six months might be. Professionally, of course, but also sexually.

Because there is no part of my body that doesn't react to this man when I look at him. The ten syllables he tossed my way over the phone today might as well have been a pay-by-the-minute sex chat. He is *that* Mount Everest attractive, and God help me, I'm not supposed to be climbing this hill.

Dr. Dom wants a wife of convenience, and I'm positive I'll find him one.

I just wish we'd met under different circumstances. Hell, in a whole different reality. Where he might be even slightly more open to being attracted to me, because my body is begging for a *something else of convenience.*

But now, he's my client. Crossing this boundary is, and always has been, a huge no-no. And after what I went through in Columbus?

The line between client and pleasure has never been bolder.

CHAPTER FOUR

It's October first when I meet London for our lunch date.

No, for our *interview*. It's an interview, which is something working professionals utilize for regular, boring, non-sexual purposes. *Not a date that will lead to kisses, heated touches, or mutual groping in the broom closet of the downtown Cleveland restaurant.*

Right. Easy enough to remember. I repeat this over and over to myself as I maneuver the tight side streets of downtown Cleveland, looking for a place to park before I meet her at a rooftop restaurant known for its spectacular view of Lake Erie. I've been here once before, ironically on one of the few dates I've managed since med school.

It was a failure, of course, reminding me of the other unshakeable truth that med school drilled into me, beyond the Hippocratic Oath: romance is a waste of time, because love is a myth.

But since I'm a man of data and evidence, I wanted to test my hypothesis before finally shutting myself off entirely. The date I brought here two years ago was someone I found on Blaze, one of those insanely popular dating apps which blew up overnight and then immediately garnered a reputation for being perfect for one-night stands. I matched with a metric shit ton of women, but only took out three. Each one was disappointing in her own way, and not a single one of them woke up the butterflies currently stalking my stomach.

Meeting with London like this was not how I foresaw the match-making process. Instead, I imagined it to be some sort of sterile, algorithmic process directed distantly by an older woman—matronly, even—who I would never cross paths with on Blaze. Someone I could see as the human equivalent of an app. Useful. Mostly updated. Slight cost to use. Can delete at any time without consequence.

But instead we have the most gorgeous woman I've ever had the displeasure of hiring, at a price tag that I can only assume is related to the fact that this venture is now labeled *URGENT*. Deleting London isn't an option, because I need her and because there's a festering curiosity inside of me that demands I learn more.

Once I park the Beemer, I assess myself one last time in the rearview mirror. I should ditch the tie. I unknot the charcoal silk and toss it into the passenger seat. I'm checking my watch on the way to the building. If service is fast and London is fast, I'll make my two o'clock appointment with time to spare. It feels weird to go out for lunch. I've eaten in my office exclusively for the past year, discounting the occasional pharma rep who sets up shop in the shared cafeteria in the clinic building.

And I'm okay with that. I get more work done that way. Work is my life. And focusing on it one hundred percent is the goal. In the foyer of the office building, I step inside the elevator and jab the up button. The elevator doors slide open, revealing the enclosed part of the rooftop restaurant. With no distractions in my life—like unnecessary lunches and an ultimately disappointing dating life—I can focus on what really matters: success.

Even though my familiar rationalizations bring back that yank in my gut that's getting harder to ignore.

I scan the area, and without realizing, without even *trying*, my gaze lands on London.

Looking all types of jaw-dropping distraction.

She's outside on the patio, sitting in a square of golden sunlight, the side of her head pressed against the encircling steel railing. The top of the railing is lined with skinny flower boxes, flower-laden vines tumbling over the edges. So not only is she bathed in sunlight and set against the impressive backdrop of a sparkling Lake Erie, she's framed with flowers and smiling up at the sun with her eyes closed.

I pause near the sliding glass door, too entranced by the sight of her to proceed. What am I looking at here? An angel? A mid-day, working woman meditation practice? A real-life Snapchat filter?

This is why London can't be the woman for the job. She wants to interview me? Well I want to interview her. For entirely different reasons than this board position and eventual notoriety. For a lot of the reasons which led me to Blaze.

A server stops at the table, snapping her out of her rooftop reverie. He's younger, bedecked with enormous ear plugs and a cutting-edge haircut. He either offers her a hilarious drink or he's flirting with her, because she bursts out laughing, and when he walks toward me, I can see the lovesick smile dangling on his lips.

My stomach churns with something I don't even want to think about. I step out onto the patio, and when she spots me, something shrouded slides across her face. She stands as I approach, and for a moment I think that maybe I'm supposed to hug her. No, I just *want* to hug her. The chocolate-brown blouse she has on today pairs exceptionally well with her sea-foam eyes, and the khaki pedal pushers highlight a tightly-packed ass I forgot to even look for the other day in my office.

"Hey, Dom." She offers a breezy smile, gesturing to the open seat across from her.

"London." Her name sounds too good on my lips. It's annoying. "Were you waiting long?"

"I actually came early so I could enjoy the amazing weather. Isn't this a fantastic October?"

I reach for the menu, ready to get down to the business of not looking at her for the next hour. This is already embarrassing for reasons I can't articulate. *Just your regular, virile male, seeking the help of the hottest woman in the world to find me a fake wife.* She knows as well as I do that the subtext here is, "Help me because I have failed with women."

"It's great." The sun is warming my back, and the fall scents in the air make me feel like I'm drunk on nostalgia and freedom. I should do this more often, but that would entail changing my lifestyle.

So that's a hard no.

"I thought this might be a nice place to come so you could get some fresh air," she goes on, swinging her gaze out toward the lake. "Seems like you don't do much, other than work."

"There are a lot of people out there who need my help."

"But you know you can't be in work mode constantly," London says.

"Nor can you be in therapist mode constantly."

When she smirks, I give her what she's looking for. "Aside from work, I go to the gym and sleep."

A sad smile graces her lips. I yank my gaze back down to the menu. It's too easy to slip up and get lost watching her.

The same server appears, London's suitor, and he looks less than enthused to see me here at her side. I order a sparkling water with a slice of lime, which earns me a lifted brow from Earlobe Man.

"Sure you don't want a beer? Or anything with some bite?" He pumps a fist for emphasis. "We have great IPAs here," he says. It's a subtle challenge to my masculinity. If we were birds of paradise, this would be the precursor to him puffing out his feathers and hopping around on a tree branch to attract attention. London is watching, curiosity sizzling between us.

"I have to go back to work," I say, coaxing my own teal feathers to lay flat.

"Oh, come on. The beautiful woman in front of you got a wine spritzer." He turns his attention to her then, squinting. "It's London, right?"

She smiles demurely. "You remembered."

"If I show up to surgery this afternoon with even a trace of a buzz, I could actually kill someone," I clarify, the smile on my face hardening. Okay, so some of my teal feathers are coming out.

"But it's worth it for an afternoon spent with London," he goes on, sending a wink her way. Gag me, already.

Still, I preen some of my bird of paradise plumage. "I'll remember that when you show up in my clinic with an earlobe injury. Those things snag easily, if you haven't learned by now."

His chin lowers. "Be right back with the drinks."

He walks away, leaving me in a cloud of just how lame he thinks I am.

London snickers. "Snags easily?"

"You must not have seen the data about how many ripped earlobe surgeries are performed yearly."

"No, I missed that memo." London is grinning like she knows a secret, her hands curled under her chin. She looks at me like we've been meeting here for lunch for years already, and this is just one more exciting date to add to the list. *Except this isn't a date.*

But the sunlight begs to differ. It bathes her blonde tresses in the same way God smiles upon creation. Her mouth, which can only be described as luscious and an impossible shade of pink, is curled up at the edges. Traces of summer linger over the bridge of her nose and across her cheeks in the form of freckles. Fuck, she's beautiful.

I would eat every inch of her, and then some. And then again, for dessert.

"Our server missed the memo, too. He was too busy falling over himself to flirt with you."

"He's a little young for me, but it's nice to know that I can still rope in the college crowd as I near thirty."

Nearing thirty. I don't know why this is titillating information, but it is. The back of my neck goes hot, and I clear my throat, studying the appetizers like there's going to be a pop quiz later.

"So let's get to the juicy details. Nancy *does* know everything about you," she says.

"What do you mean? She's been my assistant for the past three years, but she doesn't know *everything*."

"She said you'd get a sparkling water. And let me guess—you'll order salmon for lunch."

My gaze had been lingering over the half order of salmon with capers and asparagus. I quickly jerk it elsewhere, landing on the gut-busting mac and cheese in the lower left corner. "It's heart healthy. What's wrong with that?"

She snickers, idly fingering a gold pendant hanging around her neck. A breeze flutters past us, lifting the dainty sleeve of her blouse. I can't look away from her shoulder. At this point, it is the most erotic thing I've witnessed all month.

"What are you looking at?" she asks a moment later, twisting slightly to follow my gaze. I straighten, jerking my chin toward the lake just over her right shoulder.

"The lake." Like I'd admit that I was having lustful thoughts about the curve of her shoulder. I can't tell if I'm desperate or just suffering the normal consequences of not having had sex in over a year. Though when a woman's billowing sleeve is a turn-on, all arrows are pointing toward desperate.

"Do you like living on Lake Erie?"

The way she's asking sounds like she's genuinely interested, but I remind myself I just deposited my monthly installment into her bank account. *This isn't a date.* "Of course. I couldn't not live on this body of water. At this point, it's baked into my DNA."

"Okay. So I won't match you with someone who plans to move into the Arizona desert." She runs her tongue over her bottom lip, reaching for a stack of folders sitting on the table. She thumbs through some papers, looks up at me, and then launches the question. "So tell me why you're looking for a wife."

"You already know why."

"I want to hear it in your words. Right now."

I swipe my thumb along my jawline. "There's a prestigious position opening up on one of the nation's most famous physician-directed charities. I want it. I *need* it. I'll be the youngest physician to ever grace their ranks. But they are painfully traditional, and if I show up to the final interview without a wife, I'll be out of the running immediately."

Her gaze focuses on something beyond the table, and Mr. Future Ripped Earlobe comes back to drop off my drink a moment later. Our conversation is on hold while he offers to take our orders. I urge London to go first, and she orders the exact thing I planned to get. I fight a smile as I ask for the same entrée, and when the server leaves with our menus, I can't hold back the laughter.

"What?" she asks, feigning innocence. "It's heart healthy. Now tell me more about the foundation. Why do you *need* the position?"

"It's a life goal," I say.

"Okay. And you don't want to get married for *any* other reason than the way it'll look to this board of directors?"

"Well, I suppose it's time to get married, don't you think?"

"My opinion doesn't matter."

I narrow my eyes. "It does to some extent. You're the one calling the shots here."

"No, you're the one in control. I'm just facilitating your decision-making." She flashes a mischievous grin. "That's me. Just your regular old belt buckler."

"What?"

She shakes her head. "Do you believe in divorce? I mean, are you looking for this woman with a plan of divorcing her three years down the road, or do I need to find you a long-term convenient wife here?"

"It doesn't matter to me. I'll make it work either way."

"Wow. You must be very flexible in your domestic life."

I don't even know how to respond to that. I barely *have* a domestic life. "It's a non-issue. I work all the time anyway, and whoever you find will have to be fine with that. I mean, the situation is pretty black and white. Being any doctor's wife assumes a majority absence, much less one who gets called into the ER an average of three nights a week at the earliest hours known to man."

"You really get called in like that?"

I nod, reaching for my water. "Without fail. Every Tuesday, Thursday, and Friday mornings."

"But you don't work in the ER."

I offer a tight grin. "But I am the only specialist on call. It comes with the territory of being one of few specialists in the network."

"Got it. So you want someone who will ultimately approach this as more of a business relationship. Do you want kids, frequent travel, pets, et cetera?"

The mention of all of those ideas makes a strange heat float through my abdomen. Once upon a time, I wanted all of them. But since making the decision to just get lost in my work and never resurface, they feel more like outdated concepts that no longer have a place in my waking life. Like excessive luxuries I can't afford.

"Kids, no. Pets, if she can take care of them. And travel...yeah. I'd like to go to Europe at least once a year."

"Any place in particular?" She holds up a hand. "Spare me the London joke."

"I don't know. France."

"Okay. Any particular reason? Other than Paris. And again, spare the London joke."

My jaw twitches. "It's a historical gem. You really think I'm that obsessed with seeing your underpants?"

She wilts, and the daggers she sends me are deeply satisfying. "Fine. France. It made Van Gogh cut his ear off, but okay." London scribbles some things in her notepad, then her sea-foam gaze rakes up to meet mine. "Date nights?"

With you? Yes please. If this is her casual interview, I can only imagine what a relaxed evening might entail. "The bare minimum required."

She grimaces, returning to her notes. "So you want someone who you almost don't notice in the home."

"Sure. Mostly absent. Low maintenance. And beautiful, of course."

"Essentially a Barbie doll," she clarifies.

"Right."

"Is it okay if we find you a doll who speaks, or do you want her to be mute as well?"

With that grin she's clearly joking—but I smirk at her anyway.

"Well, the motive is clear. Now let's see about the rest. Your image." Her gaze snaps back to me, sweeping over my body like I'm just one among many. "Hm."

"What's that mean?"

She's scribbling furiously. "What? Am I not enunciating again? That happens sometimes—I'll try to speak more clearly."

My jaw twitches from the effort of hiding a blossoming smile. Jesus, she's snarkier than I imagined. "My image?"

"Yeah. Your presentation. I perform my matchmaking based on a twelve-point system. Your image is just one of those points. And it's mostly fine."

"*Mostly* fine?"

She doesn't falter. "Yeah."

"So what's that, a C grade on your little scale there?"

She purses her lips. "No. I don't use a grading system. Jeez, Dr. Daly, it's not like you're a piece of meat. I'm not giving you a sexability score here."

Why did she have to bring that up? Now I *need* to know how she would rate me. And how she'd rate our server. I need to know that I can at least beat that twenty-four-year-old drifter. *At least.* But that is so inappropriate, even my innate competitive streak can't convince me to say the words. "Fine. What would you improve about my image?"

Now, she gets flustered. Her blouse has betrayed her, allowing me to see the crimson creeping across her chest. "Honestly?"

"That's what I hired you for."

She waves her pen in a tight circle at me. "Undo another button."

"Not gonna happen."

She shrugs, looking back at her notepad. "You asked. I told you."

"I can't unbutton my shirt because women will fall helplessly at my feet."

She's unfazed. "Good. That'll help the wife hunt."

Silence fills the table, and the breeze lifts her sleeve again. I can't look away. Adrenaline shoots through me, and I lean forward, daring to seek out her gaze. "You said mostly fine. So tell me. On a scale of one to ten."

"What?"

"Where do I fall?"

London goes very quiet, eyes widening as if I just asked her to take her top off in public. Finally, she blurts, "This isn't about my preferences."

But would you prefer me? My fingers are searching out the next highest button of my shirt before I even make the conscious decision to follow her advice. I unbutton it as she requested and sit back in my chair, unable to hide the smirk. "What about now?"

London laughs, but it's wispy. The flush in her chest is back, and for a moment, I'd give anything to feel the pulse skating under her skin. I'm pegging her for an easy 140 bpm. If she faints, I'll be here to catch her. She reaches for her glass of water and takes a long sip. When the glass touches the table, she sends me a smile.

"You'll no doubt score a ten with all of the matches I'll be finding you."

Answered like a true professional. Not even a hint of personal preference, like whether chest hair drives her wild, as I'm beginning to suspect. These are the sort of helpful details I need to begin collecting. She barrels on with more questions about my morals, the rules of my childhood home, the types of questions that you might expect a highly paid therapist to ask.

And I answer them, as much as I can. But the back of my mind is still sizzling on the abandoned train of thought. That brief window that we both peered into. The one that I could find only because the flush of her neck guided me there.

I shouldn't want London. I shouldn't even be toying with the idea of pursuing her.

But she makes it hard not to want to try. London has a spark that illuminates the dark, echoey cavern of my heart—of nearly every man in a three-mile radius. I'm no better than Mr. Dangling Lobes over here. London wins people over in a heartbeat.

Which is the sign of a truly lovely person or a sociopath.

And something tells me she's not going to turn out to be Theodora Bundy. Which means I have to figure out what my game plan is going forward:

Unbutton more buttons, or just be smart and walk the fuck away from this bubbling attraction.

CHAPTER FIVE

It takes me a full seventy-two hours and three separate sessions with my vibrator to recuperate from glimpsing Dom's chest hair.

It was at once unruly and well-groomed. Jet black and virile. *The stuff of my fucking fantasies.*

What kind of idiot tells the hottest man in the world to do the one thing that is her kryptonite? This idiot right here. I'm still fuming over my indulgence two days later while compiling the beginning of Dom's portfolio of matches. I managed to extract enough out of him at our rooftop lunch to get a solid start.

But this man is a tough nut to crack. I need more of him. For professional reasons only, of course. Even though personally, I wouldn't mind glimpsing that chest hair again.

I clench my thighs together beneath my desk, my gaze flitting back to the printout of Dom's face that I have as part of his file. Christ, could the man be even slightly less attractive? What is *in* the Daly gene pool? There is some sort of genetic mutation there that scientists should know about. We should probably deep freeze some of the Daly sperm, too, and lock it in a vault in Norway—just in case the world is threatened with losing these blue eyes and that jawline.

I know Hazel gets me on this one. Ever since she and Grayson started hooking up, she admits that she bought a one-way ticket on the Daly Express.

And now I worry I'm doing the same. This railway is too modern; too high-speed. As soon as I step inside, I'm whisked away by a conductor who immediately leads me to a personalized cabin with a king-size bed and a life-size replica of Dr. Dom's surgeon hands.

Except I can't be boarding this train, because my career depends on the opposite. On conscious slow steps, like one would have through the shifting sands of a desert.

The thought inspires distant lyrics in my head, which prompts a spiraling internet search that lands with me blasting Seal's "Kissed By A Rose" in my office back-to-back three times. Invigorating, though not exactly helpful, because I am still attracted to Dominic Daly afterward.

I tap my finger against the U key about fifteen times, trying to figure out what the game plan should look like from here. If this were anybody else, I'd have at least three more in-person meetings planned to finalize the approach. And that's not including the post-date meetups, where we dig deep into what worked and what didn't work about each match.

But with Dom? I need to keep our meetings to a minimum. If all our information sessions are going to include me goading him to take his clothes off, then I can't be trusted to proceed.

Soon enough, I'll be competing in the match pool alongside the women I'm scouting. I might even stoop as low as elbowing one in the gut before dinner so that she's forced to relinquish her spot after spilling red wine all over her white top. *Boo hoo,* I'll tell her as she slinks out of the gourmet restaurant. *THE DOCTOR WILL SEE ME NOW!*

I rub at my face, as if this will help clear the nightmarish vision from my head. I need to get it together. ASAP.

"Willow, what would you do?" I ask into the empty office. "And don't say 'Listen to Seal again.'"

Per the ritual of asking my late sister what to do in times of distress, I listen to the silence. Looking for her voice, even though I'm not sure I'd recognize it anymore if I heard it. Looking for some internal twitch in the right direction. Looking for *anything*.

It's been ten years since my sister passed away, but I still think about her daily. I still ask her for advice *all the time,* even though she was just shy of eighteen when she died from unexpected complications from the flu. Yeah, that's right—the fucking flu.

It wasn't even one of the exotic strains that crop up each year like a fleeting fashion trend. It was just the *regular* flu. You don't think it can happen until it happens to your little sister. And then you get your flu shot every year, sometimes twice, just to be sure.

My gaze falls to the long, skinny pots lining the decorative wall of my office. They are in Willow's honor. She was a budding pottery artist, and some of my best pieces are hers, tucked away in my apartment upstairs.

"So, I shouldn't fuck him, is what you're saying," I say into the void. I can imagine her teenager squeal, imploring me to do the opposite. "Got it."

I return to my computer with a vengeance. Asking Willow is always helpful, even if my frequent pauses throughout the day might make me look crazy to the rest of the world. As I near my thirties, I no longer care. Let the people wonder why I'm smiling at the sun and taking an extra-long time as I park my car. I have no fucks to give, because Willow's departure taught me that life isn't just short, it's basically over already.

No more doubting myself, especially when it comes to this ass-hole doctor. I can hold my own around him. He's not *that* hot. More exposure to his hotness will probably help, anyway. Get my cells used to his presence, until someday soon I can be around him without wanting to melt out of my clothes and onto the nearest flat surface, legs spread and waiting for him to join me, a horny puddle of butter.

Nancy picks up the phone almost immediately when I call. "London! What can I do for you, honey pie?"

Ooh. Now we're at honey pie level. It only makes sense that the woman who is most excited about me works alongside the man who is least excited about me.

"Just calling in so we can keep this train moving," I say brightly. "Should we skip Dr. Dom and just slip this next meetup into his schedule, you and I?"

She tuts. "I can't do that. Trust me, I've tried this approach before, and it doesn't work. He's not here right now, but I think I might be able to catch him on his cell phone. Hang tight, sweets."

Ooh—now I'm honey pie *and* sweets. Soon I will boast a list of nicknames fit to open a bakery, which, of course, Dr. Dom would not patronize.

The line beeps dully every few seconds, and after a few moments I realize I'm clenching my fist under my desk. This man makes me *tense*. Just waiting to see how he'll greet me, what he might say, what level of gruff he'll sound like. Whether or not he'll hang up on me.

It's the kind of thing I could keep track of in a score sheet.

"What is it?" He barks a moment later.

I jump in my seat, my forearms going prickly. "Dr. Daly."

"Yeah, that's who you wanted, right?"

My mouth goes dry. *Damn this man.* I'm not used to the imbalance he creates. "We, uh...I need to schedule another meeting with you."

"For what?"

"For, uh...the matches." In the background, I catch hints of beeping and the murmur of other voices. I imagine him in his white coat, and I clench my thighs under the table again.

"Okay," he says in a tone that conveys just how unimportant this is.

I grit my teeth, which allows my thighs to unclench. If this man were even an iota more approachable, softer, or welcoming? I'd be that horny butter all over his toasted bread.

"What's your preference for meeting up?" I ask.

He sighs tersely, sounding more than annoyed. "Listen—"

"It won't take too long. Just tell me where you'll be later tonight or tomorrow night. Whatever works. Trust me, Dominic, I'm trying to make this easy for you. After all, *this is what you hired me to do.*"

He pauses, the beeping sounding louder in the background. Finally he says, "Find me at the gym tonight. Eight o'clock. We can chat while I get my work out in. Does that work for you?"

Does that *work* for me? It will probably kill me, but fine. It's like this man is trying to do every sexy thing possible in front of me, just to see if I'll snap. And lord help me, if he takes off his shirt tonight, I very well might. "Totally fine."

"I'll send you the address."

The line goes dead. Five points: Dom hung up on me.

While the inspiration is bubbling, I start a new Excel file and type out the title "DALY SCORE CARD". Yes, I am a shining example of professional adulthood. This is where passive aggression gets you, folks. Right here, which quickly segues into beginning emails with *per my last email.*

I spend a few minutes breaking out the infractions—hanging up without saying goodbye, interrupting, not acknowledging me, grunting like a gorilla—and assign some random point values. The highest yielding infraction, according to my new scale, is "firing me/insulting my work performance," with a hefty 55 points, which serves as the ultimate threshold of assholishness. I pray we don't reach it.

But what would the prize be if he managed to keep his score below official asshole levels? If I were insane, I'd ask for a night with Dom in bed. But since I'm sane, I'll just go with the quiet, lifelong satisfaction that I'm a nicer person than he is.

For some reason, my entire body is buzzing. With dread, with anticipation, with middle-school grade giddiness that comes from wanting the hottie asshole; it's everything at once. The irony of our meeting place tonight is almost too delicious to bear. Of course, a man looking for a Barbie needs to be a Ken doll himself.

And that's what I need to focus on. The Barbie dolls of his future. I've already started a preliminary pool, culled from the high-end dating software I'm subscribed to. But what gives me my edge in the matchmaking world isn't what app I use. It's my network.

Even though I've never lived in Cleveland, I moved here with a ready-made network that would make most PR firms jealous. It's because I never forget a name, I always make a good impression, and gosh darn it, *people like me.*

Some people are born with naturally perfect eyebrows or an ability to belch the alphabet backwards or any other number of marketable assets. But my superpower isn't a genetically perfect forehead-to-chin ratio or even a stunning ability to run long distances (I can barely jog). My superhero toolkit boasts something much simpler: I make people comfortable. I've always been able to help people calm down or open up or just feel more relaxed than before. I'm the human equivalent of a lavender-infused eye pillow. I don't know why, but this is what I've got to work with.

So while I'm populating Dom's early matches based on business-facing software, the real gems are going to be provided by my connections. The network I've built up because I love people, and

I love learning about them, paired with my intuitive and uncanny knack for matching them.

It's practically guaranteed. But the hunt still makes me giddy.

Dom can't see it yet, but I've already got his Barbie in the bag.

And no matter how much my sex drive begs to differ, that Barbie isn't me.

CHAPTER SIX

DOM

I finally leave the office that evening at seven p.m., which by all accounts is early for me. I organized it this way, because Wednesdays are my no-fail gym days.

But this Wednesday was the day from hell. Everything ran an hour behind, which is the quickest way to send me to my grave. My obituary will someday read: "An otherwise healthy guy, his early demise was caused by one outrageous traffic jam on I-480, which made him late for the OR. Family requests society review timeliness procedures in lieu of flowers."

A major surgery was cancelled last minute due to patient non-compliance, and my one actual on-time catheterization ran an hour over due to an allergic reaction to the dye. Exhaustion haunts every step toward my car, and by the time I reach my doctor-premium spot in the clinic parking lot, I make a decision.

I'm going to cancel on London.

It takes me a long time to find my keys, which were *just* in my hand seconds ago, and by the time I can gather my thoughts long enough to focus, I realize they've been clutched in my fist the entire time. Just more proof that I need to cancel on London. I can't even think straight. I need to go home and sleep for twelve hours, even though it won't make a dent in my sleep debt.

My phone dings with a new email as I'm easing into the driver's seat. Part of me is hesitant to give up an opportunity to see London, but the logical part of me knows this is for the better. I'll insist we conduct the next stages via email. It'll help me recharge for tomorrow, and honestly? The less London, the better.

I swipe to my email client, and the subject line of the new email makes my stomach drop.

SUBJECT: Final Round Consideration – Please Read

If they're imploring me to read, it can only mean something very good or something very bad. I skim the email, breath caught in my throat, until I reach the very end. And somehow, the verdict is both very good *and* very bad.

They're turning up the dial on this selection process, and they've set a date for my last interview, which will happen in roughly a month. This is the slowest-moving selection process I've ever heard of, only because the entire board is made up of full-time—and often celebrity—physicians. It's hard to get them in one room at the same time, which is why I've still not met the entire lot of them. Each interview so far has dealt with strictly business matters, meaning the enormous lie I put on my initial application that stated "Married, no kids" has still not been addressed.

There was no option for a bachelor. In fact, the only other options on the application were "Married, with kids" and "Widowed/Divorced." So it *will* come up in the last interview—it has to. Of all the bullet points we've touched on, one of the few remaining areas is personal life.

I swear under my breath as I start the car. Guess I can't cancel on London after all.

I accelerate out of the parking spot much more quickly than is advisable, white knuckling the steering wheel as I maneuver through the crush of traffic in downtown Cleveland. Dusk is just creeping into sight, the autumn hues leaking across the sky in honey and sangria. I get distracted by the colors, and then London's face creeps into my mind. That tiny smile she had on the rooftop last week lurking at the edges of my focus. She'd probably have the same smile now if she were looking at this sunset with me.

A car honks behind me, and I hurry to accelerate. Sitting on a green light in rush hour—bad doctor. This is exactly the type of distraction I can't afford to have in life. I've probably sent some other schedule freak to an early grave as well.

I arrive at the gym at ten till eight and make quick work of changing my clothes. I'm hungry, but not famished—I'll reward myself with an enormous meal on the way home. I have one hour for pumping iron, and I'm going to enjoy every last second of it. If I can stop thinking about work or this upcoming interview for even five minutes, I'll consider it a success.

I step into mesh workout shorts and free the tie that's been tight around my neck all day. Shucking the office gear is always a relief, and today more than ever. Even though it means diving headfirst into that uncharted territory of time off, which is more unfamiliar now to me than ever before. London sniffing around my personal life makes me realize just how little there is for her to dig into.

The line between regular Dom and Dr. Dom has never been thinner. To be honest, I'm not even sure what regular Dom is like anymore. Who he was, before Dr. Dom took over.

I thought I'd be happier about this shift. That was the goal, after all. But now I'm just caught in a freefall. Unsure which cord to pull to release my parachute.

Time melts away in the clanking, bleach-infused workout haven. I've just broken a sweat on the bicep curls when the big double doors slide open.

And then there she is. One of the few women in the weight room, but the only one who turns every single head in the place. She walks in like she owns the place, but not in an arrogant way. She has a subtle grace about her, confidence mixed with something else. Curiosity, maybe. Like she's sure of herself *and* taking it all in.

When her gaze lands on me, electricity sizzles through me. Bad sign. I reach for a sweat towel and swipe at my face, and when I look up she's not in front of me as I expected, but chatting with some shirtless guy with a neck the size of a tree trunk who's already way sweatier than I am.

My gaze is stuck on them. They're far enough away that I can't hear what they're saying, but I remind myself not to care, and launch back into my reps. Still, my gaze slides back to her. She's a magnet and I'm the feeble ferrite, victim to her pull. She's all smiles as he talks, and then their laughter drifts my way.

Great. They probably met in the lobby and are planning their first date before the leg machine. Do I care? Absolutely not.

I grip the handle so hard, my hand spasms. It's clear men just flock to her wherever she goes. She even made me flock myself, which is the best double entendre I'll never share with her. But that's one reason among many why I should steer clear of her. If I could isolate the synapse in my brain that is allowing me to feel attraction to her, I would burn it to a crisp. Life would be easier without this annoying pull toward her.

But I can't isolate it, so my gut turns into a pretzel as the guy reaches out and squeezes just above her elbow before they part. London breezes toward me, a silly smile on her face. It falls slightly once she reaches me.

"Hello, Dominic," she says, throatier than normal. This close, it's impossible to ignore what she's wearing. Not like I could from across the room, either. She's got on hot pink leggings that cut off right above the ankle, plastered to long curves which make my fingers twitch. She's wearing a sleeveless black crop top, which allows painful glimpses of both her teal sports bra and her tanned belly. I reach for the sweat towel again, hoping that this time I can just remove my eyeballs.

"London. You found me."

"You didn't make it easy. Next time, send me a detailed map."

"Have you never been to a gym before?"

She leans against the unused machine next to me, smirking. "This is not a regular gym. This is a luxury labyrinth that happens to have a weight room in it."

I fight the laughter heading toward my lips. "Come on. With all this matchmaker money you're raking in, you should be able to afford a luxury labyrinth."

"I spend my money on other things, thank you very much. Is this your usual gym?"

"Yeah. It's the closest to my house."

"Of course. Let me guess." She sends me a sly grin, cocking a hip. My cock twitches inside my shorts. If only she could look at me like that all the time. "You live downtown right above the clinic."

The laugh finally escapes. "Not above it."

"So you just live in your office? Admit it—you have a cot beneath your desk."

"Not that either." A grunt escapes on the tail end of my words as I bring my arms toward my body in the final rep. I release the arms of the machine and reach for the sweat towel again. "I have a penthouse on West Lakeside."

That brow arches higher. "Ah. A *penthouse*. Now it all makes sense."

"What?" I push to standing, towering over her. She tips her head back to look at me, and a hot wave ripples through me, fingertips burning with the urge to bring her against me, press my mouth to hers and see what happens.

"Penthouse-living doctor. Ritzy downtown gym." She shrugs.

"This isn't ritzy."

"They barely let me in!" She throws her arms out to her sides. "I had to provide my tax returns just to get through the door."

"Oh, is that right?"

"When they saw I made under a hundred thou a year, they turned me away. But I weaseled my way in. Even though I had to come in through the heating duct."

I fight the smile tugging at my lips. "So you just regularly carry your W-2 with you?"

She snorts, flipping her long ponytail over her shoulder. "That's the only outrageous detail you picked up on from what I just said?"

"You look like someone who would sneak in through a heating duct. So yes. Having your tax returns constantly on-hand strikes me as odd."

She's eyeing me, tongue in cheek. "How do you manage to both insult and compliment someone at the same time?"

"I don't plan on sharing my hard-won secrets." Truth is, we could stand here joking about the heating ducts for another hour. I fight to focus on anything other than her, because she is far too easy to get lost in. No wonder she and Tree Trunk probably would have been planning their wedding by the time they reached the ellipticals. I'm about ready to plan a spur-of-the-moment proposal by the dumb-bell rack. I jerk my chin toward the bench press. "Can you spot me?"

Doubt clouds her face. "How much weight are you going to put on?"

I shrug. "Two twenty."

Her eyes go wide. "Are you kidding me? That's almost double my weight! I can't catch that if you drop it."

Her reaction is deeply pleasing; I can feel my cells smiling. "Fine. Then just stand there and look pretty." *Because it won't be hard.* I bite my tongue before I can say the words I absolutely know I shouldn't say.

She crosses her arms, gaze bouncing around the weight room. Something unspoken remains between us, but I suspect it's just the weight of how badly I want to wrap my arms around her and lift her off the ground.

"So," she says, once I've loaded up the bar and lie back on the bench, "now that you're supine and vulnerable, tell me more about your work life."

I catch her gaze as she hovers above the bar, hands out like she plans to be the spotter.

"I think you know all there is to know about it," I say, wrapping my hands around the cool metal. "Are you really going to spot me?"

"I'm just acting like I know what I'm doing," she says, a conspiratorial sparkle glinting in her eyes. "If I don't, they'll kick me out, right? Am I doing a good job?"

Another laugh escapes me. "You don't have the biceps for this bar, so I'm afraid everyone in here knows you're pretending."

"You can't even humor me?"

I wet my bottom lip, forgetting what I'm supposed to be doing. Looking up at her from this strange angle makes her even more fascinating, more gut-punchingly beautiful. "You're a great spotter. Probably the best I've ever had."

A genuine smile fills her face. "I sincerely did not expect you to humor me with a compliment."

She has no idea how many other compliments I have tucked away, reserved only for her, that will never see the light of day. "If I don't humor my spotter before my workout, it could prove fatal."

A sly grin covers her face. "Don't worry. I won't let you die. I need your money."

This time, I fail to squash my laughter. I launch into my reps, the weight in my grip a welcome relief. My thoughts shrink to nothingness, for a blessed few moments. But my body doesn't forget she's here, not by a long shot. London buzzes at the periphery of the silence in my head, reminding me of things I'd long forced myself to forget about. It's been too long since I've had to keep my cool around a woman, and even longer since that woman was someone of London's level.

But what's the most striking about today is that I've already reached my goal—stop thinking about work and the future for at least five minutes. Usually when I'm here, I'm lucky to get a few minutes lost in the buzz of distraction and weightlifting. But London wipes away my stress with just once glance.

When my reps are done, I replace the bar and expel one last whoosh of air. Sweat pools at my temples, and I sit up, reaching for my towel. London claps her hands forcefully. "Come on. Next round."

"You're a brutal trainer," I crack, twisting to look at her.

"Just keeping that heart healthy. Which reminds me," she says while her gaze drifts off across the weight room. "Why did you get into cardiology?"

I toss the sweat towel and lay back on the bench. "I liked it the most during my residency."

"Did you ever consider being a different type of doctor?"

Her questions are so honest, so pure. It's like she really wants to know, but logically they have to be because of this insane task I've given her. That constant balancing act—of feeling like we're getting to know each other like two regular adults, and then remembering that I've paid her to do as much—is nauseating.

Mostly because I *want* to be getting to know her, beyond the scope of this task.

"My top three choices were pediatrics, obstetrics, and neurosurgery. But once I got to residency, none of those seemed right. One of my advisors suggested cardiology, and the rest is history."

"Oh, wow. You were almost delivering babies for a living! I can't imagine it."

"Way too much fluid for me."

"There's something powerful about saving a person's heart, right?" She cocks her head, and the air goes out of me.

"It's satisfying," I say, trying to feel as clinical as possible while her green gaze dances across my face. I'm seeing her as a patient. Not as a freckled, blonde beauty whose pink leggings are whispering at me to peel them off her. "Fulfilling."

"You know, we're both in the same field," she says, propping her hands on her hips.

"Oh? I missed the MD behind your name in your emails."

She smirks. "I've saved a lot of hearts with my services. I'll save yours, too."

"Mine doesn't need saving," I remind her, reaching for the bar. "Mine is perfectly fine."

Her jaunty comment, however well-intentioned, sends anxiety spiraling through me. Like maybe she can see beyond the carefully constructed façade I've erected. I didn't spend years building up these walls only to have everything crumble in front of a woman whose closest relative appears to be the sun itself. I'm stronger than this. I don't care about London.

But my words echo inside my head and all through the cavity of my chest, which, once upon a time, felt more in the span of a few years than I'll ever allow again.

My heart *is* fine.

But only because I refuse to open it up. Not to anyone. Not ever again.

London follows me around the weight room for my entire routine like a dutiful puppy, peppering me with questions as much as teasing me about my form. The hour flies by; it's not until I'm helping her on the leg press machine that I realize time is up. Like, way up. It's almost nine-thirty, and I still haven't eaten dinner.

"You nailed it," I say, ignoring the clock for just a little longer as she finishes her final rep. "I thought you said you don't come to gyms."

"I don't. I mean, not for anything other than the smoothie bar and the occasional cycling class."

The image of her on a stationary bike is suddenly so erotic that I have to distract myself with something else. Literally anything else. I grab for the cleaning rags.

"Thanks for cleaning up after my sweaty ass," she teases.

"It's late," I say, consciously averting my thoughts away from her ass. If this girl is a cyclist...No. Cannot think about that anymore. "I need to go."

"But you never answered my question from before," she blurts, smoothing some of the flyaways on the top of her head.

"Which one?"

"About why cardiology."

"I told you," I say, leaning against the machine. The cleanup can wait. "It was my favorite of the specialties."

"No, but like *why* cardiology? Why be a doctor?"

I pause. The original reason is less than admirable, and the recent reason is the stuff of Hallmark cards. So I give her something in the middle. "I've always wanted to help people, I guess. My father is the CEO of Bayshore Hospital, so the medical field was always on my radar. It started as a hunch that turned into a passion."

"Can you imagine yourself doing anything else?"

I scoff. "Absolutely not. Of course there are things I might change about my career…" I trail off before I can add *like finding a wife and joining this board of directors*. "But who doesn't feel that way sometimes? I've always wanted to leave an impact on the world, and there's no better way than saving people's lives."

"Saving their hearts." London's grin spreads ear to ear, which prompts something similar to happen on my face. "So why don't you want kids then? That's a pretty big impact you could leave."

My smile falls, all the way to the floor. Once upon a time, I *did* want children. But that false hope flew right out the window alongside love.

"I've never seen myself as a father." It's not the total truth, but it's not a total lie either. I could have become one, had I not been betrayed. Heartbroken. Completely sideswiped. "Besides, growing up is rough. My brothers and I fought constantly."

"You Daly boys sure were competitive growing up." She snorts. "Must be in your bloodline or something."

"Have you *met* my father?" I laugh, but it's humorless. "There's no other option than competition in my family. You play, or you lose by default. That's it."

"Is this board position part of that competition?" London asks, launching a freckled spear right into my chest.

"Why would you ask that?"

"Just curious." She shrugs, but there's so much more to it than that. I can fucking tell.

"Sounds like you're trying to be my therapist again," I say, resuming cleaning the machine.

"Therapy is one of the implied aspects of my job." She winks, and my knees nearly give out. Over her shoulder, someone is approaching us, and she must notice me looking because she turns to follow my gaze. As she does, a smooth "Hey." slides out of her.

Her sleeveless, sweat-drenched friend has returned, with even more testosterone than before. He uses the collar of his shirt to wipe at his upper lip, and they step just far enough away that I can't hear what they're talking about over the ambient rock music and clanking machines.

It doesn't matter. There's a rush of noise inside my head as I scramble to ignore the sensations flooding me. I shouldn't care. And I'm going to *not* care. As soon as I can wrap up these distracting sessions with her and get back to my regular routine.

Because that's the bottom line. Once I'm not seeing her weekly, this pesky attraction will disappear completely. And I should do whatever I can to make that day arrive sooner rather than later.

London's all smiles and sweet tones with him, rocking back and forth on her heels as they talk. He's nodding his head, saying, "Mm-hm, mm-hm," over and over again. I clean the machine three times, just so I have something to focus on. Anything other than the painful flashes of the last time I cared for a woman and what happened right under my nose with my best friend.

The adrenaline release of the past hour's workout combined with her probing has cracked something open inside me. I haven't talked to someone as a regular human in...god, I don't know how long. And I enjoyed it. Because I enjoy London. She's sweet and saucy and fun and sexier than literally every other woman I might witness in the next fifty years of my life.

Which means I need to stay the fuck away from her. I need to stop acting like flirting with her is a good idea or that any of those smiles she throws my way mean anything.

Tree Trunk was a wake-up call I sorely needed after my fantasy-filled hour and a half in the weight room with London. A reminder that what I might think I'm after with London, I'd be better off to just forget about it.

As she approaches me, her ponytail swishing, the words leap out of my mouth before I can think better of it.

"So, Matchmaker. Have you matched yourself off yet?"

Her brows draw together. "Like...you mean..."

"Stands to reason the matchmaker should have her perfect match by now, right?" I grab my water bottle and start a slow walk toward the doors. When I look over at her, she's crossed her arms, watching me with narrowed eyes.

"It's kind of the cobbler's children situation here," she says.

"I'm not familiar."

"You know. The cobbler makes his living fixing shoes, but his own kids' shoes are falling apart? Yeah. I'm the cobbler."

"So you're saying you can't even provide yourself with the same service you offer others," I say as the sliding doors whoosh open. Something urgent and hot is thumping inside me, and I can't tell if I'm going to pick a fight with her or back her up against the nearest wall. Our footsteps scuff through the empty hallway that leads toward the locker rooms. I'm not usually here this late, and the crowd has thinned considerably. Which probably means I should back her up against the wall and see what happens.

"Do you not trust I'll be able to do it?" she asks, peering up at me.

Sweet London. She has no idea where I'm going with this. She has no idea that she unleashes something that I've fought to keep under lock and key for years. It's not her fault. But it's also directly because of her.

"Wouldn't I rather choose the cobbler who can put shoes on his own kids' feet?"

She frowns. "Just because I'm single doesn't mean I don't know what I'm doing."

This is both a victory and a frustrating obstacle. She's single. Do I care? Not technically, even though this is the one piece of information I've been dying to learn.

"Still seems like a successful matchmaker would know how to match herself off by your age," I say. And those words signal my first firm steps into the side of *picking a fight* and not *backing her up against a wall with kisses.*

She snorts. "By my age?"

"What are you, thirty-five? Pushing forty?" I know full well she's close to or right at thirty.

She frowns. "You're coming through loud and clear, Dr. Dom. 'Don't trust the spinster matchmaker. She clearly has failed at love.' Well I guess it's a good thing you aren't looking for that, now, isn't it?"

I clench and unclench my teeth. I'm not done with her. I just wish I knew how to convince myself that backing her up against the wall was a bad idea. "How do I know you can get me anything I'm looking for? Your idea of matchmaking means coming to my gym and asking me questions about why I'm a cardiologist. That has nothing to do with finding me a convenient wife."

Something frightening and hard slides over London's face as she crosses her arms. "You're questioning my methods. Do you want me to reveal all my secrets here in the middle of the gym, or would you be satisfied with a summary in email form?"

My fists clench. "I'm just saying this doesn't inspire a lot of faith."

"Well good thing you don't have to do anything other than sit back and wait for me to prove that I actually know what I'm doing. Be faithless, for all I care. It won't affect the fact that you'll get exactly what you signed up for."

Lashing out hasn't helped things. If anything, it's only tangled the knot in my chest more. "Then cut the crap. Admit that today was pointless. You're just milking the invoice."

Her nostrils flare. "Wow. You know, I don't know why you had to drag it out this long just to tell me that you're unhappy with my services. If you want to end this contract, Mr. Daly, then say the word."

I grit my teeth. Firing her was not where I wanted this to end up. But taking it where I want it to go—straight to my bedroom, or, in a pinch, the desk in my office—is a non-option. Because I recognize London for what she truly is. A threat to my stability. A chance to fall head over heels.

The last fucking distraction that I need.

Besides, I know better than to chase after something that could never fit into my life. I've got one goal and one goal only: to get a wife on paper and continue my life as usual.

I just need to keep reminding myself: *this pesky distraction will be over with soon.*

"Just do the job you were hired for and get rid of the bullshit."

London's eyes narrow, turning into a gemstone glare.

But there's one problem. Even her disgust doesn't dim her sparkle or reduce the effectiveness of her freckles.

Which means I'm officially out of ideas. I can only hope that being an asshole is enough to put the distance I need between us.

CHAPTER SEVEN

It's only a few days later, but it feels like a year has passed since I last saw Dom.

A long, angry, festering year.

I've never been spoken to like that by a client. *Ever.* Not even by the client who openly groped me and suggested that my hoo-ha would serve as an excellent add on to his publicity services. He at least was sweet and cloying.

But Dominic Daly? Forget all that. He's as corrosive as acid. Which means that I officially should not care about him or his ridiculous chest hair or any of his biting, hurtful remarks.

Except I do. Not because I want to win his curmudgeonly ass over. I am enraged that he thinks I'm inflating his invoice.

It's the worst thing he could have said to me. And what's worse is that I feel duped.

Duped because I could have sworn he and I were connecting like regular adults before he pulled that graceless one-eighty. That maneuver maxed out his Asshole Score Card. It's scientifically verified, as though I needed proof. *Dominic Daly is the #1 Asshole.*

So off to the matchmaking ocean I go. For him, I'm diving so deep, I'll need to bring down an extra oxygen tank. For anyone else, I'd be able to find plenty of potential matches in shallow waters, but no—this level of asshole calls for diving into the abyss.

I called a food delivery service to transport sushi to the Mariana Trench of my matchmaking dive, scuba gear available at the front door. When I finally come up for air, I'm covered in a mystical black soot that arises as a byproduct of pairing unsuspecting soul mates.

All right, *maybe* I'm being a little dramatic. But it's all true, minus the soot. It is a deeply creative process that involves elements both physical and unknown. I'm not kidding when I tell people I'm the best in the industry, because I *am*. According to one Yelp review, I'm like an algorithm had sex with a psychic.

And I'm using every last ounce of my skills for this impossibly hot jerk who I do not still think about at all, *thankyouverymuch*. After my stint in the matchmaking trench, this portfolio I've drawn up for Dom is *fire*. I've got six bona fide love matches waiting for him that are *so good,* he's going to rethink whatever it is that's got him hung up on being a curmudgeon.

Honestly, it's baffling. The man could find a wife just by showing up at the public library and shouting, "Who wants to be legally wedded to my biceps?" Guaranteed, thirty women would show up with an engagement ring and a receipt for a wedding venue reservation.

And honestly, before he pulled the king of assholes card out of his weird doctor deck, I would have considered joining the lineup. If I could have also pretended that he wasn't already my client.

Besides, I have a vision for my future. And it doesn't involve the Don Draper of the medical world *or* faking a marriage for a board of physicians. It involves a solid dating history, a long wedding planning process, and implementing every special thing from my and my future husband's life into a carefully curated theme that I have already drawn up four prototypes for. *Yes,* I was the girl planning her wedding in sixth grade. Complete with M.A.S.H workups and all. I love *love* so much—and I want my own love story to be as romantic and epic as they come.

So really, it's a good thing the man is hellbent on rejecting love and affection, even though his workout grimace alone could convince a nun to reject her vows. As his bench press witness the other day, I can attest to the fact that I was one sweat-droplet-down-the-bicep away from ripping my leggings off and conveniently "falling" on top of his dick.

Thank God Dom showed me his true colors that night. Just when I was quivering on the cusp of *see, London, he might be the perfect man after all,* he reminded me that going after clients is never a good idea. Least of all *this* client.

Add on top of that running into my old friend Craig—the gentlest body builder you ever did see—for a fun-filled walk down memory lane to catch him up on what happened to me in Columbus, and I've racked up enough sorry memories in that stupid gym to warrant never returning. But maybe the real problem was when I agreed to get on the thigh machine. It opened up a portal that turned Dom into a raging dick. In conclusion: I probably shouldn't work out anymore. Fine.

Not like I'll be sneaking into Dom's fancy gym ever again. Hurt ripples through me again. I think very highly of myself and my work, and the fact that he so brazenly shit on my methods will sting for a while. So not only do I need to match him off for contractual reasons, I need it to happen ASAP for personal reasons.

The sooner he's out of my orbit, the better. He's mean, overworked, and too sexy. Not only that, he's fascinating, which is the most frustrating part of all. I shouldn't want to know more about the man who called our meetup *pointless.* But dammit, I do.

And the real sign that I'm a hopeless romantic matchmaker? He might not think that he needs love or romance, but I still plan to prove him wrong, even after how crappy he's been.

Although Dom doesn't think he needs anything more than *on paper*, I believe he has a shot at love. And despite how much I secretly want to climb this man like a squirrel being chased by a feral cat up a tree, I want him to find someone who is great for him.

Because over the past week of being around him, getting to know him, I see the spark in him that's been dimmed by his burnout and constant go-mode. And that spark threatens to turn into a flame the longer I pay attention to it.

Which means these matches could not have come at a better time.

All I need to do is drop off the portfolio, implore him to review the matches, and then we'll set one last meetup for us to go over the next steps in depth. Piece of not-pointless cake. This is the easiest thing I've ever had to do. My palms are not at all sweating. Why? Because my face-to-face obligations with this hottie meanie are almost complete.

I head to his office just before lunchtime, because Nancy told me that would be the best chance I'd have of finding him. My pulse starts racing as I park at the clinic. By the time I make it to the reception area, I'm short of breath. I might need Dr. Dom to examine me once I arrive. No, I might *demand* it.

But the weight of the portfolio in my purse reminds me of my mission. There are six women who are just *waiting* for him to turn that ice-blue gaze on them and light their panties on fire. He is going to make one of them Mrs. Dr. Daly.

The words become a mantra as I ride the elevator up to his floor. My legs turn to Jell-O once I push into the cardiology office, and I'm pretty sure I'm about to melt out of my clothes by the time I reach Nancy's desk. Language escapes me. I just flap my mouth uselessly as she nods, the phone pressed to her ear.

I hate that every inch of my body is anticipating seeing him—hearing him—like a fangirl waiting for Harry Styles. But I have yet to be able to reason with my innards.

"He's not here yet," she whispers while covering the mouthpiece of the phone. "But he'll be back soon."

All I can see while I pace near Nancy's desk is the gray T-shirt he wore at the gym, the sleeves straining around his biceps. I got one flash of armpit hair that night, which I've imagined no fewer than ten times since. Why is armpit hair hot? Technically speaking, it's a pretty gross area. All sweaty and warm and smelly. But on Dom? I don't even care. Give me all the Eau de Asshole.

And not only that. I would have forfeited my income from this project for just one glimpse of his abs. I would have paid *extra* to run the tip of my index finger along any grooves found therein.

The gruff undertones of his voice make me pause midstride, and only then do I realize I've been gnawing on a nail. I straighten my back, mentally preparing myself to see him again. Reminding myself of the way he called our gym date *pointless*.

I huff, trying to conjure some of my previous anger. But all my disgust dissolves when I spot him, paused at the end of the hallway, white coat in full view. He's not coming toward me. Instead, he's stopped and chatting with someone. An elderly woman, who's speaking so softly I can't hear what they're saying.

"Of course, of course," Dr. Dom tells her, nodding. I drift closer to them, unable to prevent myself from wanting to know more.

"You treated him so kindly," the old lady is saying. "And I...I can't tell you how much that means to me."

"Mrs. Wilson, your husband's health is the most important thing to me. And I mean that. I'll be checking in daily with you to see how he's recovering."

Mrs. Wilson swipes at her face—maybe she was crying. My heart hurts for a moment, but everything explodes in my chest when he pulls little Mrs. Wilson into a hug. Her voice is muffled as she mumbles, "Thank you," into his chest—the lucky lady—and then before I have time to act natural, he's heading this way, adjusting the cuff of his coat sleeve.

"Dr. Daly," Nancy begins, as he breezes past me. I grip the wall for support. He is vetiver and mahogany. Dripping with pheromones. And completely fucking ignoring me.

He heads into his office, leaving the door hanging wide open. I look between the door and her, my brows drawing together. "Does he...does he even see me?"

"I left the door open for you," Dom intones from the office. I peer inside. He's standing behind his desk, fingertips steepled on the surface, looking up at me like he can't believe I don't *get it.*

"Don't listen to the tone," Nancy says in a low voice, as if she doesn't want Dom to hear. "Just think about the words."

Whatever it takes to coexist with this peach of a man. These must be her survival techniques.

I head into his office, shutting the door behind me. He barely looks up from his desk as I approach, maintaining his stance even as I slink into the chair facing him. He looks distracted, but somehow pained.

"Everything okay?" I ask.

He blinks a few times, not looking at me. "Not exactly."

"That was a surprisingly sweet moment," I offer. "I wasn't aware that you had the capability of being nice to people."

This comment doesn't have the intended effect. His face hardens. "Are you being sarcastic?"

"I heard what you said to that woman out there." He still doesn't seem to understand what's notable, so I add, "Most doctors I know wouldn't spend even a second more than necessary with a patient. And you even hugged her. So that's like, one gold teddy bear sticker right there."

"Teddy bear," he repeats as he sits down and whatever fog that held him captive is letting up.

"Oh yeah. Trust me, you need as many teddy bear stickers as you can get."

He wets his bottom lip, which almost impregnates me on the spot. "I don't want any of them."

"Yeah, well, your general demeanor would benefit from having a couple laying around, if you know what I mean."

His blue gaze slice through me. "Says who?"

"Oh, I don't know, pretty much anyone who has to come in contact with you?" I shouldn't be talking to him about this. I should just let him be a jerk and move on with my day. But there's something about Dom that invites me to push against him. He might be rough around the edges, but I have a nail file and I know how to use it.

"The people who matter will be able to handle my general demeanor," he says, his jaw flexing.

"Great. Glad to know where I stand." I gnaw on the inside of my lip as I rummage through my briefcase for the portfolio of matches.

"I didn't say you couldn't handle me." His voice is rough whiskey. And just like that, electricity prickles through the air. I glance at him, my brows knitting together. He's implying that I'm one of the people who matter, and the insinuation pumps the brakes. I desperately need to just complete my mission and *leave*. But now, I want to follow this detour.

"Listen, I need to make this quick. I have a lot of other clients to tend to, people who are actually enthused about the work I do and the approach I take. So I'm dropping this off with you." I set the portfolio on his desk, distinctly aware of the fact that he hasn't looked away from me. Not once. And his stare is beginning to leave burn marks.

"What is it?"

"Your matches." I offer him an obviously fake smile. I'm trying to find that happy medium between professional and snarky, but he's making it hard. He blasted the door off normalcy when he took things down Dickhead Lane, so I think I'm warranted in returning what he dishes out. "Here is the fruit of all my pointless labor."

His jaw is clenching and unclenching, and I can't tell if the storm in his eyes is preceding a laugh or an insult. Maybe it'll be both. "Are you done?"

"With what? The job you hired me for? Actually, no. We still need to review these matches, and then set up the dates. I thought it was pretty clear that the job would be done once you were, you know, *married*."

"I meant done being angry at me."

I blink. "Nope. I'm not done with that either."

He finally looks away from me, the corners of his lips curling. "You're definitely going to want to drink a glass of water later."

"Why?"

"Because you're so salty." There's humor in his eyes as he looks back at me, and that immediately dissolves the hard edges of my anger. *Dammit*. He's a veteran asshole, clearly. Which means I need to barrel on with my mission.

"Thanks for the recommendation, doc. Now, let's get back to business." I slide the folders toward him. "I'd like to go over these matches with you. And"—I hold up my hands, as if warding off a *yeah but* before he says it—"I know you're busy. But even just a glance on your break or after work is all I'm asking for."

"With the thousand other things people want me to glance at."

"Now seems like a good time for your weekly reminder that *you* hired *me*."

"But I have a high-pressure schedule to work around."

"I've done nothing but work around it," I say. His attempts at dominating this conversation won't work. I'm not afraid of his hard edges and his Eau du Asshole. In fact, they only egg me on. "Every time I call in here, I ask Nancy if we can just not bother you all together, because I know you're *such* a busy man."

I might have laid it on a little too thick that time. His smile morphs into a glower. "And what do you do all day? Sleep until noon and predict who's going to fall in love next?"

I deflate slightly. *There it is.* The asshole streak. I must have #triggered Dr. Dom.

"I haven't slept until noon since college, but I'm not going to sit here and defend myself to someone who clearly just wants to be mean."

He's quiet, staring at me, clicking the top of a pen compulsively. I'm expecting an *I'm sorry*, but of course I don't get one. Instead, he says, "Tonight."

"What?"

"We'll meet tonight." His jaw flexes as he consults his laptop, clicking through something. "It's probably the only chance I'll have until next weekend. I'm on call all weekend, and honestly"—his tired gaze drags up to meet mine—"I need a fucking drink tonight."

Electricity shivers through me. "Okay. Let's get a fucking drink."

The phone rings then, and his regular Dr. Dom mask slides into place: hard, a little pissed off, the actually-model-grade medical version of Derek Zoolander's Blue Steel. He picks it up, grunts once, and then he looks at me.

"I need to take this call. I'll text you the details."

As I nod, my head feels loose, like it might bob right off my neck. He insulted my lifestyle, yet somehow I'm still at risk of drifting toward him instead of out of his office.

I try my best to exit gracefully, but I fumble with the doorknob, and something clicks. The handle won't move. *At all.*

I try to turn the knob again, but it doesn't budge. Alarms ring in my head—*you're not locked inside are you, London, did you lock the door, LONDON ARE YOU LOCKED INSIDE THE OFFICE*? I flip the tiny lock and the handle is still immobile. A nervous laugh flutters out of me.

"Um," I begin. This is mortifying. How does one lock themselves *inside* a doctor's office? I try it again, flipping the lock again. Equally as immobile. Thank God I never followed my childhood dream of applying to be on that short-lived but epic game show, Legends of the Hidden Temple–I would have been humiliated on national television. Now I'm just a late twenty-something who gets trapped inside perfectly functional spaces.

I twist to look at Dom, and his curious gaze is sizzling over me. "I can't get out."

He covers the mouthpiece. "Just open it."

This is the least helpful thing anyone has ever told me. "You don't think I tried that?" I jiggle the handle to show him, just as my cheeks turn flame red. I'm supposed to be the epitome of grace. A living, breathing example of confidence and go-get-'em attitude.

Except, you know, when it comes to doors.

Dom tells whoever he's on the phone with to hold, and gently sets the receiver down. He struts toward me, hands in his pockets, a curious smile on his face. When he reaches me, I'm bathed in his mind-bending mahogany musk. I need to save face here, but at this point, it's impossible. I've given him all the ammo he needs to continue insulting my lifestyle and now probably my intelligence.

"You have a faulty door," I inform him, crossing my arms. He reaches for the handle, his arm brushing my elbow. The mere touch is enough to send moisture to my panties. God forbid this man ever *actually* put his hands on me, because I might have a heart attack. And wouldn't that just be ironic?

He turns the handle, and it unclicks a moment later. He opens the door a few inches, the smile on his face spreading wider.

"I think you have a faulty hand." He's towering over me, that gaze nearly slicing in me two. I can't tell if I'm quivering or melting, but tectonic plates are definitely separating inside me. He doesn't move away immediately either, which makes this worse. Way worse.

"I've never had issues with any door," I say, lifting my chin, "except yours."

"Hm." His gaze washes over me, leaving aching pinpricks in its wake, and then he heads back to his desk. I scrape up whatever tiny pieces of my dignity are left and burst through the door.

"Door giving you troubles?" Nancy asks with a smirk as I hurry past.

"You need to call maintenance," I tell her. "And make sure Dom doesn't forget to put me on the schedule for tonight."

The last thing I hear as I hightail it out of his office is Nancy saying "Oooh, dinner, huh!". When the door thuds behind me and I'm in the hallway, the breath I'd been holding since setting foot in Dom's office finally escapes in one, enormous whoosh.

If you could call that "holding it together," then I am precariously close to losing my shit when it comes to Dom. And it's only getting worse. Granted, Dom doesn't know that when he brushed my elbow, I almost had to change underwear. But that is *not* the way a matchmaker is supposed to react to a client. And even though meeting him on his own turf was bad, seeing Dom loose in the wild—like at the gym, and God forbid, at tonight's restaurant—is a special type of intolerable.

I need grounding. I need guidance. I need *information.* As soon as my ass hits the warm interior of my car, I'm calling Hazel.

"Perfect timing," she says once she picks up. "I was *just* about to call you."

I glance at the clock. I managed to snag her in her daily down-time window. "Guess we needed the long-distance girl talk. What's up?"

"Oh, nothing much. Why did you call?"

"Just wanted to gab." Untrue. I want her to spill everything she knows about Dominic Daly, but I am contractually forbidden from acknowledging him. "A few days away from completing my first month in Cleveland. Can you believe it?"

"Oh my god," she says, and I imagine her slapping her hand against her forehead. "And I still haven't seen your place yet."

"Girl, I wasn't even unpacked beyond the bed-and-shower stage until last week."

Hazel snorts. "But let me guess—your office was picture-perfect?"

"You know it." I laugh. We're both perfectionist workaholics, in the best way possible. At least, we like to think so. "My apartment is looking better, but my guest bed isn't even set up. So if you and Gray come, you won't have anywhere to sleep. *Yet.*"

"Oh, that's okay. But we need to pick a date soon! And with enough time so I can just slip it into Gray's schedule without any fuss."

My heart starts thumping as I scramble for a natural segue between Grayson and Dom. *So, speaking of Gray, why don't you elaborate on his older brother we've talked about once in our entire lives?* "Is he being fussy?"

"He's just so busy with GrayWorks," she says. "You know. New business. Growing pains. Licensing issues. Blah blah blah."

"Well, he has plenty of help in the area." I run my finger along the top of the steering wheel, daring myself to go there. "You, for starters. And his brothers, I mean...aren't they helpful?"

Hazel snorts. "Which one, exactly?"

I make a display of thinking it over. "Ahh...jeez...I don't know...what's the...Dom? Doesn't he do...something helpful? I heard he lives here in Cleveland."

Hazel tuts, unaware that my heart is pounding like a jack rabbit. "The man might live an hour away from us, but he might as well be in India."

Jackpot. "Why do you say that?"

"He's just...absent. I don't know. And when he comes around, he's a dick."

My stomach pitches to the floor. I want to say, *FUNNY, he was just a dick to me too!* But I bite my tongue. "I don't remember much from high school. He was, what, four years ahead of us?"

"Yeah. He was a dick back then, too." Hazel laughs a little. "You should see the way he and Gray fight. It's fit for a reality TV show. It gets tense."

My lips form a frown, and I pick at the seam of my steering wheel, feeling let down without understanding why. "Sounds like a jerk."

"He provokes the shit out of Gray. But then again...Gray provokes the shit out of him. It's a vicious cycle in this family. I honestly can't even explain it. You'd have to see it to believe it."

"Why are they like that?"

"Their dad." Hazel's flat tone tells me it starts and ends there. "I mean, Dom probably got the worst of it, so it's not like you can blame him."

"Weird," I say, hoping Hazel can't intuit the sweat forming on my brow as I try to sound casual and non-invested. "I don't know anything about Dom. At all. Like...at all. It's crazy how little I have ever interacted with that man." Am I sounding casual yet? "Or any of them. I mean, of course, except Gray."

"Well Dom is the biggest asshole of the family," Hazel says.

I clear my throat, swallowing back the *YEAH, TELL ME ABOUT IT.* "But it can't just be because of his dad."

"Well, there was that girl."

My shoulders prickle with heat as curiosity washes over me. *Second jackpot.* "What?"

"Gray mentioned it once when we were drunk," Hazel says, her voice dropping to a gossipy whisper. "But he said that Dom used to be engaged. Dom was the only Daly brother that stood a chance of getting married, until some huge blowout happened years ago."

"Oh my god."

"He only mentioned it because we were talking about how funny it was that *Gray* was the first brother to settle down. Gray always thought he'd be the last. Or second to last, maybe."

"So Dom was almost married?"

"Yeah, but the girl cheated on him, I think. I'm not sure. I don't even know when it happened."

Hazel's insight, however limited, helps a *lot* of pieces click into place. There's a reason for Dom's romantic reticence. And it looks a lot like heartbreak. I just wonder why he hasn't mentioned it. "So Gray won the title of first to settle down."

"Yes, which he doesn't hold back from holding over his brothers' heads. Especially Connor, since he came in second."

I laugh. "Sure. But if those two have found love, which brother is next?"

It might sound like pointless speculation about people I shouldn't care about, but the Daly brothers occupied more of my conversations during high school than I care to admit. They were the ubiquitous *hot guys*, the local standard for out-of-reach sexiness that everyone just wanted to know about, even if you never spoke to them. In some way or another, I have always been aware of the Daly brothers and their general goings-on. Blame it on small-town life, but it's the way of things in Bayshore. There's fewer than twenty thousand of us, so we tend to know what's going on with everyone else while we live there.

Hazel and I chat a little bit more, and when it's time to go I can't resist cracking a joke. "So next time I call, we'll cover a different Daly brother, right?"

"Sure," she laughs. "How about Weston next time?"

"It's a date." I hang up the phone, something hot and uncomfortable pulsing in my veins. I squeeze my steering wheel, peering through my rearview mirror just to check that Dom isn't somehow magically behind my car, staring me down with those icy baby blues.

If anything, my side-swiped probing into Dom's personal life gave me exactly what I needed to know, even if I didn't plan on finding it out.

The man pushes away his family. He doesn't do anything beyond work. And though he was open to love once, he no longer is.

All of these details are, in my world, known by a different name.

Red flags.

And if I'm smart, I'll nip this silly infatuation in the bud.

Before it really grows roots and starts to bloom.

CHAPTER EIGHT

Red flags or not, I'm not ignoring this chance to dress up. When Dom sent me the location for our business dinner tonight, I recognized the name immediately. One of the coziest *and* most elegant dining spots in all of Cleveland. I've only been there once before, and unfortunately it was linked to my ex, Carl, and a random business trip. I'm more than ready to wipe his memory from this place—and my brain altogether. He's one of the only people who could make me choose the *Eternal Sunshine* procedure, hands down.

Except once he was wiped from my memory banks, there would be no way in hell we'd find our way back to each other.

Carl was—*is*—a misogynist, pure and simple. We connected because of our work, and I was enamored with his power. He was my boss, so there was something inherently off-limits and sexy about it. The company we worked for had a permissive policy about interpersonal relationships, so it seemed fine. It all seemed fine. Until it wasn't.

We had a sex-only relationship that turned into something more. In retrospect, I realize now that he'd been keeping me around for the benefits. Someone to grab dinner with. Frequent sex, but always on his terms. Willing ears to unload his anxieties onto.

But me, after a three-year dry spell post-college, I was so *ready* for a boyfriend that I lapped up his crumbs and called it a loaf of bread. It only took the "incident" in Columbus—the only way I refer to it nowadays—to help me see that Carl was a piece of shit. That our three years of pseudo-dating hadn't meant much of anything to him.

In fact, it had meant nothing at all.

To him, I was just another pair of legs that occasionally spread for his benefit. A pair of legs that he asked me to spread for one of our top clients—only after said client groped the shit out of me—so that we could keep him on the account.

I wish he wasn't one of the longest-running relationships in my personal history. I wish he hadn't blacklisted me for whistleblowing his slimy ass. I wish a lot of things. But wishing doesn't change the past.

All I can do is start over and make sure that this time around, I keep my dating life far away from the professional pool. Messing with the wrong sociopath can really set back a career. Though I don't begrudge having to start over in Cleveland. I welcome the challenge—and I like being closer to Bayshore.

Even though the move was necessitated by Carl, I'm not going to let that define my life here.

So tonight's visit to a place that I originally knew because of Carl feels a lot like a win. I'm dressing to the nines, so that I can look—and feel—a perfect ten. *Carl be damned.*

I take a rideshare to the restaurant, just in case. I have a sneaking suspicion that Dr. Dom might not be the type of man who only orders one drink. And if he wants the wine or screwdrivers or whisky neats to flow, then dammit, I need to be there beside him in his alcoholic log flume.

This is our last official required meeting for the duration of this project, so in a way, this is also a goodbye to my short-lived infatuation with him. Because after tonight, I'm laying it to rest.

Dominic will be well on his way to finding the woman of his dreams—even if those dreams are far less romantic than most sane people's—and I will be well on my way to putting Dom back in the client folder, where he belongs.

I need to repeat that thought to myself as the rideshare winds through downtown Cleveland. Amid the busy streets and the ochre hues of sunset and the building anticipation of a great meal with a gorgeous man and his acid tongue...yeah, I basically need to tattoo this reminder on my forearm.

I'm wobblier than I like when I step out of the car, and I pull my light jacket tighter around me as a cool wind billows down the street. I'm dressed sexy chic but appropriate, with a skintight black wraparound paired with a trendy black leather jacket that gives the outfit an edge. I opted for smoky makeup as well, since I'm a grown woman who does what she wants, and I'm praying that Dominic doesn't read into the clear signals I'm putting out there that I'm dressing up with the hope that he'll notice.

It's a terrible double standard, this business of being a woman. I want Dom, to notice but I don't. I want him to want me, though he shouldn't. I want him to hoist me in his arms and back me up against a wall, even though the very thought of that is the most forbidden thing in my career right now. I want to make him tumble at my feet, even though he is a jerk who does not deserve *my while.*

Warm, fragrant air envelops me as I step inside the restaurant, pure garlic and cork, and I'm immediately starving. At the host stand, I give them my name, but it's unnecessary, because my gaze falls on the bar hugging the far wall of the restaurant.

And there he is. Leaning against the wooden bar top like he's been plucked out of a movie, his charcoal button-up playing a little too well with his jet-black tresses and icy blue gaze. He sees me. I know it because goosepimples are covering my forearms and I'm drifting toward him without fully hearing what the employee is telling me. I think the host has a menu in his hand, or maybe he's telling me to go sit in the corner and wait until the last ounce of my grace is sucked out of me from looking at this gorgeous man.

I don't care. It doesn't matter. I just need to be where Dominic is.

Dominic sips from a tumbler of amber liquid, his gaze never wavering from mine. Time slows as he drinks me in, and something snaps, electric sharp, between us. It feels a lot like desire, but maybe I'm imagining it. It could be curiosity. A sudden appreciation for my outfit. Or maybe he's seeing me as the confident and successful woman that I've been striving toward since the incident. The woman I haven't felt in far too long.

It's too easy to read into his appreciative gaze, the way his attention ignites every synapse in my body. He's probably standing there, thinking about how annoyed he is that I got here three minutes late, waiting to insult some other aspect of my career. There probably isn't all this fervor that I'm feeling. All this longing and heat and thirst.

But part of me wants to imagine *what if?* What if he was undressing me with his eyes right now? What if his throat tightened at the first glimpse of me, like mine does when I see him? What if the sound of *my* voice made his thighs tense with need?

I shouldn't even go there. I know better than that. But right now, all I want to do is imagine that it's a possibility.

He lifts his tumbler in lieu of a greeting, gaze still sizzling on me as I approach. On the bar beside him sits the leather-backed portfolio of matches I gave him earlier today. *One of them is his future wife.* I need to focus on that.

"What do you want to drink?" he asks me.

"Chardonnay."

A brow lifts. "No hesitation."

"Are you going to micromanage my responses tonight?"

His jaw twitches. "That was my attempt at conversation."

"Ah. Good to know." I set my purse on the bar and begin sliding my jacket off. Once I've got it in my hands, Dom sets his drink down and quietly takes it from me. He effortlessly slings it over an arm and continues sipping his drink.

"You don't have to hold it," I say.

"But I will."

I squash the grin threatening to take over my face. Thank God the bartender chooses that moment to appear. I open my mouth to speak, but Dom sweeps in and orders "the most expensive Chardonnay back there."

"It doesn't need to be the most *expensive*," I tell him. "I didn't even look at the wine list. How much do you think it is?"

"It doesn't matter."

"Well, I mean, it matters *a little*," I tell him, though I don't exactly want to air how tight things have been these last few weeks with the relocation and the client lull. I'm not hurting, but I should be strategic. And ordering a $50 glass of Chardonnay doesn't exactly seem fiscally wise.

"I'm paying." He watches me from over the rim of his glass as he tips more of his drink into his mouth.

"Actually," I say, straightening my back, "I'm paying. This is part of the match selection process. So it falls in my domain."

He laughs a little, setting the tumbler down. "No."

I narrow my eyes, cocking a hip. "You hired me to do a job, and this is part of it."

"I suggested we come here, so it falls on me."

The energy between us spikes, and I can tell he's not going to relent. He's probably the type to pay off the server so that he never brings the bill to the table. The bartender returns with my drink, and I receive it gratefully, the chilled wine glass sticking to my fingertips.

"We'll figure this out later," I say, trying to sound *firm*. Like I mean it, which I no longer do.

"It's already figured out."

"Do you always critique the way people in other industries do their jobs, or is it a special service you reserve just for me?"

His cheek twitches, and that's when I realize what we've been toying at this whole time. Where the pushing and meanness and critiquing is truly headed. *God help us, we're flirting.*

I purse my lips at him before taking a cool sip of the wine. My eyes flutter shut, an inadvertent moan slipping out.

"Good?" he asks, as if he needs to.

"Worth *whatever* price tag it has on it."

The corners of his mouth curl as he swirls the drink in his glass. "Then we'll never know how much it was."

"Aren't you at least curious?"

"Not when knowing the price would make you stop drinking it. And you don't interfere with anything that makes a woman make the noise that you just did."

I almost choke at his words, and the smug smirk on his face sends heat to every corner of my body. I can't tell if I'm aroused or mortified. Scratch that—I'm both.

The host arrives, telling us in hushed tones that our table is ready. Dom turns, and I follow him, clutching my purse and chardonnay, watching the bob of my jacket over his arm as if it's the only life vest in this vast sea of sexual repression he just acknowledged.

I don't know what to say. How to react. Whether or not I should leave now feigning food poisoning, even though we haven't eaten a bite. *The chardonnay was bad*, I'll tell him. *Too expensive, which irritates my colon.*

No, that won't work. I smile at the host as he leads us to a small table set for two. It's intimate. I mean, we're sharing a lone half-moon booth facing outward toward the rest of the restaurant, and there are no other tables around.

The host offers to hang my jacket on a nearby hook, and I wonder if maybe I should ask for a stool. Just so I can sit a few feet away from Dom's overpowering testosterone. If I have to sit inches away from him for the duration of this meal, I'll crack. I know it. I can already feel the fissure erupting inside me, the hot gush of desire ready to break free and drown both of us.

Dom lays the leather portfolio down on the farthest point of the table away from us before gesturing for me to sit down. It feels like a trap, even though I agreed to it.

I ease into the high-backed banquette, spending too much time arranging my wine glass on the packed table of elegantly folded napkins, carefully placed silverware and stacked plates for all the upcoming courses. The seat sinks as his weight meets the cushion, and I try to ignore the goosepimples that flare along my forearms. It's a normal reaction I have to sitting in half-moon booths—nothing to do with Dom, *that's for sure.* The heat of him burns at the edges of my composure, so I reach for my water glass and sip and sip and sip.

"I requested this booth so it would be easier for us to go over the matches." The rough bass notes of his voice make me cross my legs even tighter. All I can focus on is the heat of his thigh hovering dangerously close to mine. His hand finds the white tablecloth as he toys with the fork handle.

I can't look away from his hand. Veiny, powerful somehow, and huge. This hand handles hearts and saves lives on a daily basis. I can already imagine the rough palm pushing over my bare belly, the way his fingertips would find my nipples beneath my bra. I squeeze my eyes shut and turn my head. *Focus on the job.*

"Great idea," I lie. "I take it you had a chance to look over the matches?"

He nods slowly, his gaze bouncing around the restaurant as he swirls ice cubes in his now-empty glass. "Of course."

"Any standouts?"

He frowns, shrugging. "Not particularly."

I deflate next to him, not bothering to hide my dismay. "Are you serious?"

"They all look fine," he begins, pausing just long enough to imply that there's something seriously missing.

"*But*," I encourage.

"But nothing," he says.

I'll be honest—I was really expecting more fanfare than this. But then again, he doesn't know how hard I worked on this. How proud I am of the matches that I conjured. Not just because of who he is as a person, but because of where I've been *as a person*. Starting over. In a new city. Accessing a newly growing network. I wish he'd have had *some* amount of excitement, but no.

And the fact that he's not impressed by anything I put out there makes only one thought swirl perilously close to the surface. The one thought that I will do literally anything to avoid, ignore, and squash:

If you don't like any of them, why don't you try me?

CHAPTER NINE

DOM

I've never wanted to do anything less than I want to review these matches.

Not when London is at my side, smelling like a floral wet dream, the living definition of sleek and smoky seductress.

It's like she has no idea how stunning she is, except I'm pretty sure she has *some* idea. She came out tonight looking hotter than any woman I've seen in the flesh, knowing that she was going to be meeting me.

And maybe that's the part that drives me the wildest. She made these choices with *me* in mind. Even after my conscious and repeated attempts to push her away. To show her just how little she should want me. How little I deserve someone like her. She still has that sparkle in her eye when she looks my way, and dammit, I'm not strong enough to resist it.

With this amount of whiskey in my system, I can't stop thinking that we should throw this portfolio out the fucking window and see what might happen between her and me. Sure, maybe it's because my fingers are curling as I try to repress the urge to touch her, and every time she presses a hand to her chest with a laugh, I get a little hard. My rational mind could list a thousand reasons why digging into this attraction is a bad idea.

But my rational mind isn't in the driver's seat tonight. I'm at dinner with a gorgeous woman on a Friday evening for the first time in years. *Dear lord, I'm a normal human being.* And a normal man would know how to end this night. By whisking this woman away in a flurry of French kisses that segue into so much more, topped off with a late-night pepperoni pizza delivery to replenish all the calories burned.

London is tapping her finger against the table, frowning at something I can't see. "So none of them *spoke* to you?"

"No," I admit, "but then again, I'm not in the market for any of them to speak to me."

She looks disappointed by this, running her finger around the base of her wine glass. "I know. You're right. I just...kind of thought I'd cracked the code."

A humorless laugh escapes me. "Trust me. There is no code."

Except as soon as I say the words, I know they're a lie. There *is* a code, and she's the woman who knows it. She's the first one to awaken this interest in me in fucking years. It's not just sexual interest either, though I've got that in spades. I want to invite her back to my place so we can fuck *and* talk about life.

Exactly the type of distraction I'm supposed to be avoiding.

"No, there's a code," she insists, crossing her arms over her chest, which just makes her breasts look more delectable. I can't stop my gaze from sliding downward for a tantalizing moment. A smile creeps across her face. "And you know what? I just remembered what it is."

"What?"

She shakes her head, that curious smile still splayed across her lips. "No. It's nothing."

"Now you *have* to tell me."

London draws a deep breath, then finally drags her gaze up to meet mine. "You totally just checked out my tits."

Hearing her refer to them as *tits* is somehow hotter than expected. I can't fight the grin, though, even though my cock is aching. Honestly, I'm at a loss. She called me out. "That was a clinical assessment."

She lifts her palms, as if to say *See?* "This is my point. Once you meet these women, you're going to be enthusiastic. You will clinically assess the shit out of them. I *promise* you."

"So you're saying they all look as good in a black dress as you do."

Something unreadable settles over her, and our server chooses this exact moment to arrive with a bubbly introduction. I squeeze my hand into a fist, offering her a tight smile while every inch of my body is focused on London.

I shouldn't have said that to her. But dammit, I couldn't control it.

"So is there anything else that I can bring you two right now?" The server wraps up after a spiel that I missed entirely.

"An appetizer," I blurt, eager to get her out of our hair. "Whatever the most popular one is. We're feeling adventurous."

When the server starts to talk about the menu, I interrupt her. "We'll take some time to look at the menu. When you come back, we'll be ready."

Our server takes the hint and glides away. London has a suspicious smile waiting for me.

"What?" I finally ask.

"You know."

"You'll have to refresh my memory."

"I'm not including little-black-dress assessments in the client package," she says, and I can't help but drink her in again, from her narrow shoulders down to the hint of thigh that I can glimpse before the table obscures my view. "Lest you accuse me of inflating your invoice again."

"Fine. Besides, that would be"—I struggle to find the exact word—"lecherous."

She snickers. "You are a different man once you get a little alcohol in you."

Her words rock me, because she's right, but also she's not. I am this man all the time. But what I allow the world to see is a different story. Something about her begs me to push the envelope.

"Let's not blame it on the top shelf whiskey," I say. "I'm just a regular guy who doesn't get out enough."

"I have a question for you," she says, resting her chin on her knuckles. "One of the few questions I haven't asked yet."

"Should I be nervous?"

She doesn't answer; instead, she dives in head-first. "Did you ever believe in love, or have you chosen not to just recently?"

The words are a gut-punch, and I can't entirely say why. I feel discovered, somehow, like she uncovered old high school journals underneath my bed, and the pages are full of ridiculous complaints about calculus class drama.

"This project is not about love. It was never about love."

"I know, I know," she reassures me. "But I mean, in your life. Beyond what we're doing here."

I can sense what she's getting at, and I don't want to go there. Because going there involves my history, and that is something I just don't like to get into. If there's anything ingrained in the Daly DNA, it's that we don't take kindly to failure. And I failed once, in a huge way. I chose the wrong girl. I trusted my heart with her. And she broke it beyond recognition.

That blow was the worst, but the close second was having to tell my parents we were cancelling the wedding. I'll never forget the look on my dad's face when I told him that. Like I was speaking fucking Mandarin. Because how could his golden child have performed so poorly when it came to something so important in life?

There's no humiliation more biting than being cheated on...when the other guy is your best friend. It doesn't just destroy a person's foundation in life, it completely obliterates everything they thought they knew about relationships.

I'll never make that mistake again. And the best way to avoid it is to erase it from the map entirely.

"Love...is a beautiful thing," I say slowly. "But it's too big of a risk."

"A risk?"

"Yes. Loving someone is a risk."

London's brows draw together as her gaze falls to the table. "I'd say there's a bigger risk in *not* loving."

Our server chooses to sidle back up to the table just then. "Sorry to interrupt," she purrs, "but I just wanted to check if you need another round of drinks."

"Please," I tell her, and she spirits away again.

"Did something happen?" London asks, ignoring the interruption entirely.

She's digging, and the edge of her shovel is getting close to the core. But it won't make it there entirely. "I don't know what this has to do with the portfolio."

"Everything has to do with the portfolio, Dr. Dom," she say sweetly, batting her eyes at me.

"So you *are* a therapist."

"I'm just interested in the quality of your life," she goes on, unfazed. "The women I chose for you stand a real chance at making you *happy*. If you click with them, that is. I can only do so much.

The rest, of course, is up to you and them. But I'm not just giving you some vapid beauty queen because that's what you tell me you want."

"But shouldn't you be honoring your client's wishes?" I'm ready for the whiskey to return. *Any time now.*

"I am. I'm finding you a wife. But I'm doing you one better. These women can become life partners. Someone you can grow and create with, beyond the scope of simply 'have a wife for the foundation.'"

I'm hearing her, but her words are reminding me how I'm already married to the idea of being alone for the rest of my life. Maybe not physically alone, but alone in my heart. Because opening myself up to a relationship like she's talking about can only spell disaster. There will always be threats lurking around the corner. Heartbreaks that are just waiting to etch themselves deep.

"Then I'll just have to find a new matchmaker."

Her face falls, and I realize my blow landed exactly as I intended. Maybe I played the asshole card when I should have played the coy little jokester card.

Except I don't have that card in my deck.

"You can't possibly fire me for doing an *excellent job.*"

"For going beyond the scope of our project?" I shrug. "Vapid means vapid, London."

"Oh my god—"

"But because you've already done the work, I'll hear you out. At this point, it doesn't matter."

She clears her throat, an unreadable expression wringing her features. "I'll just remember not to gloat when you're bringing this woman to the Daly-family Christmas party each year because you can't imagine it without her."

I snort. "Daly-family Christmas party?"

"I'm just assuming you do that. Your family seems like the type to get together in matching sweaters each year."

"Trust me, if we did that, we'd have the annual Christmas call to the cops along with it. My brothers and I can't do anything together casually, much less coordinate a Christmas outfit."

Her face falls, though I'm not sure why. "You guys never grew out of the competition?"

"I'd say we grew *into* it. It's stronger than ever. Which is part of the reason why we don't see each other anymore."

"I've seen Grayson with Weston and Maverick a few times," London says off-handedly, then a bright smile covers her face as the server returns with round two of our drinks. The detail makes something wrench deep inside me. Reminding me of the void that I know is there but refuse to acknowledge.

"Good. I'm sure he's reminding them that I'm an asshole."

"Aren't you reminding them yourself?"

Her sideswipe takes a moment to register, mostly because I'm shocked she went there. I'd start the slow clap myself, if we weren't in a gourmet restaurant.

"I didn't hire you to also join the I Hate Dom Club," I spit.

"I'm not in it. Don't worry." She raises her palms like reinforcing her innocence. "I was never sent the membership papers."

A laugh snorts out of me; I can't even help it. She grins, and the tension between us melts away. Still, I can tell she's got something on her mind.

"The career switch has really helped your brother," London goes on, watching me carefully. "He's *enjoying* life again. He and I were never really close, but since he and Hazel hooked up, I've been seeing a lot of him. He's a nice guy." She shrugs, a curious smile on her face. "You should try getting to know him."

"I spent eighteen years of my life getting to know him." I sip my whiskey. "That was sufficient."

Something raw and wounded crosses London's face as she reaches for her wine glass. Her gaze crosses the restaurant.

"What just happened?"

"Huh?" She snaps her gaze to me, brows drawn together.

"You just checked out. Why?"

"I didn't check out," she says.

"I practically heard sad violins playing. Now tell me why."

She crumples a little, fingering the base of her wine glass. "It just makes me sad to hear stuff like that. What you said about your brother. That's how I used to think, too. About my sister."

"Are you two still on speaking terms?"

"She died right before her eighteenth birthday," London says, her throat bobbing. "So we never got a chance to make it right. And I wish every single day that I could have just gotten over my bullshit and enjoyed the fact that I had an amazing little sister."

Her eyes are shiny as she looks at me again, and the emotion in her voice renders me speechless. *Shit.*

"I'm sorry that happened, London." Though *sorry* seems meaningless in times like these.

"It's life, and it sucks, but we all have the power to create more joy." She offers a smile, though it seems sad. She takes a sip of her wine, and in the silence, I can hear the question that she'd asked without speaking: *How would you feel if one of your brothers was suddenly gone?*

It's too much for right now. But it's something I'll need to come back to.

Once the beautifully barbed woman and warm whiskey aren't the centers of my attention.

"And you want to help me create more joy," I say slowly, getting lost in the sea-foam depths of her eyes. Though I already know how she can help me create more of it.

"Exactly. Because you deserve it. We all deserve it."

My gaze falls to the leather portfolio across the table. She must be able to sense my doubt—or the fact that I want to throw it in the trash—because she adds, "Matchmaking is an imperfect science, but a very refined art. There's always a tenth dimension to all of this—you know, that spark. The unpredictable *click* that nobody can control or even plan for. I can't tell you if you'll have that with any of them. But I'm setting you up for a good shot at it."

My whole body gets hot and noisy as she talks about the unpredictable click. Because I know *exactly* what she's talking about. I force myself not to look at her though, because if I do, intuitive London will be able to read it all across my face.

And the truth is this: I have the unpredictable click with her. And not only is it unpredictable, it's inconvenient as hell.

CHAPTER TEN

DOM

Four days later, I'm back at a restaurant in downtown Cleveland on my first date organized by the woman trying to help me *create more joy*. I half expected her to instruct me to cup the breasts of all my potential matches to see which set sparked the most joy, like the creepiest Marie Kondo method on dating. But no—I'm just waiting for my busy professional-grade blind date, determined to keep my hands to myself.

I don't want to be here. Not even a little bit. Even the fantastic wine menu, which I've been turning over in my hands for five minutes, doesn't excite me. The woman on the docket tonight is named Julianne, and she's a brilliant redheaded lawyer who's got a dirty mouth and expensive tastes. At least, that's what her executive rundown stated in the portfolio.

All I can hope for at this point is that the unpredictable click happens with one of these six women, simply so that it can override the click that I have with London. Anything to allow me to stop fantasizing about London every waking—and sleeping—moment of my life would be great.

But I have no more planned meetings with her. From here on out, it's just sterile dates with women I'm not interested in, and work. Work, work, work, date, work. Not a hint of London for the near future, save email and the infrequent phone call.

This fact makes me restless. Aggravated, actually. Sad, if I'm being brutally honest. Having her on my schedule was calming, even though my main directives were to insult her work performance.

Part of me thinks that I should somehow invent an excuse to get back to weekly meetups. Maybe the gym night could become a Wednesday tradition, except now, I'd choose *back her up against the wall* instead of *pick a fight.* Hell, we could make some sort of Sushi Sunday thing. I'd gladly keep my laptop shut for a few hours on a Sunday if it meant London would be coming over to my place with food and those breezy, fading-freckles smiles.

People approaching the two-top jerk me out of my thoughts, and I look up to see the hostess coming my way with a strangely familiar redhead behind her. Julianne. Of course. The woman I know from three photos alone. I suppose this isn't technically a blind date. It's like a late-stage glaucoma date. London would love that one, but when could I tell her? I stand and offer my hand, but Julianne wraps me in a hug.

"There you are, Dr. Dom," she hisses into my ear, and when we pull away she grips the sides of my arms, looking me up and down like an aunt who hasn't seen her nephew in a decade. "London did *not* prepare me for this."

I clear my throat, loosening my tie as I ease back into my seat. "Didn't she send along my portfolio?"

"Yes, but daaaamn." Her gaze sweeps up and down my body outrageously, like she's appraising my naked body. "Hellooo, Tall, Dark, and Handsome."

I smooth down the front of my shirt, easing back into my seat. "It's nice to meet you Julianne."

"Call me Juli." She sounds a little breathless, gaze stuck to me as she plops into the seat across from me. "You seriously are single? What's wrong with you?"

I close my fist and cover my smile. I appreciate her bluntness, at least. "I work an insane amount. What's wrong with you?"

A long, gravelly laugh spills out of her, and she touches her chest with a hand. "Oooh, Dr. Daly. We are going to get along *very well*, aren't we?" She's got perfectly manicured, nude-colored nails. Busty as hell. Filling out her business-woman-chic suit in all the right places. She's attractive. I can admit it.

But she doesn't have freckles, and if she showed up naked in front of me I wouldn't bat an eye. At least she promises to be fun.

And as the date wears on, she *is* fun. She makes me laugh a few times. She's an adventurous eater. She has some crazy stories of her early years as a lawyer, including one that involves several geese and a judge with diarrhea.

But there's no click. Not even an echo of a click. By the time we wrap up our date, Julianne is hungry for more, and I'm just ready for home.

I bow out of continuing our date as gracefully as possible, and not so poorly that I close the door to a second date. We hug, and I send her off in her rideshare before heading back to my own car. It went well. It was a precise mix of sterile and functional. Like sliding on a fresh glove prior to surgery. Someone who could be a friend and would look good on my arm as a wife. I should be excited.

But the only thing I'm excited to do is follow up with London. I dig my phone out of my pocket and fire off a quick text.

DOM: Date #1 completed. Good work, matchmaker.

LONDON: Yeah?? Did it go well???

DOM: She's nice.

LONDON: "Nice" is all I get? God. Men are so hard to please.

I smirk, looking out the window as I start my car. London would be shocked if she knew how pleased I was with the matchmaker. Appalled, really.

DOM: She's everything I ever wanted in a wife of convenience. Is that better?

LONDON: Yeah, now we're talking. Though I'm slightly concerned you're ill.

DOM: Why?

LONDON: You complimented my work. I was expecting you to finally fire me.

DOM: Too much work to find a replacement.

LONDON: So should I set up a second date or did you handle that already?

DOM: I left that for you. Otherwise what am I paying you for?

I set my phone in the dash holder as I begin easing out of the parking lot. My entire body is tense, anticipating how she'll respond. Because this is gold-level teasing here.

LONDON: Your package does include date setting as well as hand holding and ass wiping.

A laugh bursts out of me. There we go. I knew London would be up to the snark task. I pause mid-reverse so that I can respond to her.

DOM: I pay good money for VIP services and I expect you to deliver.

LONDON: At your service, sir. Now please bend over.

A car horn honks, interrupting my banter. Shit. I need to focus on getting out of this parking lot. The agitated driver barely waits for me to exit my spot before he starts nudging in, and my phone goes dark as it registers the fact that I'm driving.

But London stays on my mind. All the way home. Up into my penthouse. And into the shower with me where I fist myself into a display of fireworks behind my eyelids, imagining that little black dress she wore the other night.

And maybe, somehow, London could tell that I was conjuring her in my memory. When I return to my phone, she's texted me again.

LONDON: So I'll get you down for date #2 with Juli. Still good to try out the other ladies on the menu?

DOM: Don't be a misogynist. Women aren't food.

DOM: But yes, I'll take some dessert.

LONDON: Saucy. Or should I say chocolate saucy?

DOM: You're the pastry chef here. You decide.

I walk naked through the penthouse, rubbing a towel over my wet hair as I think about London. Really, what I'd like to suggest is that she scrub the schedule of everyone else and just put *herself* on the menu. The one drink I had at dinner is still sizzling inside me. I double back for my phone, half-decided to send her the text and suggest it.

I pick up the phone, rereading our thread. And then I begin typing out my response: *I have one request. The best desserts are made by the chef herself. Give me one night with you.*

My finger hovers over Send.

But at the last second I hold down Delete. And then I rewrite: *Though I'm open to chocolate sauce all over the pastry chef. If that's what you're thinking.*

I tut. No. Then I redo the message: *Chocolate sauce on you???*

Delete. Delete. Delete. That's creepier than I want, and hell, I'm not even certain this attraction is mutual. Worst case scenario, I'm just one more guy London has to beat off with a let-down text because he got blinded by her freckles and easy laughter.

I toss my phone onto the couch and head back into the bathroom. I'm not touching my phone again until I'm totally sober. And even then, I should never cross that line with London via text.

But in person?

My forearms prickle as the idea zips through me, like fresh drugs in the bloodstream.

Tonight might be a bad time to push the envelope. But if I know myself, I won't be able to avoid doing it.

And it needs to happen sooner rather than later.

CHAPTER ELEVEN

A week melts away in a jumble of new clients, cocktail hours with new friends, and the most minimal checking in with Dom about the status of his new girlfriends.

All in all, my life in Cleveland is *great*. Finally, both my apartment *and* my office are in perfect, organized states. All of my paperclips have one centralized location. I have a routine that includes a quaint coffee shop in my neighborhood with baristas who remember my favorite froufy drink. I know which grocery store I prefer, because I've tried them all, and dammit, I just prefer the aesthetics of the Kroger two blocks over.

I reach for my thermos of coffee at my desk and take a sip. It's damn near empty, and shockingly cold, which means I'm nearing the end of my workday. The clock surprises me: it's already five p.m. And this has been the way of things recently. Time escapes me because I get so involved in work. Two new clients signed on this week: one strictly matchmaking, the other a flagging graphic artist who needs a brand makeover.

And thank God they came when they did. I need the distraction. All of the dates that Dominic has been going on are eating away at me. And yes, I know, I'm the matchmaker who set them up for him. But I can't bear imagining how sparkling the connection must have been with Julianne, or how turned on he was when he met Riley and her *amazing* booty, or whether or not he and Geri joked about whether their future kids would have his black hair or her blonde tresses.

His text reviews of each date show promise for a love connection, even though he himself claims to not want one. I'm so sure of my subversive tactics, I'm willing to bet that he's already halfway falling in love with one of them.

I need more time away from him—that's all. More time, and I need to reactivate my Blaze profile. Because while I can be counted on for matching others successfully, I'm the last to benefit from my own services—cobbler's kid, after all.

My phone rings, and I swipe to answer without really registering the number. Thoughts about Dom have superseded all else, even my never-ending quest to avoid spam calls. And then a too-familiar bass rumbles through the line.

"London, please don't hang up."

I've permanently filed this voice in my 'Should Not Hear Again' list of human voices, and I jerk the phone away from my ear to double check the caller ID. It's Carl. Even though I deleted his number six months ago, it's 100% Fucking Carl.

"Why are you calling?"

"I miss you."

Carl was a mistake—I practically knew it from the beginning—but knowing about mistakes doesn't prevent one from making them. No, sometimes seeing a red flag just means you charge full steam ahead. Like the bullfights of Spain, Carl waved a whole quilt made of red flags, and I was helpless to resist. The only thing that allowed me to save my life from his metaphorical bullfighter antics was the fact that he sold—and whored—me out.

And I will never forgive him for that.

"Fuck you."

"London, please hear me out."

"I have no reason or desire to," I spit, and then I hang up. My heart is pounding, and it takes me a few moments to synthesize what just happened. Carl called me? Yes. Carl wants me back? Seemingly yes. Carl is ignorantly unaware of how baffling and disgusting this change of heart appears to be? Definitely yes.

The more I think about it, the more outrageous this becomes. If he were ever going to be considered a decent boyfriend or mildly engaged lover, then he would have never suggested I "take one for the team" and sleep with our largest client to retain his account. That was the last line he should have crossed, but sadly, he crossed a whole highway of lines beforehand that I overlooked or made excuses for.

Worse yet, once I blew the whistle on his unapologetically awful offer, he had the gall to blacklist me within the company and within the community at large. *Gossip, whore, liar.* All attached to my image in Columbus now. And if that isn't professional homicide, I don't know what is.

He can rot in Columbus without me.

It takes me a while to calm down from the unexpected call. I imagine fifty-five different things I *should* have said, but I must find solace in the fact that my "fuck you" was flawless. Biting, angry, and concise. I hope it rings through his head so shrill and loud that it shatters all the mirrors in his house.

I wrap up work for the day later than normal due to the un-expected derailment, and at six-thirty I'm just finishing running through my inbox. Once I lock up down here, I'll slink upstairs to my apartment, change into comfy pants, and lie on my couch until further notice, like all successful late twenty-somethings in the city.

Really, I'm itching to grab a drink after that unwelcomed intrusion from the past, but I'm not sure who I would call to invite out. Hazel is the only one who would get it, and this isn't enough of an emergency to ask her to drive a full hour.

The bells on my front door jingle suddenly, and I snap my gaze toward the door.

I gasp without meaning to when I see who has stepped inside my office. The Perfect 10 Asshole himself.

"Dom?" I ask, my mouth flapping as I struggle to form a second part to my question. All I can think is, *You're not supposed to be here. We must carefully arrange when and where we see each other or else I will unravel.*

Clearly, he doesn't feel the same dangerous desire thrumming through him, because he is fine with showing up unannounced. He can handle it. Because he's a normal person who isn't fending off these thoughts like a tourist getting swarmed by hungry goats at the petting zoo.

"Correct." He's got on a long, sophisticated coat, the type that men wear to the horse races or to 1930's-themed outings. Paired with his sharp jawline and the mahogany waves on top of his head, I'm a goner. The start of a shit-eating grin is on his face, and for a moment I wonder if I've overlooked something that we had previously set up.

"Aren't you supposed to be on a date?" My voice comes out squeakier than normal. Hopefully he doesn't realize it's related to the sudden moisture in my panties.

"She cancelled." He takes slow, purposeful steps toward my desk, and I white-knuckle my mouse, half tempted to roll up a nearby magazine and ward him off, the way one might scold an encroaching dog. *Don't step any closer or else I'll jump your bones!*

"Did you stop by to complain?"

A heartbreaking smile crosses his face, and for a moment, hesitation flashes across his face. "No. I thought we could go out instead."

It takes me almost a full minute for his meaning to penetrate the thick fog of desire. He can't mean *go out*. There must be some other meaning attached to this phrase that I'm forgetting due to the temporary ovary insanity.

"Like..."

"Like I'll take you out on the date instead."

Heat zips through me, and I'm fairly sure my entire body turns the color of a refrigerated hot dog. "I, uh..." I begin clicking through screens on my computer, though I'm not seeing a damn thing that I'm doing. "I don't think that's a good idea."

"Why not?"

"I don't date clients," I blurt, crossing my arms tightly across my chest before I do anything stupid on my computer, like delete the entire next week's schedule.

"Fine. Let's just grab a drink."

I draw a shaky breath, searching for any other excuse in my arsenal as to why I shouldn't do this. I'm not prepared. I didn't rehearse my lines in the mirror. My brain has short circuited. "I don't think—"

"Let's go over other matches and call it a work meeting." He seems unfazed by my resistance, jerking his head toward the door. "I blocked out this time on a Friday evening, and I don't want to go home. Maybe you could humor an overworked doctor?"

All the air in me goes out in one final hiss. I deflate into my chair and reach for my phone. He's talked me into it. It's not my fault. Besides, he's right—this won't be personal. It's *for work*. Maybe this will soothe the professional taskmaster inside my soul. And god, I'm ready for the distraction after that unwelcome intrusion from Carl.

"Well, I guess that sounds all right," I say in a quiet voice, pushing onto wobbly knees. I fumble with my phone, unsure what I'm supposed to do now. Do I just walk out the door with him? Go upstairs and change into sexier underwear? What about brushing my teeth in case we tongue kiss?

"Fair warning, though—I want a burger and loud music," he warns.

The last remnants of my resistance dissolve. It sounds like the *perfect* way to end this day. Even better than lying on my couch in comfy clothes and stewing over all the other things I could have said to Carl. "I think I can handle that."

"Good. You ready to go now or do you need some time? I can wait."

The idea of Dom hanging around in my office, watching me, *waiting for me*, sends anxiety snaking through me. The sooner we can get into the open air, the better. Then the intensity of his gaze won't feel so commanding.

"No, no, Dom, let me just drop everything the second you show up and do your bidding," I say, heading for the spindly coat rack near my desk. I slide my favorite black leather jacket on, moving my hair to one side. "After all, that's what you pay me for, right? To open my mouth when you say 'drink'?"

"I thought it was part of the VIP package," he returns, tipping his head to one side. His gaze makes a slow trek up and down my body, and every inch of me goes hot and prickly under his attention.

"I can feel you clinically assessing me again," I blurt, trying to make it lighthearted when it is so, so serious.

"I was just noticing your shoes," he said, his gaze stuck at my feet. I'm wearing blue suede heels today. Impractical, especially in a rainstorm. Also leaves a lot of doors open for Elvis jokes. But luckily it's a dry October evening, and apparently, Dom's not an Elvis fan. "They're very blue."

"Good observation, Doctor." I grab my purse, slinging it over my shoulder. As we head toward the door, I turn off lights and the

Himalayan salt lamp I set up next to one of the smaller vases on my feature wall. "Anything else you've noticed that you'd like to share?"

A curious smile tugs at his lips as I lead the way out of the office and onto the sidewalk. He's not saying something. I can feel it. The crisp, loamy air fills my senses, a sudden breeze moving my hair. The lock clicks into place and finally I can't bear the heavy silence between us.

"Something you want to say?" I ask, tucking the key in my purse.

"I didn't say a word."

"No, but you wanted to."

We start walking south, into the heart of the Larchmere neighborhood where all the best burger joints and bars are buried. He glances down at me, then squints out at the horizon.

"Not all observations are meant to be shared."

"Oh, please."

"Maybe once I have a few drinks in me."

Excitement tingles inside me. "So this is something for my patient folder then?"

He wets his bottom lip, and I almost eat pavement. He's not allowed to look this sexy while I'm perched on a metal spike. "Exactly."

I shove my hands in my pockets and ball my fists. What are the chances that I can cast aside my professional boundaries for the evening? Is there *any* way I can hit on this man in good conscience? I swear he was flirting with me the last time we were out, but it didn't last long, and let's be real—the man is probably a born flirt. With eyes that color, he could deliver news about my uncle's heart attack and I might still wonder if he was coming on to me. Just because that's how bad I want it.

We stroll down the sidewalk, and I pause once to fire off my last work-related message of the evening: a check-in text to Tara that says, *"Sorry to hear you had to reschedule! Let me know what works for you next week!"*. Workday: officially over. Except I have no idea what to label this next portion of my evening. A much-needed fun night out? Professional suicide? Time will tell.

As we walk, we contemplate different burger joints. I haven't been to most places and neither has he, so we make a mutual decision to try something outside of our comfort zones. That's how we settle on Zimbo's.

It's the love child of a dive bar and a gourmet restaurant. The plates we see coming out of the kitchen are Instagram-ready and elaborately arranged, yet the tables wobble and the chairs look like they haven't been replaced since the eighties. We settle into a little two-top in the back corner, by an antique jukebox with plenty of bizarre and kitschy things hanging on the wall: a doll's head, a sign telling us to "Eat, Tip, and Get Out," and seventies-style renditions of downtown Cleveland. When the menus arrive, Dom leans forward with a mischievous glint.

"I'll order for you if you order for me."

"I can't trust you. You're a doctor. You'll get me a salad."

He laughs, a dimple flashing. "I wouldn't dream of it. I know you're not the salad type."

I tip my head. "Are you trying to say something, doctor?"

"What would I be trying to say?"

"I don't know. Maybe I look to you like a girl who could stand to eat a few more salads."

He wets his bottom lip again, and the intensity of his gaze makes my throat dry. "My professional opinion is that you should continue whatever regimen you're currently on."

Satisfaction prickles through me. I can't stop poking at him. It's the only way I can feed this hunger inside me while staying within professional boundaries. "Good."

"My personal opinion is quite different," he adds, just as the server slides up with an overly-friendly introduction and list of beers. I'm stuck staring at Dom though, who just sends me an evil smile. He is withholding *so many things* from me. I can't stand it.

And he knows it.

When the server asks us if we're ready to order, Dom emphatically agrees.

"She'll be having the Zimbo burger," he says, jerking his chin at me. "With whatever your hoppiest IPA is."

My mouth parts. It sounds delicious, but it's way heavier than what I'd normally order.

"He'll take the Deluxe Zimbo Pile Burger." I hand my menu over to the server. That burger was the tallest thing I'd ever seen, with maybe three entire patties on it. "And a margarita."

When the server leaves with our menus, I send him a haughty look.

"Not heart healthy tonight," I tell him.

"It's okay. I'm due for my cardiac arrest risk to increase."

"Do you like tequila?"

"It doesn't matter—you already ordered the margarita." He leans back in his seat, his biceps straining the light gray sleeves of his button-up. His horse race coat is slung over the back of the chair beside him. But somehow, the sexiest part of what's in front of me is that quiet submission. Handing me the reins of his experience. That trust in my decision, even if it's just over dinner and drinks. Like the other night, when he wordlessly carried my coat for me. Jesus, to my parched and starving heart, it might as well have been a marriage proposal.

"Oh, I forgot something." His long, knobby fingers find the top buttons of his shirt. He undoes the first two, watching me with mischief written across his face.

And that's when it hits me. All the pieces click into place.

Dr. Dom has his sights set on me tonight.

And IPA help me, I won't be able to resist much longer.

CHAPTER TWELVE

DOM

We manage to put away an impressive amount of hamburger that evening. It's a sloppy, delicious, giggle-filled dinner. Each time London's tomato slides off her sandwich, it sets her off. And god damn, I could watch this woman giggle for the rest of my life.

I've never been able to have barbecue sauce smeared all over my mouth while feeling like the woman in front of me actually *enjoyed* the BBQ smear. Not until tonight. Her eyes sparkle every time I take a bite of my burger, and by the time the server takes away our plates, my belly is full and my heart is fuller.

This is the feeling that pushed me to orchestrate tonight's outing. It's because this woman possesses something special that brings so many parts of me back to life. I don't think about work once during dinner—not even when we tease about clinical assessments. She is like warm silk on my cheek, a breath of fresh air after holding it in for years.

And after dinner, I'm not ready to let this evening end.

"I'm paying," I announce when the server returns with our bill. I pass her a one hundred-dollar bill before London can even protest. "I invited you, remember?"

"Tara is gonna be upset she missed this," London muses. Tara, the third woman of the six that are on my match portfolio. Tara, the woman I have zero interest in meeting.

"She'll survive. Now what do you say we find some shitty bar with dollar draft specials?"

Her grin spreads ear to ear. "I'm in the mood for that. But it needs to be bottom of the barrel beer."

"Right. Total machine piss."

"This meal was so good, we really need to balance things out," she says.

"Yes. Preferably our hangover will begin while still at the bar."

She snort-laughs just as the server returns with my change. I leave everything on the table for her as tip, plus an additional twenty-dollar bill, and we stand to put on our coats. Outside, the evening has gone dark and cold. London hugs herself, teeth immediately chattering.

"You okay to walk?" I sling my arm around her shoulders without even thinking. It's an impulse I couldn't resist. "You look cold."

"I think I can make it," she says.

"I can get the car if you want."

"No, I'm not that much of a wuss." She nudges me as we fall into an easy pace. I keep her nestled into my side. I don't want to let her go, and when we choose a bar a couple blocks later, I'm disappointed. I'd carry her in my arms for another mile if it meant I got to hold her against me. My entire body is taut with anticipation. Waiting for the next window of opportunity to get a first-hand whiff of that floral nectar she wears.

My gaze drops to her impossibly sexy blue suede heels as we approach the door. Music is already leaking out, fast-paced rock music, and she tosses an easygoing smile over her shoulder as we step inside.

The place is packed and humid, with lots of groups standing around and couples cluttering the high tables interspersed around the place. The band is tucked into the back of the bar, a three-piece ensemble—electric guitar, drums, and keyboard—of twenty-somethings with long hair and questionable gender identities.

I grab London's hand as she starts to weave away from me. I want her close. Not because I think I'll lose her. Because I found my fucking window.

Surprise shines on her face as she looks back over her shoulder at me. I slide my fingers up her arm, before bringing my hand to rest on her hip. "Stay close. I don't want to lose you."

Her sea-foam gaze searches my face. "I won't lose you."

I clench my jaw, telling myself not to kiss her while she's tipping her head back to look at me, asking me all sorts of questions in the heavy silence between us. God, she's beautiful. I squeeze the top of her hip, like reminding her to move.

She stumbles into motion. I keep my hand securely on her hip as she leads us through the crowd. When my hand slips off her, she reaches behind, searching it out again. Her cool fingers lace through mine, and I watch the back of her head, studying the sparkling blonde tresses, willing her to turn around so I can give her the kiss that's dangling off my lips for her.

But she doesn't turn around. When we reach the bar, I let go of her hand and fill the space beside her. She doesn't look at me, just gets to work making eye contact with a bartender. The drummer is the only thing I can hear over the noise of my barely bridled lust. *Thum thum thum.* The singer's voice is a distant androgynous wail.

The only thing I can see is London. The heat of her hip against my hand practically left char marks. The bartender arrives and she leans forward over the bar to shout her order, offering me the tempting curve of her ass in that pencil skirt. I ogle freely. I'm way past the point where I can do the right thing.

"I'll pay," I tell her when she's standing straight again. "Just leave the tab open."

"Too late," she says, batting her eye lashes. "I got one round in on ya."

One round, which means she's leaving the door open for more. A moment later, a pitcher of beer arrives with two plastic cups. She scoops it all up and sends me a meaningful look.

"Can I trust you not to get lost in the crowd?"

"I'll follow the blue suede heels," I promise her. She offers a small smile and begins weaving through the crowd. I follow the heels as much as her hourglass figure. My cock is trapped beneath my belt buckle, and I'm relieved when she leads us to a round bar table with two high stools facing the band. She sets everything down, and I slip my coat off, draping it over the stool before I sit down.

"Drink one cup," she commands, slipping out of her leather jacket, "and then I want to hear one confession."

"One confession? Of what?"

"Of whatever you choose." She pours two healthy plastic cups of grade A machine piss. "It's your call." She lifts her cup to toast, and our drinks touch. She's got a mischievous sparkle in her eye that I could watch for damn near the rest of my life, and if being with her meant tapping into feeling like this with any regularity, I'd marry her on the spot. That would solve my problem with the foundation *and* give me the added bonus of spending the rest of my life with a witty and sparkling bombshell.

Thoughts of the upcoming interview with the foundation make my chest tighten. I take a healthy gulp of my beer, focusing on the band as they wrap up their song with a flourish of cymbals. The crowd around us erupts into cheers.

When she nudges me, I know I've taken too long to respond to her question. "Come on, Dr. Dom."

"What is this, truth or dare?"

A brow lifts. "Maybe it is."

"Then I choose a dare."

She scoffs. "Fine. I dare you to unbutton another button on your shirt."

I do exactly as she asks, and her gaze homes in on the newly exposed sliver of chest. It seems London likes what she sees. And god, I love giving it to her.

"That was too easy," I say. "And now it's my turn. Truth or dare?"

She narrows her eyes. "Truth."

I search her face as I struggle to think of the best question. There are so may inappropriate things I want to ask her. At the top of my list: *would you come home with me?* "Have you ever slept with a client before?"

Her cheeks go pink. I can't tell if that's damning or sheer embarrassment. "Never. And I never will."

Thud. That's the sound of the door slamming shut between us. Except I'm pretty sure I know how to pick the lock.

"Never say never," I tell her, tipping more beer into my mouth.

"If I want to remain relevant in this industry, it has to be never. Now you. Truth or dare?"

"Truth."

She cocks her head just as the band flares up with a new song. A throaty, rocking rendition of "Back to Black," à la Amy Winehouse. Suddenly, the lead singer is wearing a beehive wig. "Do you really want the position on the board?"

Her question is a good-natured spear lobbed into the middle of my chest. My gaze falls to the clear amber beer in my cup, and I swirl it a few times. What do I have to lose by lying to her? For once, it feels okay to open up a little. Loosen the strings that are bound around my heart all day, every day.

"No." I take another swig of beer, the truth bubbling up faster than I can control. "They're a prestigious bunch of status whores. But I'll make history if I get it. And that's what I'm going for."

She watches me for a moment, resting her chin in her palm. "What would you rather be doing?"

"No skipping. It's my turn." I've said too much, so I need to move along quickly. "Truth or dare?"

She holds her palms up. "Sorry. Dare."

"Dance with me."

Her face flushes, eyes rounding like she can't believe her ears. "What did you say?"

"Let's dance." I stand up, offering a hand so she doesn't mistake my intent. Couples are hanging off of each other around the bar, including a small cluster of people right in front of the band. We don't have to go far. I just need to touch her, in any way possible.

"We only said goodbye with words. I died a hundred times," the singer croons.

Her brows draw together as she sets her cup down and slides off the stool. She places her small hand in mine hesitantly, and I bring her against me until our chests touch.

"Don't worry; I'm not going to do any ballroom dancing," I murmur into her hair above her ear. Her sweet floral scent fills my senses, and for a moment, my entire body is buzzing and hot, anticipating more. I push my palm over the small of her back, and she melts into me, our fingers lacing together as we start a slow back and forth dance.

"I definitely wouldn't have pegged you for a ballroom dancer."

"Didn't Gray tell you? Our mom signed all us boys up for dance lessons when we were younger." The feminine curves of her body pressed to mine send blood rushing to my groin. I push my hand a little lower, needing to eliminate any vestige of space between us. She tips her head back to look at me.

"What was your specialty?"

I grin. "Polka."

She snorts. "Seriously?"

"I did a polka competition one year. I was ten. She and my grandma Ethel wanted me to."

"Did you win?"

I jerk my head. "No. I came in second. My dad was pissed. Second place in the Daly family just means first loser. Grayson teased me about it for a year after."

"So you two have never gotten along."

"We always got along by not getting along, if that makes sense. Competing was still our way of bonding." I pause, more words burbling up inside me. I shouldn't admit this stuff, but it feels good to get it out. "And it's better than resentment and silence, which is what we have now."

"You can change that, you know."

I'm getting lost in her pretty green gaze. Because it's too easy to fall headfirst with her. Because I'd do damn near anything she asked of me at this point.

"So you never answered my question," she says suddenly, the heat of her breath hitting my chin. Our lips are so close, I could lean forward and coax a kiss from her. My heart is pounding, every inch of my body alert and wanting her.

"What question?"

"What would you be doing now if you could?"

My gaze drifts past her as the music crescendos in the bar. "*And I'llll go back to...*"

"I'd open a clinic in Bayshore," I blurt. I've never said these words out loud, but it's a thought that has returned to me more times than I care to mention. "Just a part-time thing, maybe."

A secret grin tugs at her lips. "Aww. You miss home."

"It's an underserved population in Ohio," I say, but when I catch her narrowed eyes, I add, "And maybe I miss Bayshore a little."

"Sometimes the penthouse just doesn't cut it, huh?"

The music stops, and cheers swell around us. She had no idea how right she is. My penthouse is a sad excuse for a home. But with no one to fill it with—no warmth or traditions or fucking *time*—there's not many other options.

We slow our movements, but I don't let go of her, and she doesn't step away. I release my fingers from hers and wrap my other arm around her, unable to stop myself. A breathy sigh escapes her, and she clutches the backs of my arms.

The penthouse doesn't cut it. Just like not having London in my arms doesn't cut it anymore.

"I'm thirsty," she says suddenly, slipping out of my arms. Cold air replaces her, leaving me feeling empty somehow. She slides onto the stool, sending me an apologetic smile before she tips some beer into her mouth.

I clear my throat, sitting at her side. I'm not wrong about what I'm feeling between us. I can see it in the guilty glances. The way she plays with her necklace. Her flushed neck and the exact number of times she drags her teeth over her bottom lip.

She wants more, but she won't let herself have it.

Except I plan to show her there's nothing she needs more.

CHAPTER THIRTEEN

LONDON

"Last call!"

I clutch Dom's arm as the announcement shudders through me. I show him wide eyes. "Are they serious?"

We finished our pitcher a half hour ago, but we've just been talking and laughing ever since. I thought it was only midnight. Dear God, please tell me I'm not closing down the bar on a work night. Not when I have the feeble, hangover-prone constitution of someone on the cusp of thirty. I fumble to find my phone.

"I don't think they'd pull our leg on this one." He twists behind him to look at the bar. "Last call is no laughing matter."

"Look!" I show him the screen, which blatantly displays one thirty a.m. "I haven't been out this late since college."

He rubs his face. "Do we really have to go?"

The sentiment makes me grin, and I just know that it's the silly kind. The type of smile that I've been delivering to this man *all night* as we alternated between hilarious stories about our respective childhoods and intense thoughts about adulthood.

"We aren't in our early twenties anymore, buckaroo," I remind him, slipping my jacket on. The clamor of conversation reaches new heights as the drunk crowd around us shuffles to the bar for their last orders. "I already know I'm going to have a hangover tomorrow."

He smirks as he comes to standing, sliding his coat on. "Weak."

I shove his shoulder before grabbing my purse. "Like you won't?"

"No. Because I'm going to drink a gallon of water before I go to bed. And so will you."

I snort, because it almost sounds like he means that we'll be going to bed *together*. And lord above, that is exactly what I want. I drank enough beer to effectively ruin my morning tomorrow, which is just the lubrication I need to ruin my professional boundaries as well.

"How will you know if I drink a gallon of water?" I zip up my jacket, sending him a haughty look.

"I'll make sure you do," Dom says, placing his hands on my shoulders and tuning me around so I'm facing the door. "Now let's go."

We're dancing a very fine line between temptation and propriety. I know that he wants more. The only thing holding me back is my final shred of professional dignity, which I effectively dissolved with the liter of beer I consumed.

It doesn't take long for his palms to travel down the lengths of my arms and settle onto the tops of my hips. My core clenches with need, yet another gut punch of lust pummeling through me.

Sleeping with a client actively seeking a wife is not just stupid, it's confusing. He's supposed to be initiating relationships with the women in his portfolio, not starting the process out by having an affair with the matchmaker. This is already a situation destined for Jerry Springer.

But if we keep it to a one-and-done slip?

Then maybe that'll lessen the guilt load—and up our chances of being picked for Springer. After all, I just need to get this out of my system. Dr. Dom has been the looming, unattainable cardiac king for too many weeks. If I dip my toe in the water, I'll feel refreshed and ready to forget all about him.

We burst through the front door of the bar and into the crisp night air. Dom immediately scoops me against him, his arm hugging my shoulders.

"Are you cold?" he asks.

"Not with you wrapped around me like a big bear," I tease.

He grunts. "Little London needs a bear."

"Sounds like an inappropriate children's rhyme," I crack.

"Little London needs a bear," Dom begins. "A big man to carry her everywhere."

"Keep going."

"She wooed the men with long blonde hair, and always knew the best heels to wear."

My grin spreads ear to ear. "Am I wooing you?"

He grunts again, tightening his grip around me. "You have no idea."

My heels click on the sidewalk as we hang a right at the next block to head toward my office. My heart is pounding as I anticipate the next ten minutes. How I'll maneuver him into my bed without feeling like a matchmaking failure. Whether or not I'll be able to look him in the face ever again.

"Is this how you plan to seduce your matches?" I ask him, my cheeks heating up.

He scoffs. "I can't answer that. It's been so long since I've tried to seduce anyone. I don't even know how anymore."

The space between my ears grows raucous. Every cell in my body is urging me to hop onto this train of thought and ride it all the way into the station. "Oh, come on."

He's quiet for a moment, and the only sounds between us are our feet scuffing along the sidewalk and our soft breaths. "Why don't you tell me if I know how?"

"What," I ask, "like, give you feedback?"

"How about I run through my game plan, and you tell me if you're seduced or not," he says, like the diabolical sex god that he is. "But only if you want to."

Yes. I want it so much. "Yeah, let's hear it." I gulp, the words escaping before I can convince myself otherwise. "Seduce me, Dr. Dom."

He wets his bottom lip, glancing toward either end of the side-walk. We're on the same block as my home, just four doors down from my office. Dom steps toward me, steering me toward the brick wall of the nearest building. He backs me up until my jacket is pressed against the gritty wall, his palms pressed to either side of me.

"My first step," he says, a sexy growl edging his voice, "would be to take you out to a brand-new burger joint and order you the sloppiest fucking thing on the menu."

I bite my bottom lip, holding in a laugh.

"And then I'd take you to a bar so we could drink and have a good time and listen to a local band butcher our favorite songs."

The laughter is fading. Because hang on. This means that Dr. Dom wanted to seduce *me*. From before he even showed up to my office. "Go on."

"While I was there, I'd somehow convince you to dance with me and pray to God that you couldn't feel how hard my cock was as we swayed back and forth to a surprisingly good Amy Winehouse mix."

My eyes widen at the dirty word rolling off his lips. This is already so much better than I anticipated, and we haven't even kissed. I might not survive foreplay with this man if we ever make it to my bed. He was already too hot to begin with, but now he's revealing a dirty mouth that might just unravel me.

"Once I talk myself down from making out with you in the middle of this bar full of college students and young professionals, I'd walk you home and push you up against a brick wall just before we make it back to your office. I'd tell you all about the dirty fucking thoughts I've been having about you for the past three weeks. How many times I've imagined kissing you. All the different sexy dreams I've had starring your perfect ass bent over my knee."

He clears his throat, opening up his coat suddenly and pulling me into him. A gasp escapes me as he closes his coat around me, inviting me into his radiator-grade warmth inside. His arms close around me, forming a seal between our bodies.

And that's when I feel it. The hardness pressed into my lower belly. That thick ridge that I've dreamt about the same way he's dreamt of my ass. My knees go weak, but he doesn't let me fall.

"I've imagined fucking you in every position possible," he whispers into my ear, his breath hot and provocative against my head. "I would eat your pussy until you turned to Jell-O. And fuck, London, I want you to forget for one night that I'm your client. I know you want this as bad as I do. Listen to yourself."

God, he's right. I'm panting like an animal in heat. He grips my chin between thumb and forefinger, tilting my head back.

"And then, just to make sure the seduction is complete," he whispers, his lips so close to mine it actually makes me angry, "I'd kiss you until your lips go numb."

I suck in a breath just before he bridges the infinitesimal distance remaining between our mouths. His rough kiss claims my mouth, all his restrained hunger and passion and lust leaking out of him and into me. I push onto my tiptoes, needing more of him, needing everything he has to offer.

Because he's right. It's beyond decided. I'm erasing the professional line for one night.

Tonight.

His lips are softer, the kisses needier and hotter, than I could have ever fucking imagined. I wrap my arms around his neck as one kiss bleeds into a second. A second bleeds into a million. We are making out hot and heavy on the sidewalk, in plain sight, and I can't force myself to care. Not even when a moan bleeds out of me and into the night.

His tongue pushes into my mouth, and I wilt against him, fisting the front of his gray button-up. My fingers drift toward the exposed patch of hair that has been teasing me all night, slipping beneath the starchy fabric until I find the heat of his skin. A chill races through me, and a triumphant sense of relief fills my limbs. *Finally.*

Because for how wrong this is, it feels too right.

We kiss until he finally breaks for air, looking up and down the sidewalk. When he assesses me next, his eyes are hooded, lust shining in his icy blue gaze.

"So," he says, his voice husky, "are you seduced?"

I shake my head vigorously, my lips buzzing. "Unclear still. I think you need to expound a bit more on what would happen after the kiss."

A shit-eating grin stretches from ear to ear. His big palms make a hot trek down the small of my back and over the curve of my ass. Something primal slides over his face as he grabs my ass cheeks in each hand.

"Once I kissed you until your lips go numb, I'd take you upstairs to your cute little apartment."

"How do you know it's cute?"

He smirks. "Because it's your apartment, so it can only be cute."

His comment makes warmth trickle through me, though I'm not sure why. "Smart man. Go on."

"And once we get upstairs, then I'd lay you out on the nearest flat surface. Doesn't matter what it is. Kitchen countertop works just as well as a bed. And I'd start taking every piece of clothing off your gorgeous body."

My vision goes cloudy for a moment as he gives my ass another healthy squeeze.

"And then," he continues, "I'd kiss every inch of you. Starting with the tips of your perfect breasts, all the way down over your belly, until my lips found your dripping…juicy…pussy."

My eyes flutter shut, and I wilt again. It's too much. I can't take it. I want him so badly that my brain is dissolving. I'll have to donate my sexually crippled body to science, so they can study the ways in which my Dom-inspired libido caused my demise. His arms go tight around me.

"I'd kiss your clit until you come. Then I'd fuck you with my tongue until you come a second time. And then I'd ease myself inside you so slowly that you come a third time before I'd even buried myself inside of you."

I gasp without meaning to, my eyes shooting open. Dom is watching me with the satisfaction of an expert seducer who knows that he's not only hit his mark, he's reduced his target to a willing puddle of goo.

"Now tell me, London," he says, his deep voice scraping through me, "are you seduced?"

"Oh god," I pant, squeezing my thighs together. I don't even know if I have it in me to lie. "I—"

"What if I were to slip my hand underneath this skirt," he growls, his fingertips trailing up the side of my hip, "and push a finger beneath your panties? What would I find?"

I swallow hard, hardly able to form thoughts anymore, much less words. My panties are a sopping mess, and I need this man more than I've needed anything else in my entire life.

"London," he prompts, when I've taken too long.

"You would find," I force out, my voice husky and foreign to my own ears, "the wettest, most willing, most seduced vagina of your medical career."

A laugh escapes him, and he looks so boyish and joyful in that moment that I think I'm not just horny anymore, I'm actually in love. He grabs my hand and pulls me into a quick walk beside him.

"Do you have your key?"

"Of course I do." I pat the front of my body, forgetting where I put my purse. Where my keys are stored. What my fucking name is.

"Get it out. Because I can't wait another second to get you laid out and screaming my name."

Heat shudders down my spine. Like hearing *that* is supposed to help me think clearly.

Dom smiles over his shoulder at me, equal parts mischievous and tender. The type of lusty look that washes over a woman and makes every inch of her feel alive and desired.

This is the sort of thing I could get used to.

Except I could never get used to it with Dom.

Because this attraction we're diving into can only last for tonight.

CHAPTER FOURTEEN

LONDON

I lead Dom through my dark office and toward the back hallway like we're thieves heading for the getaway car. Our footsteps clang up the back steps to my apartment. Once I push past my heavy front door, Dom is all over me. He cups my face in his big, warm hands, his lips gliding over mine like it's been years apart from me instead of minutes.

We bump and thud our way down the hallway, me halfway guiding him through my apartment, halfway blind and useless from the mind-numbing kisses. I should give him a tour, but how can I concentrate on anything while he's got his mouth against mine? When there's a pause, I manage to say, "Here."

He breaks apart long enough to smirk. "Yes. We're here." He looks around, nods, and adds, "Yeah, this is totally cute."

I'm glad he notices. I put effort into my new home. But now's not the time to talk about my interior decorating choices or the extra fluffy rug I just couldn't say no to at Target. I tug at the lapel of his coat, urging his mouth back toward mine. He gladly resumes kissing me, shrugging his coat off at the same time. Once the heavy wool crumples to the floor, he begins easing me out of my own jacket, without missing even one French kiss.

And lord, how I needed this. The strong, measured movements of a man rocked mindless with desire for me. How long has it been since I've felt this? I can't even remember. Possibly never, if I'm being honest.

Dom has desire written all over him. In his quiet push to speed things along, in the growls that escape him as he tugs at my bottom lip with his teeth. And damn, it feels good to relish this sizzling attraction for a night. A woman *should* explore a connection like this at least once in her lifetime.

I'm full of rationalizations now that it's happening. Because there's no way in hell I'm letting this stop.

Dom peels my coat off and drops it to the floor. He breaks for air, looking around long enough to set his sights on something. "Here we go."

He hoists me then, slinging me over his shoulder like I'm a rag doll. I giggle, kicking my feet. His hot palm glides over my ass and down my skirt until his fingertips scorch over my bare calf. He removes one heel—it drops to the floor with a *thud*—and the other. He sets me down on my square black dining room table, and the evil glint in his eye tells me exactly what comes next.

"Nearest flat surface?"

"Mm-hmm." His eyes are hooded as he unzips my skirt and starts easing it over my hips.

"You know, my bed is right over there."

"We'll get there. Don't worry."

Every inch of my body is tight and expectant as he tugs the skirt over my ankles. His gaze lands on my sheer black panties, nearly setting fire to the fabric. And then he presses his lips to the inside of my knee. Coaxing my legs wider, seeking a path up the inside of my thigh. My fingernails curl against the table, my lower belly taut as his head creeps closer to my pussy. The barely-there scruff of his face stubbles against the sensitive flesh of my inner thigh. When he reaches the seam of my groin, his breath coming out hot against the crotch of my panties, I'm a fucking mess. And he hasn't even properly touched me yet.

"Dom," I whisper, my voice hoarse.

"London." He drags his teeth over the crotch of my panties, which have to be embarrassingly damp. Like, just-throw-them-in-the-trash-already soaked. My legs are trembling. If he breathes right against me, I might come.

"Do you want me to keep going?" he asks, his voice like rough velvet. He nuzzles my inner thigh, which makes my entire body jolt.

"Oh, God, yes," I moan, firming my palms against the table. He grips me by the hips, jerking me closer to the edge of the dining room table. My knees bend, heels dug into the edge of the table. With the way he's crouched in front of me, we look like he's doing a back alley gynecological exam. A laugh rockets out of me, and he sends me a quizzical look as he hooks his fingers under my panties.

"Miss London. What is so funny?"

"This is like, getting back to your first love, right?" I can barely form words, much less make sense right now. Not with all this unbridled lust streaking through me. "Back when you wanted to be an OB-GYN."

He chuckles, sliding my panties down my legs. They drop to the floor a moment later, and his heated gaze finds the crease of my pussy.

"I can't respect the doctor-patient boundaries when your legs are spread like this," he says, palming the thick ridge tenting his charcoal gray dress slacks. He wets his bottom lip, shaking his head. "Good thing you never showed up during the one week I shadowed that GYN."

I giggle as he presses kisses along my inner thigh again, heading for the dripping core of me. "So no examination today."

He grunts, his mouth stopping at my mons. He drags his chin over the tightly trimmed hair there. "Oh, I'll be examining. Just not medically."

A shiver of anticipation races through me. I've never hooked up with a doctor before, and I didn't realize it would be *this* much fun...and a turn-on.

My thoughts dissolve when his crushed velvet lips press to the lowest point of my mons, and then his thumbs are spreading me open, apart, baring all for him to see. But I don't flinch. I don't even mind that he's opening me up and looking at my most intimate parts. Because there's hunger in his gaze. He's ravenous, and the meal of his life is right in front of him.

Dom covers my clit with his plump lips, pressing slow, lazy kisses to my needy nub. A strangled moan escapes me immediately. It's exactly what I need, but I need so much *more* of it. His lips close around my clit again, and he sucks. And as he does, he eases one knobby finger inside me. My pussy makes a juicy sound as he sinks his finger inside me, and then a second one.

"Ohh, my god." I sink back onto my elbows, unable to keep myself up on my palms. My thighs are shaking as his tongue takes another lazy pass over my clit. A noise I've never made before slips out of me. Something between a grunt and a hyena laugh and a sob. It's unattractive, but I can't even care.

"Jesus, you feel amazing." He pushes his fingers into me, swiping his tongue back and forth over my clit. I sink all the back onto the table. I'm done. He'll have to collect me here later. "How are you so fucking juicy?" He slurps at me, his thick fingers pumping in and out of my dripping slit. My legs are totally splayed open. He runs his teeth along the stiff bud of my clit, and I cry out.

"Dom!" I reach for something, anything, and my fingers connect with his thick head of hair. My thighs go around his head, because he should absolutely *never* leave this spot.

He says something, but it's muffled between my legs. It doesn't matter. Not when he's creating these sensations in my limbs. Making me useless and dumb with bliss.

He sucks at my clit again just as he fills me again with his thick fingers. The delirious combination sends me over the edge in a free-fall. Fireworks explode behind my eyelids, and I'm screaming, unable to control it or stop it or do anything other than ride this orgasmic wave.

My pussy pulses while he continues dragging his tongue back and forth over my clit, the evilest glint in his eyes. He groans, gravelly and low, nuzzling the crease of my thigh. "Fuck, London."

"What...What's wrong?" My chest is heaving. Having an explosive orgasm is tough work.

"Change of plans." He stands up, the tenting in his pants even more impressive than before. His belt buckle clanks as he undoes it, and then his pants *whoomp* to the ground. His deft fingers make quick work of his button-up, and then the fabric falls away, revealing his abs the color of steamed milk, and that delectable tiny forest of chest hair.

I reach for him, because I fucking need him on top of me, filling me, consuming me. He knows what I need because he scoops my ass cheeks into his hands and brings our groins crashing together. His cock slides hot against my primed and dripping pussy. He groans, his hips rocking in a slow circle.

"I wanted to eat you out until you came three times and *then* fuck you mindless," he says, voice gritty. "But I'm impatient. I need you wrapped around me, London." He thrusts, his swollen cockhead nudging my clit. "Right fucking now."

"You are such an overachiever," I tease, but my voice comes out weak. He's drained me of most of my energy, and he's about to drain what little remains. "And I'm not complaining."

He grunts in response, working his jaw back and forth. "I don't have any condoms."

I squeeze my eyes shut. Oh, right. That little detail. "I don't have any either."

He keeps my pussy pinned against the nuclear heat of his cock. I can't keep myself from bucking against him.

"I'm on birth control though," I offer.

His tongue traces the outline of his lower lip. "You don't mind?"

"I'm not gonna lie, going bareback on the first date isn't exactly my style," I say, my voice sounding flimsy and distant. "But I'm so down if you are."

He sets his jaw, surging forward to capture my lips in a kiss. That's the final confirmation. The password to allow the next span of time to unfold. While I'm lip-locked and lost in the heady scent of man and cedar and sweat, Dom hoists my hips. With the backs of my knees hooked over his wrists, he is part stirrups, part Kama Sutra. He is the sexy union of clinical doctor and sex god.

Then he's easing himself into me, throbbing hot and iron hard. My mouth parts and everything inside my body goes bright and loud. The unsheathed feel of him is raw and naughty and too fucking right. Too fucking real. My fingernails sink into the ropy muscle of his sides, searching for a place to anchor while he buries himself.

Once he's claimed every inch inside me, Dom scoops me up into his arms and kisses me. Not distractedly, or hurriedly, or as an after-thought. He *kisses* me, thorough and deep and passionate. That alone combined with the throbbing steel inside me brings me perilously close to the edge. Because despite the fact that we're breaking the rules tonight, I have a too-soft spot in my heart for this man.

Because Dom, for all his assholishness and lack of sentimentality and fractured family dynamics, is the man I want. There's something so tender and wild that pulses between us, and the truth of it is unavoidable now that he's buried balls deep in me.

And what do you know? The overachiever is right.

Just from easing himself inside of me and kissing me like no one else pushes me over the edge into another orgasm.

Dom simply holds me and smiles through the kiss.

CHAPTER FIFTEEN

DOM

I've never been this turned on in my entire life. Every muscle in my body is demanding release into the silk wonderland that is London's pussy.

But I want this to last. I'd draw it out for a year if my dick would let me. If we wouldn't be driven mad by peripheral needs like eating and showering.

London comes for a second time, her pussy quaking and quivering around my cock as she does. It takes all my strength not to join her. Because I'm in my mid-thirties, dammit. I'm not a high schooler who comes within the first three minutes.

But it's been awhile, and I wasn't expecting to get this far tonight. My dirtiest fantasies have come true. But they're even better than I imagined.

I scoop my arms underneath her and bring her body crashing against mine. She's a limp noodle. Wrung out with satisfaction. Her arms flop around my neck as I hoist her, my cock still buried in her.

"Where are we going?" she murmurs.

"To your bed." I measure my steps, trying not to stumble while her weight is pooled on top of my cock. A grunt escapes me as I head toward a partition in the studio apartment. Just behind the elaborate woven wall, a perfectly made king bed awaits, topped with a white down comforter and about thirty teal and pink throw pillows.

She laughs as I ease down onto the bed, my forearms shaking as I lower her weight without breaking the seal of our bodies.

"This is why you work out, huh?" she teases.

The air slides out of me as I fill the space between her legs, this time on a much comfier surface. "The one and only reason."

She tosses her head back and laughs, and I seize the opportunity to bury my face in the hollow of her neck. The floral and amber scent shoots through me like a drug. I press my lips to her collarbone and she writhes beneath me, languid and loving it. I dip down and take a pebbled nipple between my lips, which causes a gasp to slice through the air. She arches her back.

"Jesus, Dom," she cries out. "Do you ever stop making me feel amazing things?"

That's the feedback I like to get. "Stopping wasn't part of the seduction plan." I swipe my tongue across her nipple, then switch to the other side. Her thighs squeeze around my waist, the most delicious pressure. I want to be buried between her legs for as long as humanly possible.

"So we'll be fucking until daybreak?"

"I'll fuck you until my dick falls off," I tease, pressing kisses to her jawline. Her body rocks with laughter.

"'Dick falling off' isn't usually a selling point," she says, "except in this instance."

My laughter turns into a groan as I pump in and out of her. Her breathy panting dials me up to level ten horniness. Hell, it's practically hypnotization. I could be in the middle of a catheterization and if London showed up, sounding like this, I'd drop trou immediately. It's dangerous, really.

I slip out of her, because the orgasm is knocking on my door like an impatient Fed-Ex guy. I want to draw this out a little longer. I gently bring her legs together, and she watches me with a dazed expression.

"What..."

"New pose. And I need a breather or I'm going to qualify for premature ejaculation."

"We wouldn't want that," she murmurs, looking more than content as I urge her to flip over onto her belly. I nudge her legs apart with my knee, and then lift her by the hips. She slides back so her ass is in the air and her cheek on the comforter. The sight alone is almost enough to undo me.

"There we go," I whisper, pressing kisses along the bumps of her spine. She is lithe lines and golden skin. Freckles and softness. Silk and sensual. And I already know that tonight with her isn't enough.

I need this every night of my life.

"You aren't..." she trails off.

"Not unless you want me to," I say, pushing my fingertips over the slippery folds of her pussy from behind. My middle finger finds the tight bud of her clit, and she jerks forward. My fingertips slip back and forth over her swollen clit as I ease myself back into her. The extra deep angle is even more fatal to my composure. A long, shuddery moan slides out of her as I bury my cock in her velvet depths again.

But this time, I can't keep myself in check. The walls of her pussy clamp around me, and everything inside me is ready and begging to come. I start a fierce rhythm, one that has her fisting the comforter, alternating between screaming my name and shrieking. My head is spinning. Sweat collects on the tops of my shoulders, and I grip her hips for dear life as I fuck her exactly the way I've been imagining for weeks.

Time folds to a blissful, tense burst of moments: London wailing 'fuuuuck yessss' while her pussy turns into a vice around my cock; the deep churn of pleasure that shoots like fireworks through my limbs; and then finally the powerful rounds of my orgasm bursting out of me.

I slip my cock free, because it seems wrong to come inside her on the first date, even if we're barebacking it already. A gruff cry passes my lips as my cum arcs through the air and right onto the small of her back. She's already collapsed on the bed by the time I can catch my breath to say anything.

"Hang on," I tell her. My heart is racing so fast I feel like I might pass out. That's how good the sex is: nearly fatal. God forbid "Amazing sex after a two-year lull" be the cause on my death certificate. "Let me get you cleaned up."

She laughs weakly, and I find the bathroom after stumbling around for a minute. I bring back a damp washcloth and wipe her down, as gingerly as I can. My cock is still hard and throbbing, as though I hadn't just given it the workout of its life.

"Sorry," I say once I'm lying beside her. "Should have warned you."

"Next time, you can come somewhere else," she says with a grin and closed eyes. Like she's still floating in outer space. But what I hear more than anything is that she wants there to be a next time.

"Where, like all over your dining room chairs?"

Her laughter is sharp, and she rolls onto her side, reaching for me. I bring her against me for postcoital cuddling as if we've been doing it for years. Her warm body tangles into mine, smooth thigh pressing between my legs to find a comfy resting spot. But it's not until she buries her face into my neck and sighs that the hot tendrils of satisfaction begin unfurling inside me, dangerously slow, with roots exposed.

London makes it too easy. To be with her. To know her. To want to dive headfirst into this lagoon that I honestly believed had dried up.

She smooths her lips against my collarbone, and I respond by pressing a kiss to the top of her head.

But the matchmaker has shown me that the lagoon wasn't dry at all.

I was just wandering the desert.

CHAPTER SIXTEEN

LONDON

The scent of coffee is the first thing that registers. I crack open one eye and then the other, the wash of bright light filling my apartment feeling like an attack. My coffee pot gurgles, and that's when the questions arrive.

How the hell is my coffee maker on?

Has it been brewing since last night?

Is half of my kitchen on fire and I'm unaware?

Why does my pelvis feel like I was attacked by a battering ram?

I groan and roll onto my side. And then I hear humming. Low hums, a distracted accompaniment to whatever is going on out in the kitchen. The realization hits me as a quick punch: Dom is here.

He is the battering ram.

Dom pokes his head past the partition a moment later, his blue eyes landing on me. And suddenly, all my qualms disappear. The man stayed the night, *and* he made me coffee the next morning.

He is already a thousand steps ahead of most romantic rams—er, partners—I've met in my life.

"Morning," he chirps. The man is an early bird. I grope for my phone, squinting at the numbers. It's eight a.m.

"Grrrnnnngh," I say.

"I hope I didn't wake you up."

"No, my hangover did that all on its own," I tell him, collapsing back onto my bed. A dull throb punctuates each breath. "But the promise of coffee is reassuring."

"Coffee and *eggs*," he clarifies. "Hope you don't mind that I raided your fridge."

He disappears behind the partition, and his shadow returns to the kitchen. I burrow into my covers, savoring this unexpectedly perfect Saturday morning. Sexually sated. A gorgeous man who *wants* to be here. A homemade breakfast awaiting me.

I relax, buried in my bedcovers, until the lure of caffeine is too great. I tug my sheet off my bed and wrap it around me, since the thought of finding any clothes—much less putting them on—makes my headache throb to life.

But I'm not prepared for what I find in the kitchen. Dom is naked except for his tight green boxer briefs, which cling to his sculpted thighs. He hums absent-mindedly as he hovers over the sauté pan, my trendy plaid dish towel slung over one shoulder. He turns toward the cupboards, rummaging for plates like he's done it a thousand times before.

"You sure know your way around my kitchen already." My voice sounds like a bullfrog as I shuffle toward the stools lining the kitchen island.

"I'm a good guesser," he says. "There's only one logical option for your plates based on where your sink and countertop are."

I nod, my eyes turning to slits. "True. Never thought about it like that before. Though I kind of liked imagining you taking notes about my cabinetry before I woke up."

"Oh. Right. I totally did that." He sends me the type of grin that could stop a human heart. And if mine were to stop right now, he's the first and only man I'd want reviving me. He's finishing up the eggs, and my gaze drifts over the stove top.

"Wow. You even cook like a doctor."

"What's that supposed to mean?"

"You have everything laid out like surgical instruments." The chef's knife exactly parallel to the spoon, which is exactly parallel to the stovetop. Two bowls sit on the cutting board, equidistant from all edges of the cutting board.

He smirks. "I can't even deny that. It's force of habit."

"Just don't get confused in surgery. You don't want to scoop out somebody's heart and accidentally taste test it."

He snort laughs, which feels like a victory somehow. This man, whom I'd met in a peak state of assholishness and distraction, is now relaxed and nearly naked in my apartment.

Though the nearly naked part is the opposite of a victory. In fact, it's a symbol of my professional failing. My *moral* failing. The truth trickles through me, tugging my mouth into a frown. How low have I fallen?

Apparently not low enough to repent. The boulders of his biceps snag my attention as he pushes two exactly equal portions of eggs onto the waiting plates. The memory of him—both buried inside me *and* wrapped around me last night—shivers through me, warm and inviting. Sleeping with a client shouldn't feel *that* good.

"Hope you're hungry," he says, setting the pan back on the stove. He garnishes the piles of eggs with shredded cheese, his flourish equal parts chef and surgeon, and then pushes my plate toward me. I can't fight the grin taking over my face.

"This is certainly a surprise."

"No, the real surprise is that you don't have an espresso machine," Dom says, pouring a steaming mug of French pressed coffee. He sets it in front of my plate. "Do you take cream?"

"This is perfect," I say, my eyes stuck on him as he walks around the kitchen island to sit beside me and enjoy his own breakfast.

He tugs at my bedsheet as he settles onto the stool. "Why are you hiding all this gorgeousness?"

My cheeks flush, though I can't say why. He's seen every part of me and more. His lips went where my ex's ventured too few times to count.

"Because if we *both* have breakfast while naked, the balance of the universe will become disrupted. Or something super serious like that," I crack before I shovel a mouthful of eggs past my lips. They are perfectly salted and fluffy. My eyes flutter shut.

Damn this man.

"I'm willing to risk it," he says, turned toward me as he smooths a palm over my covered thigh. His breakfast is totally forgotten, and I look up guiltily at him. This would have been easier if he was on the same page as me. That page being, "Why don't we just pretend we didn't violate all the client/provider boundaries last night?" which would lead to him disappearing in the night.

But no, he has to be Mr. Secret Thoughtful. You can't count on outward assholes to also be *inward* assholes, which is the most confusing part of the dating game.

He's fishing for the edge of the sheet, the unmistakable fire of lust burning in his gaze. Even after all the postures and moaning and grinding we did last night into the wee morning hours.

"You really want me to eat breakfast in the nude, huh," I murmur, already willing to do whatever he asks of me. As long as he keeps looking at me like I'm the only thing he wants in the entire world.

I swear my body might combust with the intensity of his gaze. I've never been looked at like this. By anyone. Ever.

He nods slowly, tugging expertly at the edge of the sheet. The fabric crumples around me, exposing my naked body. A satisfied grin stretches across his face.

"Much better."

"Now I'm going to drop scrambled eggs in my vag."

"Then I'll just have to eat your pussy as part of breakfast cleanup."

I dissolve into laughter at that one. He looks particularly pleased with himself.

"Dirty doc," I tease, shoving his shoulder. He finally turns toward his plate, his big hand moving to his groin to adjust himself. His boxer briefs have tented slightly, and I have to admit—even though he fucked me into next year—just knowing that he's already aroused by me *again* has desire prickling beneath my skin. Maybe we can have one last romp before he goes. To celebrate the decision that this will *definitely* never happen again.

My phone chimes from my nightstand, and I scoop another forkful of eggs into my mouth before I head over to get it. Sunlight fills every inch of my apartment. The wood floor practically sparkles in the sun beams, all the cozy corners of my home illuminated in brilliant beauty. A contented sigh escapes me. Between the light and the amazing breakfast and the hottie doctor in my kitchen, my hangover is already a thing of the past. Maybe I've attained perfection for this fleeting moment.

A text from Hazel is waiting for me: *Are you up?*

LONDON: Yeah girl, what's up?

My phone rings a moment later, just as I'm sliding back onto my sheet-draped stool. I tuck the phone under my ear as I answer her call.

"Jeez, Hazel, that was fast."

"Well, great ideas call for fast acting," Hazel intones. The sound of her voice makes me smile, but I can tell that Dom has stiffened at my side.

"What's the great idea? Do tell."

"Grayson and I realized we have an unexpected night off tonight, and we want to come see you in Cleveland!" she gushes. "If you're not booked already, that is. I want to see your place, and we can go get dinner and drinks and do whatever. What do you think?"

"Oh my god, that's perfect!" I glance at Dom, and the frown on his face makes me wonder if he can overhear her. "What time do you think you'll get here?"

Hazel and I set a time for the visit, and when we end the call, Dom looks as sour as the day I met him. I set the phone down, elbowing him lightly.

"Why the long face? You sad you can't join us?"

He hefts with a humorless laugh. "Not exactly."

"You have to admit, a night out on the town featuring dinner and drinks sounds like a suspiciously familiar good time."

He smirks. "Fair enough. But not when Grayson is there."

"Are you talking about the contract we signed?" Our NDA is burning bright in my mind. "I promise I won't leak it. Hazel's my best friend, but I'm not going to say anything."

"Well, I'd hope not. But that's not exactly what I'm getting at."

"Oh." I push eggs around my plate, the cool air making goosebumps flare on the tops of my thighs. "You mean because you'd be in the same room as Grayson."

"We can be in the same room," Dom says, "but not for long."

"So I take it he won't be coming to visit you while he's in town?"

"Definitely not." Dom takes a swig of his coffee. "When we were in Bayshore for our grandmother's funeral, we didn't exactly have an easy time. And that was after a full six years of not seeing each other. At all."

My shoulders slump. Their fractured relationship shouldn't bother me, but it does. Partly because of the hollow parts that Willow left in my heart. Partly because I know how great Grayson is—at least how great he is with my best friend. And I'm beginning to see how great Dom is. At least how great he is with *me*.

And those two individual equations seem like they should add up happily in the middle somehow.

"Listen, we've never gotten along, and I'm sure that's never going to change," Dom says, a hard edge to his voice, like he's wrapping up a meeting with unruly employees. "Besides, he's happy with Hazel. He has everything he needs now. He's never going to see me as anything other than his arrogant older brother."

I blink rapidly, unsure which part to begin dissecting first. "Wait, you're calling yourself arrogant?"

"Well, yeah. But so is he." He tips more coffee into his mouth. "We all are."

"Then you should all understand each other better than anyone else in the world," I say, poking his arm. "So why don't you meet up with him sometime? He's your family. He's your *brother*. Life's too short for silence and resentment."

I'm using his own words against him. He straightens his back, crossing his arms over his perfect chest. I'm trying to keep this friendly, but I mean the words more than he probably imagines. Sure, he knows about Willow, ever since I told him that night we reviewed matches in the restaurant. But I never told him how deeply her death still cuts through me. How much my regret stains the edges of my happiness.

"Sometimes people just don't get along, London," he says, his knee bouncing. "And part of being an adult is accepting that."

My pulse picks up. "So my encouraging you to make up with your brother is childish?"

His warm hand finds my knee. "That's not what I meant. I'm saying that not everyone in a family gets along. It's part of life."

"But don't you ever feel like trying?"

Dom removes his hand from my knee, presses it to his own. He begins shoveling eggs into his mouth. I can sense that I've gone too far. Big surprise. If there's one platform in my life, it's reminding others to love their family. And after all I've learned about Dom, the gaping hole in his life is more than obvious to me.

I just wonder if he actually sees it.

We eat in silence for a few moments, alternately slurping coffee. Once I clear my plate, I squeeze his elbow.

"Thanks for breakfast. You're a real sweetheart, you know that?"

He pushes away his cleared plate and then turns to me, his low belly crinkling. "Normally I wouldn't accept a title like that. But when you say it, I'm tempted to get it tattooed on my forearm."

A giggle slips out of me as I turn to face him. "Tattooed on your forearm? Would the league of cardiac surgeons allow it?"

His warm palms slide over my knees. "Absolutely not. But I'd do it anyway."

Something deep inside me is throbbing. The sincerity in his blue eyes combined with the warmth pouring out of him makes me want to pitch forward and do a nosedive into this man.

And the urge to fall headfirst works like a reminder. I snap myself out of it. I slide off the stool, busying myself with collecting our plates and cleaning up the kitchen. While I wash the dishes, I ask, "So what's on deck for your Saturday?"

He taps the screen of his phone, frowning. "Hospital. In fact, I needed to leave five minutes ago."

Our reverie is coming to an end. The realization sends something cold and twisty through me. Despite how much this needs to end, I don't want it to. Once he walks out my front door, I'll need to redraw those crisp, professional boundaries. Even though forgetting about them for a night allowed me to break in my new Cleveland apartment in an epic fashion, orgasms blazing.

"Even on a Saturday?" I ask.

"Especially Saturdays," Dom says, heading to collect his clothes from the far reaches of my apartment. "But being late today is worth it."

His words thrum through me as he picks up his clothes and dresses. I just wash dishes in the nude, glancing over my shoulder at him like some sort of nostalgic housewife.

Once he's back in his dress slacks and gray button-up, he's grinning at me like he knows a secret. He approaches me at the sink, his rough palms finding the dip in my waist.

"Do you know how hard it is to walk away from you right now?"

"It's just because I'm naked," I tell him, tipping my head back to drink in those baby blues.

"Among other things." He gazes into my eyes for a moment and then presses a spine-tingling kiss to my lips. He grips my chin between his thumb and forefinger before ripping himself away from me. "Zimbo's later this week?"

All I can do is grin like an idiot. He winks at me before he lets himself out of my apartment, and I stand in blissed out silence for minutes or maybe an hour. I can't tell. It's only the buzzing of my phone that brings me back to Earth. I half-expect it to be Dom, or maybe Hazel, but it's neither.

Tara, the woman who cancelled on Dom yesterday, has finally replied to the check-in text I sent her yesterday.

TARA: Yes, I'd love to set up another date. But I didn't cancel on him. He texted me to let me know that he couldn't make it because of work. I was bummed!

I have to reread the text a few times before the meaning clicks into place.

And when it does, it lands like a boulder.

Dom orchestrated last night. As romantic and thoughtful as that is—all the ways it makes me want to swoon right into the wood floor—I need to read it for the sign it is.

Dom's chasing the wrong woman.

And if I know what's good for me, I won't let him snag me a second time.

CHAPTER SEVENTEEN

DOM

I should have known that shutting the door to London's apartment would mean shutting the door on a chance with her.

A little voice whispered it to me that Saturday morning as I left, but I figured I was overreacting. She agreed to a second date at Zimbo's, for God's sake. That's practically a notarized letter of deep personal interest.

But as the days wear on, the evidence piles up around me. She confirms it by ignoring all of my flirty postcoital texts and reaching out—via email, like a true professional—only for agenda-related matters. Avoiding everything that doesn't directly connect to our formal end goal: me sharing my life with someone who isn't her.

I shouldn't be surprised. I signed up for this shit.

But what surprises me is how much the personal ghosting hurts.

I can't get thoughts of her sun-drenched apartment out of my head. They haunt me every day at work. Through each new date I go on. I just want to be *there*. Back to the first bit of warmth I've felt since...fuck, I don't even know when. My heart has been a barren wasteland for years, but London has shown me that the soil is still fertile enough to grow something.

The only question is: what seeds do I plant?

And what do I do when I want the gardener, but she refuses to tend my plot?

Life barrels on despite not having answers. Office hours, surgery, ER, sleep, gym, and dates. That's all I'm doing anymore. Minus the dates, it's all I've ever done. But the whirlwind isn't half as satisfying as it once was.

I try to convince myself that this is just post-sex hysteria resulting from too long without *getting some*. So all week, when she emails me about date follow-ups, I ignore my own urges to remind her how many times she screamed my name last Friday night or to slip into our email a casual, "Fun fact: the memory of eating you out on your dining room table is making me hard right now," which seems less like an email signature and more like something an online predator would say.

But once next Friday hits, I need to hear from her. We had a standing date to Zimbo's, for god's sake. I'm ready to redo our whole magical, sensual, hilarious evening. But if she won't agree to that, then I need to at least see what she would be willing to do. Maybe we can work out a compromise—just see each other once a week for the rest of the contract, and then once we're done...what? Nothing really makes sense, but I can't stop myself. By the end of the workday, I'm dialing her number without even realizing it.

She picks up just when I think the phone is going to click over to voicemail. "Hello?" She sounds suspicious.

All my thoughts dissolve. I can't remember what my reason for calling is. Other than I need to hear the sound of her voice almost more than I need air.

"Hey." I search my desktop for something. A clue. A prepared speech. *Anything.* The only thing on my mind is: *Are you thinking about our night together as much as I am?* "Uh...I'm surprised you answered."

"Well, why wouldn't I?" Her tone is sugary. The type I heard her use with an annoying guest at the bar last week. "You're my client."

"Yeah, well, you've just been kind of...unresponsive." My palms go damp. I should have thought this through more. I feel like she's caught me with my pants down, even though I'm the one who wandered her way.

"What do you mean, 'unresponsive'? We've emailed this entire week about your dates."

I press a palm to my forehead, willing myself to just say it already. Just slice my chest open and bleed out and be done with it so I can move on and forget that I ever fell headfirst again, despite knowing better. "I mean, you've been unresponsive about what we did last Friday." My tongue finds dry lips. The silence on the other end of the phone is deafening. "You remember, don't you?"

"Why do we need to acknowledge it?" she finally asks. "We both know it for what it was: a drunk night that shouldn't have happened."

My thumb and middle finger find the indentations of my temples and dig in. This was a horrible fucking idea. Because not only *should* that night have happened, it should have happened six times since then.

"Yeah," I manage to say. "You're right."

"I know I'm right," she replies, her tone razor sharp. "And it won't happen again. It's just not a good idea for the situation we're in."

So apparently a Zimbo's repeat is out. I clear my throat, willing myself to ignore the memories bubbling to the surface. All the little signals I got from her that she was just as into it as I was. The sweet smiles and the soft caresses. I need to forget they ever happened. Because this won't go anywhere.

London herself won't allow it, and it's time for me to get on board.

"Don't you think?" she asks, after I'm silent for a while.

"Yeah," I say, straightening my back. I take a deep, cleansing breath, trying to reorient myself to the rational world. The world that doesn't involve sex comas or passionate nights or so much laughter that I feel like my heart had finally been put back together after an intolerably long and dark night of the soul. "I just, uh..." I don't know how to cover my tracks after this one. How to make myself seem like I'm not limping away. "It had been a while for me, you know. So that's why it was, you know, noteworthy."

"Noteworthy," she repeats.

"But don't worry. You found me some great matches. And the sexual chemistry is there with all of them," I say, the words just rolling off my tongue. "So it won't be long before there's more noteworthy evenings."

"Right," she says.

"With other women," I clarify. "Who aren't you."

"Yep. That's the plan."

"So you were sort of the appetizer," I say. "Better meals ahead."

She sighs. "Don't be an asshole."

"Come on, London. You know better than to tell me that."

I hang up the phone before I can say anything else ridiculous. I pinch my eyes shut for a moment, and the whole world falls away. My medical degree, my board certification, my application for the foundation, every single prestigious thing about me dissolves, and all I can feel is this prickling hot embarrassment. Humiliation. I should have never called her, but more than that, I should have never allowed myself to get swept up in the fantasy that we'd shared anything more than great sex last week.

I know better than this.

And my only recourse is to get lost in work. To bury myself so deep that I have no bandwidth to think about London or her breezy, freckled smiles.

I go into deep hyper-focus mode, a skill learned in residency. Hours drift by. When I finally pull myself out of it, I find a new email waiting for me from London. She is all business and perky exclamation points outlining the next round of dates for the upcoming week.

"This is exciting!" she writes in the last line of the email. "You're getting closer to The One!"

So why am I not even slightly relieved?

CHAPTER EIGHTEEN

LONDON

November in Cleveland means two things.

One, football season is in full swing, which means I avoid First Energy Stadium on game days like the plague—unless I have tickets, of course. Two, the weather has transitioned into full autumnal glory: fluttering golden leaves and chilly winds, which require oversized knit sweaters and unnecessarily long scarves.

What do both of these things have in common?

It's Boyfriend Season. The best time of year to have someone warm to snuggle up with. Nothing combats a perpetually losing football team and crisp breezes like the hulking warmth of a hottie on your arm.

And I swear, this is the *only* thing I'm telling myself I see in Dom as I trudge through the days after our accidental—er, intentional—hook up. I'm repeating this shit like a mantra: It's just science. Basic math. Cold weather plus slight frame equals an unnatural obsession with the nearest available warm man in your vicinity. *That's it.*

Because I can't have a crush on Dom, even though I most definitely, scientifically, verifiably *do*. If I can just convince myself that my attraction has everything to do with his proximity, then distancing ourselves post-fuck-fest will cure the problem. And trust me, I'm doing everything I can to keep myself on track.

Up to and including slamming the door shut in Dom's face when I know he's willing to go for round two of our inappropriate yet dually confirmed sexual chemistry.

I need to stay away for more reasons than just client-provider boundaries. If I ruin this man's shot at finding his convenient wife, then I have blown my first profitable gig in my new territory. Furthermore, I don't want that stain on my conscience *or* my track record, even if it's only between us. That's not how you karmically start out a new chapter in your life. Even if I've already gone and gotten chocolate all over the opening pages.

I still have a chance to minimize the damage and keep this to a one-off, totally understandable, it-happens-to-everyone slipup.

Besides, there's no way in hell I could truly fall for a man who is so unromantic that he honestly thinks he'd be happy with a stage wife. Or a man who has no interest in mending fences with his alive and healthy family. He's got the world at his fingertips, and he barely notices it.

Willow's death taught me a lot, first and foremost that I'm never going to ignore the wild, vibrant world in front of me.

It's why I've amped up the volume on my Cleveland immersion plan. In the past two Dom-avoiding weeks, I've accomplished the following: joined the Rotary club, sampled four new yoga studios, volunteered at a soup kitchen, volunteered at a winter clothing drive, signed up for a spring 5k that I am already resigned to walking the entirety of, and made a list of sip-and-paints that Hazel and I want to drunkenly attend. I am living the bachelorette dream life.

But there is a boyfriend-sized hole in my Cleveland life, made slightly larger by the fact that it's Boyfriend Season. This hole reaches car-swallowing depths because dammit, I'm ready to find my happily-ever-after. Despite this bizarre sinkhole of desire, one truth remains.

I can never be someone's stage wife. No matter how hot and fun and occasionally assholish he is.

Furthermore, no amount of losing football teams or chilly, autumnal winds would ever drive me back into the arms of my smarmy, misogynistic ex. The man who believed a client—and prioritized the account—over me. It's been two weeks since I've gotten his sorry phone call, which has now been followed by several emails—which I absolutely did not respond to—and I'm still just as baffled and outraged by it.

If anything, it serves as a yellow flag. A bucket of ice water on top of my roiling, unchecked desire for Dom.

And God help me, I'm going to survive this ice bucket challenge. Even if I have to get crafty. Which is why I've scheduled my please-God-let-this-be-the-last meeting with Dom on *his* turf. No more rooftop restaurants (too cold), gym-time meetups (too sexy), or fancy after-work dinners (too easy to be seduced again). I'm going straight to Dom's office, where Nancy will be sitting six feet away, and I'm going to do it in the middle of the day.

No chance of "staying late." No accidental hooking up on his desk. Not unless we want to scar Nancy for life, which is *not* something I want on my conscience *or* resumé.

When Nancy calls me at noon, just as I'm preparing to head out of the office for a quick lunch down the street, I'm equal parts hopeful Dom cancelled and scared that my plan is already unraveling.

"London," she says, in that familiar warm, excited way. "I have some bad news, but it's not terrible. Dr. Dom was called to the ER this morning—"

My breath catches in my throat, wondering if our appointment is a thing of memory now.

"—and we had to jam an emergency surgery into his office hours in the afternoon."

She goes on to explain the details of this situation, and the more she talks, the clearer it becomes. Dr. Dom wants to meet, but he can't until around four. I swear under my breath. That is pushing us perilously close to "let's just go grab dinner together" territory after our meeting, but I'll have to make it work. After all, Dom didn't orchestrate this emergency.

Even though he *did* orchestrate that cancelled date two weeks ago. Heat flushes through me, reminding me of just how not calm and detached I am after our two weeks apart. I'm more jittery than a piano player on recital day. This is going to be the performance of my life. Acting purely professional and *meaning it* in front of him, after mind-blowing sex that I still fantasize about *on a daily basis.*

Ugh, that's the sort of thing I don't want to admit. Because it would be one thing if I hooked up with my client and it sucked or I never thought about it again. But it's entirely different when he becomes the new standard for masturbatory fantasies forevermore.

I grab lunch and reorganize my afternoon to accommodate Dom's emergency surgery. When I'm heading downtown at a quarter till four, I'm white-knuckling the steering wheel, and my legs are clamped together. I should have worn a chastity belt, for God's sake. Not to protect myself from Dom—to protect him from *me.*

I park my car, float into the clinic, and when I get up to Dom's floor, my body is on high alert. I look for him everywhere. Trying to spot him before he sees me. Remembering how he scooped me up into his arms and carried me across my apartment, the hot steel of his cock buried deep within me.

"Is it too hot in here?" Nancy sounds genuinely concerned as I roll up to her desk.

"No, I...sorry, what?"

"You're all pink."

I shouldn't tell her it's just me blushing all the way down to my liver from memories of fucking her boss. "No, I'm fine. It's this jacket." I slip off my vintage tweed bolero jacket, laying it over my arm. "The seventies was an era of warm fashion. Thanks for checking, though. Is Dom ready for me?"

"No, honey, he's not out of surgery yet." Nancy offers a pained grimace. "But do you want to go see him in action?"

That sounds a lot like watching Dr. Hottie in the middle of Hottie Surgery, and every inch of me wants to gracefully bow out. But before I can say a word, Nancy adds, "The OR is right down the hall, and we don't even have to scrub in. It's so interesting, I promise."

I smile politely in return, dropping my jacket over the armrest of a nearby chair. I'll need as few layers as possible for this. I should probably just strip down to my panties now. "I'd love to."

Nancy encourages me to leave my things at her desk, and then ushers me down the part of the hallway that I never venture down. I follow her sure strides, my forearms prickling with anticipation. I feel like I'm surprising my boyfriend at work, which is absurd, because I have firsthand evidence of how many women consider Dom their boyfriend right now. And I am not one of them.

He is closer than ever to selecting his wife, having his final interview with the foundation, and living unhappily-ever-after. It's high time I start letting my heart know the decisions my brain is making.

"You know, Dr. Dom has been uncharacteristically happy since you came into the picture," Nancy says as she leads me through bright white hallways. "It makes me happy to see him so happy, you know?"

"Well, he's closer than ever to finding the woman of his dreams."

"I think he found her," Nancy says.

"Oh?" I can't ignore the pang of disappointment that shudders through me. The distant heartbreak. The infuriating jealousy. "Did he share with you which one is the winner?"

"No, we don't talk that intimately," Nancy dismisses me with a wave of her hand, "but I can just tell. Someone has changed him. I started noticing it about two weeks ago."

Hmm. My own basic math skills tell me that my own psychosis started about two weeks ago as well. But why listen to facts when I can create a perfectly fabricated reality instead? I focus on the symmetrical patterns of the hospital tiles. "He's been seeing a lot of women. He's probably having a great time out there, figuring out which one is Ms. Right."

Nancy laughs, pushing through swinging doors into a narrow hallway that doubles as an observation room into the OR. And suddenly, we have front row seats to the Dr. Dom Show.

My throat seizes as I take him in. He's in light blue scrubs—covering his body, his hair, and most of his face—and flanked by colleagues. I can't hear what's happening, since the hospital had the huge oversight of not installing Dolby surround sound speakers for this little observation area, but I get the sense that it's *really serious.*

Dom moves methodically, exactly the way he did in my kitchen that morning. Except then, his boxy frame was naked. God, I wish I had my own face mask to hide my burning cheeks.

"It's an open-heart surgery," Nancy whispers, though there's no reason for her lower her voice.

"Jeez." I rub my hand over the back of my neck. I'm remembering all that tenderness that Dom holds for his patients. The way he's sacrificed his entire life to tend to strangers. My *coldhearted anti-family man* excuse is crumbling, and I desperately need as many excuses to avoid him as possible right now. "Just a regular Friday afternoon, right?"

Maybe this area isn't soundproof after all. Or maybe Dr. Dom can just sense me nearby. His eyes flash up to the glass partition, zeroing in directly on me. My entire body goes hot, and Nancy whoops a moment later. She's holding me up. I've stumbled in her direction.

"You aren't getting queasy, are you?" she asks.

"No, no. No. I'm fine." I can barely breathe. Dom straightens, his ice blue eyes still fastened on me. His high cheekbones shine from the top of the facemask, and I can just imagine the scowl on his perfect lips. Dear Lord, my panties are wet. Somebody save me. "I've just never seen a surgery like this before."

Dom twists toward a colleague. He must bark out something because the other man jumps like he's been scolded and scurries toward the instrument table. Nancy and I watch—or pant, depending on who you're talking about—for a few more moments before she guides me back through the hallways.

"He's almost done," Nancy murmurs reassuringly. "So we should be ready for him."

Funny of her to say that. I don't think I'll ever be fully ready for Dr. Dom. Still, I follow her back to the office area, braindead and drifting. Why is he so mind-bogglingly hot? I can't think of anything but turns of phrase involving Dom, his scalpel, and the specific cracking occurring within my chest cavity. Nancy and I spend the next ten minutes chatting casually—well, it is most likely casual for *her*. She clearly is accustomed to witnessing a heart-stopping example of a heartbreaker playing with hearts, which is the best doctor pun I can come up with in my feeble, horny state.

When heavy footsteps sound down the hall, I don't need to turn around to know that he's near. The bass notes of his voice reach me next, sending a delicious thrill up my spine. I twist and see him talking with a med student, but his eyes are on me. Icy blue and hot, practically burning a hole through me.

They wrap things up, and the student leaves. Dom heads my way, following the tractor beam he's got me paralyzed in. My whole body is tense, waiting for something. Anything. Anger or indifference or more of his assholishness, maybe, since I drew the line in the sand between us so deeply. Instead, he heads for his office, something lackadaisical in his gait. He pushes open the door and holds it, looking at me expectantly.

I can only watch him, unsure what I'm witnessing. Dom clears his throat just as Nancy sends him an unreadable glance.

"Come in, London," he says, his sexy rumble almost bringing me to my knees.

I almost can't believe it. Who *is* this man? He's finally acknowledging me in his workspace. Greeting a newly arrived person like a regular human. I'll have to knock off a few points from his asshole scorecard. I never planned on him racking up points in the sweetheart direction.

My legs are moving toward him, taking me closer to his tall, boxy frame. Every inch of my body is taut with need as I behold him. His broad shoulders strain under the pressed, light blue fabric of his button-up. He has somehow gotten beefier in the two weeks my eyes have avoided looking at him. Maybe he's pumping extra iron in an attempt to woo his future wife. Which is not me. *You are not his future wife, London. DO YOU COMPUTE?*

He smooths a palm down the buttons of his shirt, and I remember how it felt to drag my own hand over those washboard abs. I press my index finger to a temple. Everything is whirring and wild. I don't know if I can keep this façade up much longer.

"Are you okay? You look a little flushed."

His question sends a streak of desire through me, and when I catch the beginning curl of a smile on his lips, I know exactly what he's thinking.

"Yeah, I'm okay. But I think I'm coming down with something."

He nods, easing into his chair, his gaze heavy on me like a dare. But I won't meet his eyes. Because if I do, I'll crumble deeper into the truth of what's pulsing between us.

Meeting him on his turf wasn't as neutral as I imagined. Because what I'm coming down with has a wide variety of symptoms, but only one main cause.

I fell for Dr. Dom.

CHAPTER NINETEEN

LONDON

I check my phone as discretely as possible while Dom takes the fifth phone call that has interrupted our meeting. I'm not miffed. The frequent interruptions help me restock my dwindling supply of cool.

It's taking my everything to keep things light yet professional. To avoid the breathtakingly large elephant in the room with a sign around its neck reading "Sexual Tension." I came here to work, and that's what I'm going to do, dammit.

I've cobbled together an additional PR plan for Dr. Dom for the next phase of his career. A five-year community reputation outline that details ways he can deepen his standing in the community once he snags the board position. It looks a lot like what I've dabbled in over the past two weeks but drawn out over years to allow for a doctor's lack of free time. It involves ample galas and charity events with his soon-to-be wife on his arm, whose name I excluded from the work-up, because I still don't know who he's leaning toward.

And would you believe I can't find it in me to ask who's in the lead?

"Okay. Sorry about that." Dom sets the receiver down, reaching for a prescription pad. He scribbles a note.

"Are you writing yourself a prescription for Xanax?" I ask.

He smirks. "Sometimes, I wish that were the answer. But no. I ran out of sticky notes."

"Nancy can help with that, I hear."

As if on cue, Nancy pokes her head into the office. The door has been ajar since we set foot in here, since I'm taking the inverse of the mother-of-high-schoolers approach.

"Dr. Daly, it's time for me to leave."

"He needs sticky notes," I say, pointing at Dom like there's some confusion.

"Why don't you go buy them yourself?" Nancy asks, looking at him. Dom rolls his lips in, looking at me as if to say *Happy now?*

"Thanks, Nance. Have a good evening. I'll see you Monday."

She sends us both a sugary smile. "Don't you two stay out too late."

"We're almost finished here—"

"We'll be good," Dom interjects. "Like always."

I wait until Nancy leaves the office area to twist his way and send him a sharp look. "Did you have to add that?"

"It's true." A shit-eating smile has started a slow slide across his face.

"Actually, it's not. Unless you mean from last Saturday morning onward. Because yes, we *will* be good according to that criteria."

"Jeez. Get your mind out of the gutter, London." He sniffs, leaning back in his chair, his eyes going hooded. "I meant we'd be good, focused colleagues. Which we always have been."

Heat prickles across my shoulders. "Sure."

"Where were we before the call?" He clicks the top of his pen, his gaze settling on the outline I brought for him.

"The charity balls."

"Right." He frowns. "We might have to edit this."

"Why?"

"There might be a...conflict of interest, let's say."

My heart rate picks up. The ideas presented in my outline are vetted and solid. There's no way I overlooked a conflict of interest. "Sorry, what? I don't follow."

"My soon-to-be wife. Well, one of them, at least." He hefts with a laugh, but it seems empty. "This first gala you have listed here is sponsored by Murray Law Offices, but since Julianne works for their largest competitor, I don't think that'll go over very well."

My stomach thuds to the floor. So it's Julianne. "Oh. Well, you know, I didn't realize that she was the top contender." My mouth is dry. I can feel a big, plastic smile creeping onto my face. The type that tries too hard to show everyone how much of a smile it is. "I can modify this if she's...you know...The One."

Dom's face is expressionless. He blinks once. Then again. "What do you think?"

That you and I fit too well together. "About Julianne?"

"Yeah."

"I think it's a perfect match." I attempt a breezy laugh. "It's why I matched you."

Dom nods, still studying me in a way that makes me wary. "You're a horrible liar, you know that?"

This time, I feign shock. "What?"

"Yeah." He clicks the pen maniacally. "You think I should be with someone else."

I tut, willing my cheeks not to flame. "Like who?"

He doesn't answer, but his gaze darts back and forth across my face. His chair creaks as he leans his elbows against the desk. We're too close to the forbidden zone. Even though every cell in my body is craving it. He's not answering my question, just staring at me as if we're fluent in telepathy. And I think I'm catching hints of what he's trying to say with that gaze.

"I'll fix the proposal," I blurt, looking away, "but I think the rest of it stands, unless you had any other issues?" I need to bring us back to the present, platonic moment.

He rubs his forehead, nodding. Suddenly he looks tired. No, exhausted. Like he hasn't gotten a good night's sleep in weeks.

"No issues," he says. "Thank you." When his hands drop, part of his mask falls away. Something naked and vulnerable is facing me, and I can't avert my eyes.

"Long day?" I ask, standing as I repack my briefcase.

"I was on call last night," Dom explains, leaning back in his chair again. He loosens his tie, and his winding down movements have me itching to curl up in his lap and relax along with him. "I started working today around three a.m."

I grimace. "Ouch. Did you at least get a cat nap?"

He sends me a heavy grimace, which I take to mean "no." The exhaustion radiating off him reminds me what a grueling schedule he keeps. Not to mention I witnessed the tail end of him saving someone's life earlier.

"Is there anything I can do to help?" I ask, even though I absolutely should not have offered.

He tilts his head as he rolls up each of his sleeves to mid-forearm. I squeeze my thighs together, forcing myself not to notice the bulging veins that I love so much. *Like.* I do not love this man or anything about him, I just appreciate him.

"Dinner would help immensely," he says, looking around his office like he misplaced something. "You should join me."

I freeze. I knew this was coming. I smelled it a mile away. And dammit, it's almost six thirty. I was hungry a half hour ago.

Dom stands and walks around to my side of the desk, leaning against the edge. He's so close that his arm brushes my shoulder. I roll my lips inward, starting a quiet stream of counsel, as if he's a slowly approaching rabid raccoon as opposed to an overworked, undersexed doctor: *Stay cool, London. Just back away slowly. But dinner does sound nice. Maybe he wants sushi.*

"Dinner, huh?" The most original response of all humankind.

"Yeah. But don't worry, I won't bother lying to you about my intentions this time around."

Goosebumps flare across my forearms. I snap my gaze up to his and find his icy blues sizzling on me. Waiting for the green light.

"Let me guess. You said you want dinner but really you want breakfast?"

"Cold."

"You already ate fifteen granola bars behind your desk, but you just want an excuse for someone else to cook."

He smirks. "Getting warmer."

"You have another staged lonely Friday night lined up, and you need me to fill in for a date that you cancelled yourself."

Something in his gaze flashes, and I can tell part of him has unhinged. Maybe it's the sleep deprivation. Maybe it's the fact that he was fondling a heart less than three hours ago. Whatever it is, Dom is equal parts raw and passionate.

"How about I just tell you? I want to take you out to dinner, but this is in no way related to our professional lives. I didn't cancel on anyone. No going over matches. None of that. Not even a little bit."

His sexy I'm-the-boss-here voice is back, and it has me tingling all over. Fuck, this would be better if he could press me up against that brick wall again. Heat is pouring off him, muddying my senses, making it hard to think straight. All I want to do right now is drape myself over him and listen to his heartbeat.

"Um," I begin, forgetting why this is a bad idea. It's just dinner. We're being clear with our expectations. Is that so wrong?

"But I'm not going to beg," Dom says, standing suddenly. The loss of his body heat sends me off balance. I grip the arm rests of the chair, stopping myself short of reaching out for him as he walks away. He goes over to the coat rack by the bathroom door and slips that long wool coat on. When he returns, he packs up his briefcase wordlessly.

Every step of the process is fascinating. His jaw flexes as he pops the lock on his briefcase. I watch his knobby knuckles as he sets some folders and his laptop inside it. Every inch of me is taut and expectant. Waiting for more of him.

Who am I kidding? I can't leave this office without a piece of him. It feels wrong. Sacrilegious, even. But I've been quiet for too long. When Dom looks at me, there's something sad in his gaze.

"I'll take your silence as your answer, then."

"Wait." I hold up a palm, my heart racing. I think I know one final loophole. "Truth or dare."

He pauses. "Truth."

"Have you slept with any of your matches yet?"

My heart pounds as I await his response. This, right here—this is the murky underbelly of sleeping with a client. Because if I'm doing my job well, then I have created six brand new enemies. I'm not here to be competing against the women who are interested in this man.

"Would it change things between us if I had?"

It shouldn't, but it would. "Just answer the question."

"No. I haven't slept with any of them." He lifts a brow. "Only you."

A breath I didn't realize I was holding escapes me, and my decision is made. I'm not stepping on anybody's toes—yet. I can give in to this passion one more time. Sure, I might hate myself a little bit more. But *this* is the last time.

"Truth or dare," Dom blurts.

I squeeze my eyes shut. Both options are fraught. "Truth."

"What would you say if I said, 'Screw dinner—all I want is you, naked, in my apartment, riding my cock until morning'?" He pauses. "And, you know, some takeout."

A shiver courses through me, winding and delicious. That's all I've wanted since our last time together. And it's somehow relieving that he's on the same page. "I'd say, 'Let's hurry, because I'm starving.'"

The tension snaps between us, and Dom leads the way out of his office. "For what? My cock or food?"

"Both."

A sexy smile stretches across his face, and after he shuts the door, his free hand finds mine. He guides me through the halls of the clinic, our fingers laced together.

It shouldn't feel so right, but it does.

CHAPTER TWENTY

DOM

Physical exhaustion is a thing of the past as I pull into my apartment building's underground parking garage. London pulls into the spot next to mine, and I'm practically stumbling over myself in my hurry to get this woman up to the penthouse.

My shoes scuff over the smooth gray cement as I lock my car and close the distance between us. She's got a silly, sparkling smile on her face as I swoop her up, pulling her into my side. My heart pounds like we're teens sneaking out to go on a secret date. I don't know why I can't resist this. Resist her. It's just that everything inside me is telling me to try. To go for it. Even though London is right: I *should* stick to the matches. We *shouldn't* make this unnecessarily complicated by hooking up again.

But hell if I care about the shoulds and should nots right now.

I guide us into the elevator, her hand clasped tightly in mine as I jab the P button. Once the doors slide shut, I cup her heart-shaped face in my hands, claiming her lips. One kiss turns into another and another, and something deep inside me begins to unravel. Like a cord that's been wound tight in her absence, and finally being in her presence again allows it to unfurl.

London smiles through the kisses, looking as blissed out as I feel. She feels it too. I know she does. That doesn't make this any less confusing, though.

"Did you decide what food you wanted to order?" she mumbles through a kiss.

"Your pussy." I press my tongue past her lips, and a gravelly groan escapes me. I back her up against the wall of the elevator. The time apart didn't help things. It just made this desire worse. More unwieldy. More difficult to contain.

"I need something to eat, too, you know," she says, sliding her palms over the tops of my shoulders.

"My cock."

I run my hands down the length of her body, feeling all the dips and curves that I've been fantasizing about since our last time together. When the elevator opens at the top floor, I guide her, lip-locked, out into the short hallway. My door is one of two up here. I fumble to find my key fob in my pants pocket. London is practically purring, hooking her chin on the side of my arm to watch my struggle.

"Can't find your keys?" She pushes two fingertips along my belt, heading for the obvious tenting between my legs.

I grunt, stalling my search as her hand reaches the bulge in my pants. She looks up at me, mischief written across her face as she palms my cock through my pants.

"Fuck, London." I draw a fortifying breath, then finally find my keys in my coat pocket. I swipe the fob, and the door clicks open. I push inside, leading her into the expansive depths of my dusk-lit penthouse. Windows line the entire western wall, and the remaining burnt orange rays of sunset fill the cavernous living room, glinting off the chandelier over the dining room table. London's mouth turns into an O as she beholds my home.

"This is pretty," she breathes, head tilting as she takes it in. "Did you just move in?"

The question is a gut punch. It feels like I've been outed. "No. I've been here for about a year."

She spins in a slow circle, still clasping my hand. "Then why are there so many boxes left?"

It's easy to overlook stuff like that, when I'm barely here and I never have the energy to fully settle into this place. "I'm hardly ever home. It just keeps slipping by."

"You could hire someone to help you finish up, you know." Her heels click on the hardwood floor as we wander into the kitchen. Lake Erie sparkles in the distance, past the rooftops of other high-rise buildings. An interstate bridge cuts across the eastern half of our view. I love this place and the view. I just wish it felt half as welcoming as London's home.

"You don't even have any art up."

"Hey, I have three pieces of fake fruit, and those count as art." I jerk my thumb toward a decorative bowl on my enormous kitchen island. A pear, a banana, and an apple sit there permanently, gleaming at all hours of the day. Glancing at the fruit reminds me of my grumbling belly. I guide her toward the dining room table, which is a rustic set fashioned from upcycled, reclaimed wood, and encourage her to sit. "Let's figure out what we want to eat. Besides your dripping wet pussy."

A blush creeps across her cheeks. "You pick. I'm down for anything."

"All right. We're going to play delivery app Russian Roulette. First thing I find, I'm ordering." While I scroll, she starts fiddling with my belt.

"Good idea. Otherwise you'll be stuck deciding for hours. Like trying to find a movie on Netflix."

Then my pants crumple to the ground. London is nuzzling the crotch of my boxer briefs, purring like a kitten.

"Mmm. I hope you take longer than a Netflix search down there." I wet my bottom lip, unable to focus on the restaurant options on my screen. She laughs and places her mouth over the outline of my semi-hard cock, smiling up at me like she knows a secret.

"I'll take so long we decide not to watch a movie after all," she threatens, sliding her cool palms up along the sides of my thighs. She hooks her fingers over the edge of my boxer briefs and tugs them down. My cock springs free, bobbing heavily in the air between us. It grazes the velvet of her lips, and my abs go tight.

"Oops. Slapped myself in the face with that." She laughs, her hooded gaze stuck on my cock. I lower my phone, the image of her distracted by my cock too sexy to ignore. But her eyes snap up to find mine. "Hey. Don't get distracted. You need to eat. Order that food."

"Yeah, yeah. You're just making it a little hard."

She giggles. "Obviously."

And then her hot breath brushes the tip of my cock. She's brought her teasing game, and at this point, I can barely even see the screen of my phone. I grit my teeth, looking down at the glossy blonde top of her head.

"London," I urge, flexing my hips ever so slightly.

"What?" She looks up at me, my cock veiny and straining toward her. Her open mouth is dangerously close to the tip of my cock, and she leans forward just enough to take my cockhead between her soft lips.

A groan rockets out of me as her tongue swirls over the army helmet, and then she pulls back. "Order."

"I am." Except I'm not. I begin swiping screens again, trying to remember where I was. I'm selecting things without realizing. Her fingernails scrape up my thighs as she presses soft, languid kisses along the length of my dick. I grunt, thrusting my hips. I need more. I need her swallowing me whole.

"What are you getting?"

"I don't know yet," I admit with a laugh. I've made it to a final screen, and I'm beginning to digest words when she wraps her lips around my cock and swallows my length. My phone falls from my hands, clattering to the floor. I can't even care. Her silky mouth is God's gift to humanity. To *me*.

Fuck all the other women she's trying to set me up with. I only want her.

She pulls hard at me, and then disconnects with a loud *pop*. "Did you order?"

I grunt, fisting the front of my hair. "I don't know. You make it hard to concentrate."

She chuckles, handing my phone back to me. She plays with my balls while I make one last attempt to comprehend technology. Finally, I press ORDER and then drop the phone to the dining room table.

"Done," I wheeze, just as she takes me into her mouth again. Her green eyes find mine as she takes long, intentional pulls at my cock. My abs go rock hard as she slurps and slobbers all over me. "Jesus, London. I didn't know you were this hungry."

She moans from around my dick.

"I would have let you have a taste in my office." I tilt my head, watching as the waning slivers of color glint against her blonde hair. "If I knew you were starving."

"Fucking ravenous," she mumbles from around my cock.

"What's that?"

"Ravenous," she repeats louder, drooling all over my junk. I heard her the first time. I just like to watch her try to talk when she's got a mouthful of me.

"Gonna have to speak up, beautiful." I run my palm over the top of her head, and then take a firm fistful of her golden tresses. "Can't hear you around my junk."

She dislodges again, licking her lips as she eyes my dick. "You just want to hear me say dirty things."

I groan. "*Yes, please.*"

London smirks, looking equal parts girl next door and kinky angel. "Fine. Your cock is so big that I was sore for a full week after we fucked. And I'm pretty sure you just massaged my tonsils with this thing."

"Not what I was expecting, but hot nonetheless."

She giggles, returning to the work at hand. She jacks me off at the same time she's sucking me, and my balls are tightening within seconds. She's heat and heaven and so fucking sexy, I could melt. I fist her hair again and flex deeper into her mouth. The orgasm is churning, and there's no way I can stop it. Not when I've been imagining her on her knees in front of me daily for the past month.

London takes one last draw, and I pull myself out of her mouth, shooting my load in an epic arc across the dining room. She wipes her mouth, nodding.

"You got some real range on that one," she comments, as if this were a spectator sport.

"Come here." I tug her to standing and pull up my pants. I need to be buried inside her, because even though I just came, I'm ready for more of her. "I'm not done with you."

I hoist her over my shoulder, landing a sharp crack against her ass as I haul her off to my bedroom. Inside my slate-gray haven, the only remainder of the sunset are mauve bands near the horizon, bleeding into inky black. I toss London onto my king bed easily, with views of Cleveland sprawled all around us.

"This is impressive," she says, her voice breathy as I'm shucking my button-up.

"I know, the view is great."

"No, I mean, this." She traces a wide circle with her fingertip in my direction. "You're bulking up."

"Burning off all this sexual chemistry you refuse to acknowledge," I say, stepping out of my pants. "It drives a man to extreme fitness."

She laughs, but it fades quickly. "If that's your dirty talk, it's different from last time."

"No, that's just real talk. I have plenty of dirty things lined up for you, don't worry." I make quick work of her black slacks, sliding them down her legs, popping off her heels at the same time. She sits up long enough for me to slide the teal blouse over her head, revealing the plaid bra beneath. She helps me unclasp it, and when her palm-sized breasts are exposed, I scoop them up in both hands.

"Let's hear it then," she says, something in her tone giving away how fucking bad she *wants* this.

"Why the rush?" I bring my lips to one pebbled nipple, then the other. "You've been dying for it, haven't you?"

Her head tips backward as a I flick my tongue over each nipple in turn. "Hm."

"Fuck, London. You can't lie to me. Don't forget that."

A shudder ripples through her, eyes drifting shut. "I don't lie. I'm just...repressing."

A grunt escapes me as my kisses drift down over her belly. There aren't many people that I'd beg to hear everything they have to say, but London is definitely one of them. "You shouldn't do that. It's bad for your health."

She wriggles beneath me as my lips approach her pussy. I can already see how swollen she is. How she's fucking begging for it, without even saying a word. Seeing her laid out like this, hungry for me, even when every bit of her is trying to deny the attraction, sends me into a tailspin. If I were smart, I would stay away from her. But I'm powerless to say no to this.

I brush my lips over her swollen clit, and she arches beneath me. "Now, London." My lips touch her clit as I speak. "What are you repressing?"

A throaty chuckle slides out of her. "We're not playing therapist right now."

"No, but this is the erotic extension of our little truth or dare game." I flatten my tongue over her clit, and she moans, fisting the comforter. "Now what are you trying to keep inside?"

"Nothing." She's panting now, probably because I've slipped my middle finger inside her. She's velvet and juice and the most delirious heat. I'd do anything for her right now, and she doesn't even know it. Jump off a bridge? I-71 is right outside, so that's easy. Quit my job? I don't love the clinic most days; I'd probably find something else within a week. Drop the foundation? I'd send an email right now, rescinding my interest.

But she doesn't ask any of that. She doesn't even want me, not technically. I'm just aiming to change that.

"You were hiding something from me in the office," I say, drawing teasing circles with my tongue around her clit. "And again now. So let's just hear it. Otherwise, I might not give you what you're looking for."

She grunts. "Stop it. You can't use my orgasm as a bargaining chip."

"Too late. Already did." I ease a second finger inside of her and pump them in and out, gloriously slow. She's writhing now, bucking against my hand.

"Dommm."

"How many times have you touched yourself, thinking about our night two weeks ago?" I press a soft kiss against the stiff tip of her clit.

She groans. "Enough."

"Daily?" I ease in a third finger, and she sighs.

"Yes, Dom."

I suck hard at her clit, and she cries out, bucking against my hand again.

"Me, too," I admit, nuzzling her inner thigh. My hand drifts to my cock. I'm already begging for another release, and it's been less than ten minutes since I came. "Do you have any idea how hard you make me? Fuck, London."

"Why don't you show me?" she breathes, arching again as I slurp at her clit. And she's right. I *should* show her. I certainly plan to. But I need to know something first.

"You'd like that." I bury my fingers in her again and keep them still. "But tell me one more thing, London. And I want you to be honest." I flick my tongue back and forth over her clit. "If we didn't have the matchmaking thing between us, would you give me a chance?"

Her face scrunches up, as if she's unwilling to let the answer out of her mouth. Deep inside her, I begin curling my fingers. Her lips part, and she drapes an arm over her eyes.

"Yes, Dom. We'd be dating and fucking on the daily and visiting Zimbo's every Friday." It all rushes out of her in one long, hot confession, warming me to my core. I dip between her legs and lavish her clit with the attention I'd been denying it. Her fingers tangle in the top of my hair, and she rocks against my face, urging more friction, more passion.

I give it all to her. Because I got what I wanted. I fingerfuck her with the force I'd been restraining, and she unravels around me while my lips are covering her clit. She jerks once, and then again, moaning my name over and over again.

While she's twitching and sated, I cover her body with mine, pressing a soft kiss to her lips. Her eyes drift open and shut, but clarity zips through her gaze as my cock nestles into the folds of her pussy.

"Still not done with you," I murmur into her jawline. My lips drag up to her earlobe.

"Mmmm." A smile crosses her face.

"Exactly." I wedge myself between her legs, my cockhead finding the damp heat of her pussy. She inhales sharply, fingernails digging into the ridge of my shoulder. Darkness has descended on the bedroom, the only light streaming in from the world beyond the floor to ceiling windows. Our union is backlit by amber and gold city lights, casting a dreamlike net over everything.

Her breathy pants punctuate the still air as I curl my fingers into the flesh of her ass cheeks and surge forward. The first moment of filling her makes everything fall away. A quiet, burning bliss fills me from head to toe. It feels too right. *She* feels too right.

Something low and guttural tumbles past her lips. Everything inside me goes tight, waiting for our next release. Together. I sink into her, deliciously slow, enjoying the way the light glances off the curve of her breast, the tip of her nose. Once I'm buried to the hilt, I scoop her up in my arms and flip us over, so that I'm lying on my back.

She pushes onto the heels of her palms, looking at me with a drugged gaze. "Dom. Why do you feel so good?"

"I could ask you the same question." I kiss the tip of her nose, helping her sit up. My cock finds the last millimeters of space inside her, and a grunt rips out of me. Her head lolls to the side as she sits back on her heels.

"Ride me, beautiful." I tweak a nipple, and then rest my hands at the swell of her hips. "Enjoy the view."

"Oh, I am." Her gaze is stuck to my chest.

"Talking about the city again."

She laughs, dragging her gaze to the windows behind the bed. She gasps, pressing a hand to my chest. "Holy shit. I didn't even notice it got dark."

"That's ten points for my pussy-eating skills," I tell her.

"More like therapist negotiation skills." She rocks her hips back and forth on top of me, starting a slow but glorious rhythm. I assist her, bucking from beneath, so hard that her breasts jiggle each time I thrust upward. Her breaths are wispy, fragile, almost. It won't be long before she tumbles back over the edge.

I know it won't be long for me. Not when she's stretched like hot silk around me, her freckled smile burned into my memory. I slide a palm up over the curve of her ass, along her waist, finally cupping a breast. Her eyes drift open and shut as we find an intense but tender rhythm. Heat prickles inside me. A warning sign.

"I'm not going to last much longer," I warn her.

"It's okay." She sounds like she's a thousand miles away. Her hand covers mine on her breast, rooting me to my spot. "I want you to come inside me."

Hearing those words alone is almost enough to push me over the edge. I drive into her again from below just as she arches against me, causing a girlish gasp to escape her. I play with her nipples as she rocks back and forth, and soon, my abs are tightening, and it's all over for me.

I let out a gruff cry as the pleasure assaults me. London rocks against me again, her pussy turning into a vice around my cock as our orgasms wreak havoc at the same time. She throws her head back and moans, while I dig my fingertips into her ass cheeks as if she might float away if I don't.

The bliss is blinding—overpowering—as I pump my rounds inside her. We turn into a sloppy, sticky, sated mess. But she doesn't move. She just sits there and watches me, grinning like she's the happiest woman in the world.

I recognize that glow. It's burning bright inside me too.

And for right now? I'm the happiest man in the world.

CHAPTER TWENTY-ONE

LONDON

Penthouses don't allow much sleeping in. Not when floor-to-ceiling windows aren't covered with good blackout curtains and the following Saturday morning is the brightest on record for all of civilization.

Dom must be a perpetual early bird or a sadist. Or perhaps both. I check the clock on the nightstand—seven thirty. Jesus. So much for sleeping in on the weekend.

As I come to consciousness, I realize I'm alone in the bed. The sheets are rumpled all around me, and for a moment, I'm sad. I wanted to wake up nuzzling into Dom's warmth and that brand-new six pack I've been fawning over since yesterday.

His dark-haired head pops into the doorframe, hair tousled and the shadow of his beard sprouting across his jaw. God, this man is gorgeous. The sight of him steals my breath, and for a moment, I can't think or say a thing.

"Morning, beautiful."

"H-hi. How did you know I just woke up?"

"Had a feeling." He walks into the bedroom, holding a spatula. "Also, I've been checking every three minutes."

I fling my arm across the bed. "I was sad you weren't here to cuddle with me."

"Hang on." He races out of the bedroom, and from deep inside the penthouse, I hear a brief clanking sound. Then he returns, sans spatula.

"Had to turn the stove off," he explains as he climbs back into bed. His warm body meets my naked flesh a moment later, and he scoops me into his arms. He kisses the top of my head and everything inside me melts. Again. For like *the billionth time*.

"That was fast-acting cuddling."

"When a woman like you asks to cuddle, it's been my experience that you comply. No matter what."

I grin, tracing invisible patterns over the ridges of his abs. It feels like we've been doing this for years, even though it's been less than weeks. "I could get away with a lot, then."

"You have no idea."

There's something very serious behind our lighthearted conversation. Something that I consciously looked away from last night. Something that he forced me to dive headfirst into.

The fact that we are fucking falling for each other.

I thought it was just me, but it's more than obvious he's on this crazy train too. When our food order arrived last night, we ate in the nude on a bearskin rug in front of the crackling fireplace. Okay, I put some panties and one of his old college T-shirts on. But *he* was naked. And we were on a bearskin rug. And I'm not giving him back these clothes. Does it get much more romantic than that?

I'll overlook the fact that he ordered two sides of potato salad and one giant roast beef sub. Because, well, I was giving him head when he ordered, so he can't be held responsible for what showed up at the door.

"Have you always been this romantic?" I ask the question casually, but there is something deeper thrumming through me. He's made me fall at his feet without even trying.

"What do you mean 'romantic'?" He's dragging his fingertips in a lazy pattern over my forearm.

"We ate potato salad on a bearskin rug last night," I remind him.

He laughs. "That's not romantic. That's food delivery Russian roulette."

I nuzzle deeper into his side, relishing the scent of him. The mahogany-tinged manliness has mingled pleasantly with sweat after all our activity last night. I could get lost in his scent forever and still want more. "But it *is* romantic. Just like when we went out the first time. You orchestrated that whole thing to get me to go out with you."

"Some would call it slightly creepy."

"Or what about the breakfast you made me two weeks ago? That was very romantic."

"It's what one does after waking up," Dom insists.

I sigh, shaking my head. "What were you doing out there right now?"

"Making pancakes for you."

"For *me*." I can't help the grin that covers my face.

"Yes. Because it's what one does after waking up." Now the grin has spread to his face, and we're facing each other, foreheads pressed together like teenagers in love. In *like*. Because I don't love this man. I'm just...experiencing chemical reactions inside my body. That's all.

"You can't help but be of service, can you?" I murmur, searching his clear blue gaze. It all makes sense now. He's constantly *serving*. It's his love language. He'd probably be making me a bookshelf or something if breakfast wasn't the easiest and most practical option.

"I don't see how this relates to being romantic. Which I'm not."

"Okay. Then define romance. What would you do if you were trying to be romantic?"

His gaze shifts down and he's quiet for a moment. "I don't know. Probably...get an expensive suite somewhere and line the jacuzzi with rose petals."

"Hm. It's romantic by default. But I'll tell you what. The whole 'surprise nights out' and 'pancakes for breakfast' approach wins a lot more points."

"Oh yeah?" He presses a soft kiss to my forehead. "So how many points do I have now?"

"Too many."

The satisfied smirk that stretches across his face makes me equally upset and head over heels him. "How many more do I need to convince you to make yourself my number one match?"

The question thuds through me, burning hot and chaotic. I'm so stunned, I can barely speak. Of course I've entertained this idea. *Of course* I've already imagined what it might be like to date Dom. But the fact that he's also seriously entertaining it feels like even more of a failure.

Because not only have I led him to believe he might have a chance with me, I've failed in setting him up with someone else who would claim his attention.

"Dom," I start.

"I'm serious." His rough palm swirls over my low back.

"But you're looking for a wife. You're trying to get married."

He doesn't look fazed. "So why not to you?"

The response makes me weirdly sick to my stomach. I shake my head, rolling onto my back so I can use the unmarred white ceiling as my anchor. "That's not how I want to do things, Dom. I know you're looking for a wife of convenience, and I'm trying to facilitate that. But I'm not going to be somebody else's wife of convenience. I deserve more than that."

He props himself up onto an elbow, looking down at me with something tender written across his face. "You do. And I'm not asking you to do that. I just think that...we have something. Don't you?"

"Yes. And we absolutely shouldn't." I sit up suddenly, my chest feeling tight. This cuddle fest took an unexpected turn.

"Well it's there, regardless," he says, reaching for my wrist. He swipes his thumb back and forth over my pulse. "Whether you like it or not."

A humorless laugh escapes me, and I twist to look back at him. "Yeah. What do you think we should do about it?"

"I want to be with you," Dom says. There's no hesitation in his voice. Not an inkling of a waver or anything. He's boring into my soul with his crystalline blue eyes, and it's taking every ounce of me to stay strong. To remember why being with him is a bad idea.

"But you want to be married by next month so you can get the position with the foundation. There's no way for *us* to advance, with that in the mix."

He's quiet for a moment, but his gaze never wavers from me. "We can figure something out."

"What? What on earth could it be?" He doesn't answer right away, so I continue. "Maybe we can write into the marriage vows that you'll be a doting fake husband to Julianne while maintaining your side bitch. That the legal marriage will always entail one additional girlfriend. It's all so modern and progressive. Because if the marriage of convenience thing isn't going to snag a lady, the matchmaker girlfriend on top of it will surely seal the deal."

He's frowning now. "Funny."

"No. It's not funny. It's needlessly complicated." I sigh heavily, my gaze wandering to the delicious lines of his abs again. "If you want to be with me, there's only one direct route that I can see. And it looks like getting rid of the obstacle that you brought to my doorstep."

His frown deepens. "I'm so close to the position I can taste it. I can't back out now."

"I'm not asking you to. I'm just telling you one possible solution. Maybe the *only* solution."

He rakes a hand through his hair. "Well it's a non-option. They're going to offer me the position. I know it. And not only will I have job security for the rest of my life, I'll be making history. How can I walk away from that?"

I shrug. "You're not supposed to. You know what you want. And it's the prestige."

His eyes narrow. "It's more than prestige."

"You're right. It's prestige and a loveless marriage and the perfect cardiological façade."

As soon as the words leave my mouth, I know I've gone too far. Dom's gaze drags razor-sharp over me, and I can tell I've activated something inside him.

"It's not a façade. It's my fucking end goal."

"An organization that you yourself called a prestigious bunch of status whores."

He scoffs. "What non-profit isn't that way? It's called playing the game. I don't make the rules, but I know where I want to end up, and I know how to get there."

"And I respect that. But your game will lead you and me in opposite directions. It's just a fact. Because I'm not going to sacrifice what I deserve just because you need to have a wife by next Tuesday."

"Noted. And now we know what happens when the world's two most stubborn people try to make something work," he mutters, pushing to standing.

"There are plenty of other fish in the sea," I say, even though it feels like a big lie. I'm sure I'll be repeating it to myself for the next few months. Even though Dom is the only bull shark I want.

"There's that romance you're looking for." The sarcasm is dripping from his tongue. "You know, I was going to say that you didn't even tell me if you wanted to be with me too. But I realize you made it more than clear."

He stalks out of the bedroom, leaving me in a tense, amply lit silence. Everything inside me feels misplaced and odd. Even though we're at a dead end, I don't want to leave things like this between us. I roll out of bed and use his bathroom to wash my face and get ready for the day. I slowly redress in yesterday's clothes, and the smell of pancakes fills the air.

When I walk into the kitchen, Dom is preparing breakfast with a scowl. He's made up two plates, which dissolves the hard edge of the lingering tension.

"Just so you know," I begin, sliding onto a stool at the kitchen island, "I do want to be with you. A lot. Like, way more than I want to ever admit to another human being. Okay? For being the most arrogant, work-obsessed, anti-social, basically-estranged, non-family man I've ever met—"

"Are those all my flaws?" he asks.

"Yes. And despite them, I still want to be with you. But you and I both know that we've come to a dead end here."

"Marry me," he says, so tenderly that for a split second, I actually consider it. "That way, we can both have everything we want. You and I can be together. It's just a piece of paper, London. It doesn't mean anything. I'll get the position, and we can keep dating."

My throat tightens, tears threatening at my composure. Jesus, he really is the least romantic man on the planet. This is not at all how I envisioned my proposal story unfolding: in a desperate race against the non-profit clock. True love forged from a deadline.

No thanks.

"We've had sex twice and you want to get married."

"We've had sex way more than twice, and yes, I knew after the first time that you were it for me."

I pinch my eyes shut. It's hard to stay grounded when he peppers in little details like that. *Because I feel the same way about him.*

"So, we just date while married until we realize six months from now that we were wrong about each other? Usually when people stop dating, they don't need to hire a lawyer. But in our case, it would mean getting a divorce."

"Who cares? I have the money to pay for it." He's pushing tiny pancakes onto two plates. Maple syrup is already on the island, and he fills the rest of the plates up with scrambled eggs. "If it comes to that."

The food looks and smells amazing, but it does nothing to sweeten the pot. I pour an overly generous amount of syrup on my pancakes as I mull over my response. His idea makes a snakelike anxiety slither through me. And for some reason, it all just seems like a slap in the face to the vow I made my dead sister.

"Go live life to the fullest," doesn't start with a sham marriage.

Or does it?

"Just think about it," he urges.

I'm ready to tell him no, but when I catch the sincerity slashed across his face—the raw edges of his feelings for me—I can't find the words.

Instead, I swallow the knot in my throat and nod.

CHAPTER TWENTY-TWO

LONDON

Dom and I wrap up our weirdly non-romantic morning together—a couple's fight, followed by a sham wedding proposal, rounded off with his grandmother's recipe for cinnamon pancakes. His idea sits inside me like a questionably fresh sushi roll. Will I be ill in an hour, or will it turn out that the eel roll was actually fine?

I need a second opinion. Hazel's, to be specific.

Not having signed the NDA would be great, but I'm stuck in that no matter which way I turn. This just means I need to be extremely dodgy while laying out all the specifics of an intimate relationship. No big deal. I'm sure Hazel will have no problem with this scenario.

I wait until I'm back home in the golden warmth of my apartment, nestled into my favorite armchair with a furry blanket draped over my lap. Hugging a steaming mug of coffee, I call Hazel on speakerphone. When she picks up, I dive right in.

"I'm about to tell you something that might sound a little crazy, but I need you to hear me out." *Like I'm fucking your boyfriend's brother, and he wants to make me your future sister-in-law.*

"Okay," she says slowly.

"I need romantic advice."

She snorts. "Is that the crazy part?"

"No, it's just—" I falter, pinching the bridge of my nose. "Here goes. I started seeing a client."

"Oh, wow. You're seeing someone? And a *client*?"

"Like I said, just hear me out. I tried like hell to avoid it, but this man..." A sigh escapes me.

"Who is it?"

I roll my lips inward. *You already know him.* "I can't say. For legal reasons."

"Oh my GOD, are you dating one of the Cleveland Cavaliers?"

I snicker. "No. But that doesn't sound like a bad idea. It's just...the professional side makes things weird. And we're in the middle of our contract. So I can't say a damn word about who he is."

She heaves an annoyed sigh. "How am I supposed to give you advice if I don't know who it is?"

"You wouldn't know him anyway." White lies never hurt anyone, right? "It's just part of our contract."

"Can I at least get a physical description?"

I smirk. "Tall, dark, and handsome."

"The most cliché description of all time. Fine. Go on."

I run through the brief history of our meetups, and the fact that he needs to get married for unspecified, urgent reasons. When I tell her that Mr. TallDarkHandsome wants to marry me instead of one of his matches, Hazel gasps.

"Are you going to?"

"I don't know. I shouldn't. And especially not when there are many other routes we can take to being together. None of which he considers an option, of course."

"Hm. Well, while I wouldn't mind a quick Vegas wedding getaway to be your witness, I see your point."

"He's dragging me into his complications. Life is too short to do something you don't want to. I should be 1000% on this. Not 85%."

"But you think you could be serious about him?"

"Yeah. Probably. I mean, I'm falling fast for him, Hazel. I'm not gonna lie. I just don't think it's fair that my only option to continue seeing him is to marry him or...nothing."

"You're right. And you know what? If he feels so strongly about you, he should be moving mountains for you. It sounds like he's got his priorities elsewhere. It would be convenient if you fell in line and allowed him to have his cake and eat it too. But that's not what you're looking for, babe."

I squeeze my eyes shut, pinching a tear out. I don't know why it hurts so good to hear that. Maybe because I needed to hear my best friend's wisdom to remind me that I'm not insane for not offering up my ring finger when Dom says, "Marry me."

We chat for a little bit longer, the conversation drifting to a sip-and-paint that we have planned for an upcoming Cleveland outing, and then we hang up the phone. Resolution is burbling inside of me. I'm going to let Dom know I made up my mind. That the ball is officially in his court, but I cannot become Mrs. Daly. Not now. Not under these circumstances.

My fingers are shaking as I write the text. I don't know why, but it feels like we've been dating for years. Like I'm walking away from something huge. Like maybe I really am dumb for rejecting his offer of marriage as a temporary solution. Maybe it *would* give us everything we wanted.

Willow, what would you do?

I can see my little sister in my mind's eye, the same as the week before she passed. Long, blonde, flowing hair, her dimpled grin both innocent and mischievous. I can imagine her urging me to marry him for the shock value of it, just so she could be the flower girl.

I hear the whole conversation in my head—Willow suggesting I divorce him a week later, only to find a new urgent husband, followed by another divorce, followed by another husband. But then I imagine Willow's face going serious. Her reaching out to touch my shoulder. Saying, "You don't want to have that many weddings, though, do you, sis? You should just do it once. To the guy you love like crazy. The one who's gonna last forever. The way you've been imagining it since forever."

Tears are pooling in my eyes as I type out the text. It shouldn't be this serious. But for some reason, with Dominic Daly, it is.

LONDON: Dom, I can't marry you.

LONDON: I know it's not what you want to hear. I hope you believe me that I want to be with you. Just not enough to sacrifice my sacred vision of what my future marriage will be. I deserve a chance at that, at least. Maybe you don't get it. I know it's just a piece of paper to you. But I have higher hopes for the love of my life.

I check my phone every ten seconds after those texts, waiting for a response. For an emoji. For fucking *anything*.

In the back of my head, I'm praying that Dom will find a different solution for us to explore this crazy connection between us. One that looks a lot like allowing things to take a natural course. Without constraints or timelines or faking a marriage for a board of physicians.

When Dom doesn't answer that evening, I'm not surprised.

When he doesn't answer the following day, I begin to understand.

And when Monday rolls around and he still hasn't written back, I realize he's made his decision.

CHAPTER TWENTY-THREE

DOM

It's nine a.m. in Chicago the following Friday. My plane landed at ten o'clock last night, and even though I only packed a carry-on, I brought enough anxiety to fill at least three checked bags.

It's the day of the final interview with the Physicians Guild. I'm 100% certain they're going to offer me the position, until five minutes passes and I'm feeling 100% certain that this was a massive waste of my precious time.

Not only a waste of time, but a waste of energy. Energy that I could have spent convincing London to stay.

It's not time to think about London. And definitely not about how she should be in your life. Get your head in the game, Dom.

Not an hour has gone by that I haven't reread her text in my mind. I'd be lying if I said I didn't consider dropping my quest to snag this position. I've thought about it too much, in fact, starting from the day I brought her back to my penthouse. But stewing over it that long allowed my rational mind to surface for one last, gasping breath to remind me that I was acting fucking crazy.

Dr. Dom, renouncing his goal just because of a couple amazing dates? That's not me. That's not the man I've been struggling to become. And if anything, London has made me realize why I'm becoming the man I am. Why it was important to begin with.

Because what happens when a man chases a woman the way I was tempted to do mere days ago?

Everything crumbles. I've already lived it. I already know how that story ends. And hell if I'm diving headfirst into it again.

Realistically, I should be happy that London helped me wake up. Instead, I am the opposite.

I am—in a word—butthurt.

"Dominic Daly." The sound of my name in the cavernous foyer jerks me to attention. This is fucking it. I stand and smooth the front of my nicest dress pants, adjusting my tie for maybe the fiftieth time since seven a.m. A featureless woman leads me into a board room with an incredibly high ceiling and a conference table that could host an entire royal family dinner.

However, instead of a dining monarch and his clan, there are seven very stern looking physicians. I swallow hard, butterflies staggering to life in my gut. This is somehow worse than my board exams.

"Dr. Daly. A pleasure to finally meet you." The monotone voice of the board president, Dr. Humphrey, fills the room. He's an actual celebrity in the medical world, having been named the country's top neurosurgeon for the past seven years. The other doctors I only know from photos, when I did enough covert research to warrant browsing in Secret mode. He gestures to the lone chair facing them.

"A pleasure hardly covers it." My voice rings false in the room. I wonder if they can tell. If maybe all the men showing up to this final interview today sound the same as me. "I've been looking forward to this moment for years."

Dr. Humphrey and the other board members smile, but it's the polite kind, like the Queen of England might use. Because these men *are* royalty in the medical world. And I'm closer than I've ever come to being knighted.

"Your application has shown amazing promise. We've all been quite interested to meet you in person. It seems you're doing innovative work in your region of Ohio."

"Innovative, yes. Consistent, as well."

Dr. Humphrey and the other members have papers in front of them, which they refer to at random. It must be my application or some sort of summary featuring my merits. I squeeze my hands into fists below the table. I can only imagine what a most recent breakdown of my merits might look like. *Top skills: open heart surgery; spicy scrambled eggs; chasing the one unavailable woman in Cleveland.*

"Dr. Daly?"

I realize one of the other board members has asked me a question. I don't even remember what we were talking about.

"I'm sorry, could you repeat that? I'm hard of hearing on this side." It's a lie, but a convenient one. Better than the truth, which is that I'm being derailed from the biggest meeting of my life by thoughts of a woman who would rather chase a fantasy than be practical. What I offered her was practical. A promising relationship that satisfies everyone's needs.

How could she not see it the way I do?

Our interview trudges on, full of empty platitudes about service to the medical community and inquiries about my long-term vision of improving medical care. I'm able to bullshit with ease—a master, after all—and I can tell that the board is pleased, though it's hard to tell just how much behind those most-likely-surgically-altered stern expressions without a hint of forehead wrinkle.

In fact, all these men are oddly smooth. Like some sort of reptilian alien species came and chose *doctor* as their disguise du jour. The costumes are passable, but just a few details are off.

That's something London would have liked to hear. I'll have to tell her.

Except I won't ever get the chance to.

"...and honestly, Dr. Daly, in full confidence, you are at the very top of the list at this point."

I tune in just long enough to catch this quiet vote of confidence. Dr. Humphrey is grinning.

"Now, you said that you're married, no kids." He shuffles some papers. "Hopefully children are on the table by now. Will your wife be available to attend the acceptance gala?"

Anxiety constricts my chest. After such a successful interview, I'd been lulled into a false sense of security. Maybe they wouldn't address the one area I still haven't figured out in my life. But of course they did.

"Gala?"

"You know that we host an annual holiday gala to welcome new board members and thank our donors. Will your wife be present at the event? It's imperative that wives attend the biannual celebrations each year."

"I, uh," I clear my throat, lacing my fingers together on the table. This might be the moment where it all falls down around me. "This was one aspect of my application that we haven't had a chance to clarify. I'm not married *yet*. My fiancée and I have a winter wedding date set."

The lie burns through me. The board members consult each other with doubtful looks.

"I do suppose this is part and parcel of me being potentially the youngest new inductee. My fiancée and I wanted to wait until our careers were set before spending so much money on the lavish celebration that we deserve. But she's one hundred percent committed to this organization as much as, if not more than, I am." If this is the case, then my wife can *never* be London. "You can absolutely count on her being there."

My heart pounds with the falseness of it all. And in the back of my mind, I'm just hoping they don't ask me what her name is. Because I don't know. I'm just hoping this buys me more time to convince London to see me one more time because I'm jonesing for her, or to finally cut out my attraction to her like a malignant growth. One of those has to happen. Immediately.

"You raise a fair point," one of the board members rumbles. "Today's world is different than when my wife and I married."

The board members briefly confer about my fudge on the application where I selected "Married, no kids." They decide that it was the only valid option for me to select, given my intention to marry during the current fiscal year. As my father always said: Ask for forgiveness, not for permission. I hedged my bets correctly.

After a few wrap-up questions, I am on my way out the door with a bright promise that I'll be hearing back about their decision within four weeks.

On one hand, four weeks is an eternity. We'll be in December by then, for God's sake. I just want the notoriety already, but this new timeline is the ticking clock on finally biting the bullet. The thing I've been expertly avoiding for the past God-knows-how-long.

Post-interview, I lunch at a Chicago-style pizzeria with views of the river. I walk down some streets before grabbing a ride to the airport, and I stumble upon an artisan pottery store of all places. The pieces are gorgeous and thoughtful. Exactly the kind London would have hanging around. I buy a smaller vase without thinking twice.

It's a bright and sunny November day, and the chill in the air reminds me of how much I'd like to have London tucked into my side...or maybe even pulled into the front of my coat, like the night we went to Zimbo's.

My heart clenches strangely. The proud side of me refuses to lie down for someone who wouldn't do whatever she could to help me achieve my goal. London knows that this is what I've been dreaming of and reaching for. So why not just make my life easier so we both get what we want?

I'm mulling over this predicament nonstop, even when I'm napping on the plane, or otherwise trying not to think about it. My flight lands in Cleveland by eight o'clock, and I'm home in bed by nine.

Nothing feels quite right. Going ahead with Julianne feels unattractive in a way I never could have predicted. Backing out of the running still seems like a non-option, even though more and more I am thinking about when London confronted me about my own words: *prestigious bunch of status whores.* Not only are they status whores, the most pressing part of today's interview was whether or not my model-worthy wife would be on my arm at the gala.

I wish I could tell London how right she was to call me out, but that's also a non-option. I'm still going through with it. I've had my eye on it for too long to back out now, and I am if nothing else a man of his word. My father might have been a competitive slave driver to me and my brothers growing up, but he instilled some basics in all of us that still keep us on track. And one of those basics is that stability is the foundation to success.

I am as stable as they come. I can make the bedrock of the Rocky Mountains look like a flaky bitch. I am not only stable myself, I stabilize others—during heart attacks, in catheterizations, and more.

So this board position is the natural extension of my stability. It's like carving my name into the ancient rock bed so that future generations can also know how stable I was.

I barely sleep that night, and the whole rest of my week is pretty shitty too. The office is busier than normal because of the holidays: everyone's trying to get seen before we break. Usually for Thanksgiving, I stay home and take a rare *me* day that involves lounging on my couch while indulging in maybe one movie before eventually turning my laptop back on to catch up on work. I haven't gone home for Thanksgiving in three years.

But this year, everything feels disjointed. Scattered. Maybe *imploded* is the right word. London haunts me more than I can explain—more than seems logical—and amid all my confusion, it seems like going home might actually be the only step that makes sense.

I call my mom the Monday before Thanksgiving, once I've finally accepted that a trip to Bayshore is right. I haven't been back there since my grandma Ethel passed earlier this year in June, where I saw all my brothers at once. Staying in the Daly childhood home was a difficult walk down memory lane, mostly because Grayson and I were at each other's throats immediately, and Connor kept me up most nights while he incessantly fucked his girlfriend Kinsley. I spent a long weekend there, but it was enough to tide me over for the year—or so I thought.

But this time, the prospect of a walk down memory lane is less off-putting. Something about Bayshore is calling me. I can at least go there for an evening to see what this pull is trying to tell me.

An email from London arrives on Tuesday. We haven't spoken for weeks, even though she sent me a follow-up email last Monday that I ignored. The sight of her email address in my inbox makes my stomach drop to my feet.

Hey again! Just wanted to check in on your progress. I'll take the silence as a good sign, since I'm sure you're out there working on your new relationship! I really hope things are going well with Julianne. Just give me an update when you can for my records. You know, with the holiday coming up, it would be a great idea to take her back to Bayshore so she can meet the family! That way, you can establish even more legitimacy before the board decides who to pick. As I promised, I'm seeing this through to the end. I'm invested in the happily-ever-after you're going after, so you can count on me if you need anything until you set the wedding date.

Best,

London

I scowl at the email for a full ten minutes. I haven't talked to Julianne in a week and a half. At this point, she's on stand-by, and she knows it. I was brutally honest with her about what I need and how things might progress, and she was still somehow down with it. I think she's more excited about using me as arm candy. And isn't that just perfect?

But what doesn't feel perfect is how London has reverted so quickly back to business-as-usual. And that's the root of it. What I felt burbling to life inside of me doesn't allow for business as usual. While it's my fault for even allowing it to happen, I can't deny that she woke me up to something I had decided to leave in my past.

She clearly wasn't affected the same way. She could walk away. She could turn down a perfectly logical proposal, even when it made all parties happy.

It's my turn to forget what sprang to life between us, since she clearly already has. And sitting in my penthouse over Thanksgiving isn't the way to do that. I need to be distracted by new and different methods.

My head needs some fucking clarity.

And my heart?

It only needs London. Which I need to fix. Immediately.

CHAPTER TWENTY-FOUR

LONDON

I'd be lying if I said I didn't reconsider Dom's least-romantic-of-all-time proposal to me on the daily—sometimes hourly—for the two weeks after he made it.

I'm as incensed by the marriage proposal as I am inclined to double back and accept his offer. Not like it's still valid. I'm sure that my break-up text to him was enough to drive Dom away forever. And really, that's what I wanted. That's what I was shooting for. So why aren't I happier about the distance?

I thought two weeks would break me of this unnatural infatuation with Dr. Dom. I thought his proposal alone would be enough to show me that we're on different pages and that we can't continue reading this book together. But these details only prove to me that I am hopelessly lost.

Forget my happily-ever-after. Apparently all I can focus on is the unhappily-ever-practical of Dom's obsessive quest to medical stardom.

So more time. That's what I need. Two weeks is nothing in the spectrum of nursing broken hearts. I need to let two months roll by, and *then* see where I'm standing.

Operation wait it out: activated.

Operation fantasize about Dom's dirty mouth: cancelled.

Dom's radio silence has been a pretty clear signal that he's either still pissed about that text or has solidly moved on with Julianne, or maybe both. And goddammit, I wish I could talk about *any* of this with Hazel. But I've reached my limit of faceless advice-seeking. At this point, my issues involve aspects of Dom that are heavily Daly-centric. I can't fathom explaining the family dynamic of the Dalys using anonymous identifiers, only to chuckle with her about how similar it sounds to Grayson's family.

Surprise, Hazel. All this drama revolves around the man who made your boyfriend's adolescence a living hell.

All this ridiculous lovesickness would be enough. But Carl hasn't stopped emailing during the two weeks leading up to Thanksgiving. I've read most of them, out of morbid curiosity, but the recent ones I haven't bothered opening because his earlier emails made his thoughts clear. He still thinks I was wrong about what I did. Carl wants to "put the past in the past" and "move beyond the professional suicide," because he believes he can "help me rebuild." He hopes I "recognize his forgiveness," because not every lover or employer would be willing to do the same.

His words look less like forgiveness and more like a reminder that he's the big man doing *me* a favor. Which is what it always was with him. Always.

How many more weeks will it take to wait out these unwanted spam emails? I can't be avoiding two different men for two different reasons for the rest of the year.

Thanksgiving is going to be a welcome disconnect. I built out my week so that I can head to my parents' house in Bayshore on

Wednesday and stay through Sunday. Not like I need to stay so long when I live just an hour away, but I'm treating it like a mini-vacation. No work.

Just friends, family, and food, as God intended.

Hazel is the first person I see when I get into town. I go straight to her office, in fact, walking down the sidewalks of downtown Bayshore with childlike wonder. They put the Christmas decorations up early this year—usually they wait until *after* Thanksgiving—but I'm not mad about it. Right outside Hazel's office, they hung an enormous wreath that says *Tis The.*

Hazel is seated at her desk, typing on her computer when I walk in. A big grin lights up her face. "There you are!"

"Finally. Hey, did you know your wreath only says 'Tis The'?"

Hazel snorts as we meet in the middle of her office for a hug. "That's a city-supplied wreath, I'll have you know. I would never leave my seasonal greetings hanging like that."

"Maybe we should finish it for them. I'll find the materials and fix it and then bill the city." I follow Hazel toward her desk and sit down in the plush chair facing her workspace. "Except the message might be different when I'm done with it. I'm thinking, 'Tis the Sneezin'.'"

"In honor of flu season," Hazel confirms.

"Exactly. Now tell me, O Master of Real Estate. What are our plans for tonight?"

A mischievous look crosses her face. "Well, you know how downtown goes wild on the night before Thanksgiving. There are a few cocktail parties I've got my thumb on. I think we should have a healthy sampling of all of them."

"I *love* healthy samplings. Whatever you choose, I'm there. Just tell me the dress code."

"I think we should go all out."

"Does that mean we dress like actual turkeys? Because I didn't bring that onesie with me."

Hazel snorts. "Do you really have a turkey onesie?"

"Target," I say. As if that needs any additional explanation. "So you're saying heels, enormous earrings, and my tightest dress."

"'Tis the Sneezin'," she confirms with a wily grin.

"Oh, please. No flu season for me tonight. I need to look good enough to snag Henry Cavill while also honing my spinster vibes." My cheeks flush at the inadvertent celebrity-lookalike reference to Dom. Ugh, if only they didn't look so similar.

Hazel's face softens. "I take it that thing with the mystery Cleveland Cavs man didn't end well."

"You could say that." I sigh, absentmindedly fiddling with the decorative bolts along the arm rest of my chair. "I just want to have a great night out with my girl...and her soulmate, of course."

Hazel bites her bottom lip. It's so funny how she gets coy about her and Grayson still. Like she hasn't seen it coming for approximately, oh, her entire life. "We're going to have a *great* night. And you're going to forget all about that stupid man you're contractually forbidden to mention by name."

Dom. His name is Dom. The words run like a marquee through my head, as I'm sure they will all night. Hell, all weekend.

Seeing Grayson so much is only going to remind me of his older brother. But I can at least feel confident in one thing. That stubborn, nearly estranged mule is tucked into his penthouse in Cleveland, counting his awards or hearts saved or whatever it is he does in his nil free time.

I have no chance of running into Dom while I'm home.

And I don't know if that makes me relieved or unbearably sad.

CHAPTER TWENTY-FIVE

I don't think anyone in my family is as surprised to see me walk through the front door of my parents' house as Grayson.

Honestly, the genuine confusion that wrenches at his face could have won the grand prize in the Great Sibling Estrangement Race. The runner-up is when he says, "Dominic? Is that you?"

"Not sure who else it would be." I set my overnight bag on the floor before I head to greet my family in the kitchen. Mom is there, as well as Grayson, who looks like he just lost a battle with a paint roller, and Maverick.

Grayson follows me into the kitchen. "There's just no way it would be Dr. Dominic Daly. He doesn't leave his golden Cleveland skyscraper for *anything*."

My teeth clench. Shots fired, and I've been here thirty seconds. Mom shushes him and sweeps toward me, pulling me into a hug.

"We're so happy you're here," she murmurs into my ear. Patting my back, she squeezes me one last time before pushing me away to get a good look at me. "I thought you weren't coming until tomorrow."

"I was able to clear my schedule," I say, glancing at Grayson. I have a hundred evil things I could shoot him down with, but the acidity dissolves before I get a chance to. "I thought I'd enjoy some extra time at home."

A weird silence settles through the kitchen. Grayson's brows draw even closer together.

"Okay," he says.

"Good luck actually enjoying it here," Maverick mutters, and then disappears down the hallway.

"I think it's *wonderful*," my mother oozes, with those Mom-grade earmuffs that allows her to ignore all the bullshit coming from her spawns' mouths. "What's new, honey? Is work still going well? Dad said you had some big news coming up."

Of course he said that. Because I've been spoon-feeding him the highlight reel of my career, waiting for...something. I don't know what. An award that says, "Congratulations, you're definitely the best of all time, so no need to keep trying anymore," maybe. A trophy securing my place as the eldest *and* most successful Daly brother. In the worst-case scenario, a pin that says "#1 SON."

Thanksgiving is *the* ideal time to dangle this accomplishment over my brothers' heads. To elicit gasps and delight from Mom while my brothers watch Dad nod approvingly.

But I'm missing my usual verve for one-upping, for showing Grayson he's not as great as he thinks he is. Maybe it'll come back to me once I figure out why I should give a shit about the board position these days.

While I'm silent mulling over my response, Grayson chimes in. "Big news, huh? Let me guess. Lifetime Achievement Award for Arrogance."

I narrow my eyes. "Good guess, but wrong. They only give that award out once. And if memory serves correctly, you were the recipient last year, Mr. Bigtime Banker."

He frowns. "Ex-banker, thank you very much."

"That's right. Banker turned Tim 'the Tool Man' Taylor." It's a low blow, but I've spent my life sending out the barbs without considering the consequences. But this time, something deep inside me wrenches. Not sure what that is, though. Maybe my anxiety is breeding indigestion now.

"Wow. I can't believe you just used the show *Home Improvement* as an insult. Thanks, *Wilson*."

"Boys," Mom says.

"Wilson was a source of guidance and inspiration," I remind my brother, "so thank you for the compliment. I'll be sure to get it printed out and framed so I can hang it alongside the one other compliment you've paid me my entire life."

Grayson props his palms on his hips. "There is something seriously wrong with you."

"Do you two have to be at each other's throats like this the second you're in the same room?" There's a tinge of desperation in her voice that gets both of us to look her way.

"It's just hard for me to believe that Mr. Know-It-All gives a damn if his lowly little tool man brother pays him a compliment," Grayson goes on.

"It's less about receiving a compliment," I clarify, "and more about receiving anything that isn't actual piss out of your mouth."

I can see his hackles rise—I'm good at making that happen. The slump of my mother's shoulders combined with the skyrocketing testosterone in the room reminds me suddenly of London—*basically-estranged non-family man*—as if her words haven't been ringing in my head since she spoke them. And here I am, proving her right.

"You are one to fucking talk—" Grayson begins.

"Listen, I piss out of my mouth too. It's whatever. Can we move on now?" It's my best on-the-fly attempt to smooth things over. Is this a baby step? My heart is racing, and I'm tense, as if waving a tiny white flag has somehow outed me a wuss.

"There we go." Mom sends us both a strained smile. "An odd way of saying 'welcome home,' but I'll take it."

Grayson seems slightly subdued, so maybe I made the right move. Maybe he's just planning his revenge, like that time he waited in my closet for *four full hours* just to snag the perfect chance to jump out of my closet in full gorilla regalia, in the hope that I'd piss my pants.

I didn't piss my pants, but I did trickle. He never knew that, though.

"I've gotta get back to work," Grayson says brusquely. "Thanks for lunch, Mom. Thanks for nothing, Dom."

He storms down the hall before I can respond, and when the front door slams, my mom and I simultaneously sigh.

"Just in case you forgot what it was like to have your two eldest sons in the house," I tell her, squeezing her arm.

"Thanks for the reminder." She sends me a wry sidelong look. "If I'd known you were coming, I would have waited to have lunch with you. What do you have planned for this afternoon?"

"Nothing," I admit, and the confusion on her face echoes the confusion inside me. I don't entirely understand why I've taken time off to come home early. Nancy was thrilled—with me taking time off, sure, but more because I'd be going to the same place *London is from*. Like I wasn't from Bayshore first. I'm four years older than London, for God's sake. But Nancy has been gaga for London since the first time they emailed. Their sisterhood would delight me more if I weren't so hellbent on removing London from my headspace.

"Well let's do something just you and me," my mom says, a big smile stretching across her face. "How long has it been since we've had the chance? Probably almost a decade. God, how time passes." She sighs, and then gasps, grasping my forearm. "I know! Let's go see your inheritance!"

"My inheritance?"

"What Grammy Ethel left you, silly." She swats my arm, and that's when the pieces click into place. I'd forgotten about the inheritance. *All* about it, actually. Mom told me after the funeral that Grandma had bequeathed me a piece of property downtown, but I bolted back to Cleveland the first chance I got and never thought of it again.

"That sounds great, actually." I wouldn't mind visiting downtown, spending some time just being a person again, out with his mom. "Want to go now?"

Mom grin and pinches my cheeks, just like she used to when I was a boy, and scoots off to find her coat. When she's bundled up in a sleek pea coat, I offer to drive.

"No, let's walk. I want to see the water."

No complaints there. It's a decently warm day, especially for Thanksgiving, which is always a fifty-fifty chance between outright blizzard or 60-degree heat wave.

The sidewalks are still cluttered with fallen leaves, but I can tell that the city leaf collection has been around at least once or twice. The piles of leaves lining the streets are thinner; all the big oak and maple trees are now completely bare. The air holds something crisp and invigorating—slight decay mixed with the freshwater breeze.

Our footsteps scuff down the sidewalk as we head toward the boardwalk, which wraps around the lakefront toward downtown. Being this close to the lake feels better than I anticipated. Sure, I live less than a quarter mile from the lakefront in Cleveland, and I look at it every day from the penthouse. But this feels different. Maybe because I'm here without a to-do list. Maybe because I'm searching for something. Maybe because I'm actually giving myself a chance to unwind, however it ends up.

By the time we make it downtown, Mom has made it her new job to act as my official Bayshore tour guide. She's pointing out all the new developments—a lash and brow bar that she visits with Hazel for their girl dates, a Vietnamese restaurant, a bakery that specializes in Instagram-worthy cookies that has gone viral twice since opening. They've redone sidewalks and updated planters. All the Christmas decorations are out in full force too, which is disorienting, because in my mind it's still June.

We've walked almost the entire width of downtown Bayshore, lost in conversation and nostalgia, when suddenly my mom stops and grins up at a dilapidated building.

"Here it is," she says, gesturing toward a forgotten wooden door with a grime-caked window looking into an abandoned showroom. The navy-blue paint is peeling off the door, and you can still read the faint outline of the letters that used to be painted on the window: "Heineman's Photography."

I'm so underwhelmed by this building that it takes me a moment to put two and two together.

"You mean this is what I inherited?"

Mom nods and fishes a key out of her pocket. The front door opens with a painful lurch, and Mom leads me into the cool, musty front room of the building.

"Your Grammy Ethel was the landlord of this place for the past fifty years. She always wanted to pass it on to her eldest grandchild. She viewed it as a business venture that she wanted to pass along."

I blink, taking it all in. I can't imagine what on Earth I'm supposed to do with this place other than get rid of it. "But...why not sell it?"

Mom shrugs, our footsteps echoing through the cavernous space as we go deeper into the building. The walls are a mix of dusty plaster and peeling wallpaper. If I had to guess the last time this place was inhabited, I'd say pre-nineties.

But the ceilings. Oh, lord, the ceilings are gilded and exquisite and easily fourteen feet high. I stop walking to crane my neck and stare. The geometric designs are mesmerizing up there.

"Holy shit," I murmur.

"Yeah. Just wait until you see the back part." Mom leads me down two steps and through a small doorway that opens into a long room with bay windows overlooking the lake. Natural light fills the space, and I gasp.

"This is a nice surprise," I say. "Wish my office looked like this."

Mom chuckles, and the idea hits me like a sack of bricks. My office. This could be *my office.*

At my Bayshore clinic.

My throat catches, and I actually need to take a few breaths to calm the sudden surge of excitement. I spin on my heel to look at everything again. My low-income clinic could fit *perfectly* here. Walking distance from several senior living centers. Accessible by residents of any part of the city via the Bayshore bus system. I swallow a knot in my throat and head back into the main area, scanning things with the clinic in mind.

"What used to be here?" I ask, trying to sound casual and not like I just stumbled upon a piece of my personal puzzle that I'd been missing for the last five years.

"Oh, it used to be a lot of things. Back in the fifties, it was a legal office. At some point it became a yacht showroom."

"In here?"

"The yachts weren't *in here,*" Mom clarifies. "But you could browse their catalogs and hear a spiel from a guy with a bad combover."

"I take it you were approached by a yacht salesman."

"I dated one," Mom confirms wryly.

I can't believe I've never known this juicy little detail before. "Who was it?"

She frowns slightly, her gaze moving toward the back of the building. "Kinsley's dad."

My mouths rounds, but I don't say anything. The whole thing is still kinda wild to me—not only that Connor dared to date a Cabana girl, but that it's lasted this long. Much less with someone as...well, *odd* as Kinsley.

"He had a combover in the seventies?" It's the only thing I can think to say.

"No, but his boss did." She laughs. "God, I hope that family doesn't become related to me by law."

I can sense we're stumbling into awkward territory. "You think Connor and Kinsley are going to get married?" If so, then my whole get-married-before-the-others window is shrinking way faster than I bargained for.

She lobs a sigh, shoving her hands into the pockets of her pea coat. "I think it's coming. Connor hasn't proposed yet, but he and Kinsley have started that business together."

This is news to me. Guilt trickles through me. Connor took the entrepreneurial leap, just like Grayson, and I had no idea.

"I had no idea they started a business together. Why didn't you tell me?" It's hard to keep the accusation out of my voice.

"You're able to talk to your brothers on your own, you know," she shoots back. "Besides, would you have cared?"

The question is a dagger in my chest. Because she's not wrong. About any of it. I wouldn't have cared. But for some reason, I do now.

"I care now," I say, my voice sounding weird and distant to my own ears. God, have I ever said these words to my brothers? "I think that's great. I'm glad for him."

Mom offers a small smile, taking one of my hands in both of hers. "He's doing extremely well. And the business is taking off. They're making it work. And if they can make something like that work, I can only imagine that marriage will be the next step." She heaves a sigh, like she's preparing to unleash something from the depths of her soul. "Kinsley is really good for Connor. She's a sweet girl, even if she has an unfortunate last name."

We take our last looks at the space, I snap some pictures, and we lock up before heading back across town. Our conversation is ringing in my head.

I don't quite understand it, but I want to be the third Daly brother to join the entrepreneurial ranks. I'll even cede bragging rights about being the first to do it. The only question is when.

If I want to be smart, I'll wait until the board makes their decision. I'll figure out my marriage conundrum, finish out at least another two years at the clinic, and then tackle launching something as big as a clinic of my own.

This building has been hanging around since my great-grandmother's time. I'm sure it can wait a little longer.

Mom pauses at Hazel's office when she notices that Hazel is inside. We push into her warm, cinnamon-scented office, and—surprise, surprise—Grayson is there too.

"Hey, guys!" Hazel sends us a red-lipped smile and comes toward my mom like they're BFFs 4EVER. They hug like they haven't seen each other in years, though I suspect it's maybe been a day. "Dom, you're in town! What a nice surprise."

Grayson remains annoyingly quiet in the background.

"I was missing Bayshore," I say, the words feeling bulky in my mouth. But it's true. God, it's actually true. "Your office looks great. Amazing location."

"As a realtor, those are the two best things you could tell me," she says with a laugh. "Are you excited for Thanksgiving?"

"Mostly for Mom's famous corn crap," I say, which elicits an enthusiastic *Fuck, yeah!* from Grayson. He's crept a little closer. Maybe Hazel is the mediator here.

"I've never had it," Hazel admits, pulling my mom into a side hug. "But believe me when I say there's nothing I'm looking forward to more."

"As soon as we get home," Mom says, "I'm going to start preparing."

"I can help," I blurt suddenly. I think the last time I helped Mom prepare for Thanksgiving was when I was twelve.

"Oh, no, honey. It's the night before Thanksgiving. You should go out and do something," Mom insists.

"Yes! Dom, why don't you come with us?" Hazel grips my arm like it's the most exciting thing she's ever conceived of. Grayson is already protesting.

"I don't know about that—"

"There's this amazing private cocktail party we're going to tonight," Hazel gushes, looking between me and my mom. "It'll be so fun. And I bet you'll run into a ton of your old classmates there."

"Honey, you should go with them," Mom urges.

"I'd really rather stay and help you, since I doubt any of your other sons will stick around." When I sense Grayson's mouth turning into a scowl—which, I assure you, is something I can just *feel* energetically, without witnessing it—I hurry to add, "And I've shirked my Thanksgiving prep duties for long enough. It's my turn."

Hazel sags a little. "Well, if you change your mind, you're welcome to join. My best friend London is coming, too, and—"

My gut clenches. "What time are you planning on leaving?"

She shrugs, looking back at Grayson. "Around seven thirty?"

My heart is thumping in my chest, and all I can hear in my head is *this is your chance, this is your chance.* "How about this? I'll help out Mom until then, and then I'll head out with you guys for a little bit."

Grayson sighs, but at least he's not fighting it. Hazel claps her hands together.

"Great! We'll have so much fun. There's so much to catch up on."

She's got that right. Like the fact that I've fingerfucked said best friend into a messy-haired sex coma on more than one occasion, the memory of which I literally cannot move past.

Mom is grinning mischievously as we say our goodbyes and head back out into the cool November air.

"There's something different about you, Dominic," she muses as we return to the boardwalk and stroll our way back to the neighborhood.

I say nothing. Because she's right. I'm not sure what's different...but I am sure of *one* thing.

It has something to do with London.

CHAPTER TWENTY-SIX

LONDON

I'm not gonna lie. If Henry Cavill showed up tonight, I might be the first woman he noticed.

I went *all out.* And no, not a turkey onesie in sight. I got my roots done. My lipstick be poppin'. This dress? Don't even get me started on this dress. It's made of gold shimmer and sequins exclusively and has been hanging in my closet practically since the start of the year. Just *waiting* to be flaunted at some unnecessarily fancy event featuring olives as the main dinner course.

And here I am. Popping olives and sipping the driest martini a girl ever did taste. I'm tucked into a lushly curtained corner of the reception hall of the Bayshore Theatre, where this string quartet is playing what I'm pretty sure is a rousing, classical rendition of Journey's "Don't Stop Believin'." Gorgeous, truly, but unexpected.

Hazel and Gray are supposed to be here around 7:30, but because I was eager to get a head start on my seductress strut, I got here at 7:20. Not that I plan to seduce anyone. The only man I want to seduce doesn't believe in romance, and he's safely tucked into his scrubs in the hospital, or beneath his scrubs-lined sheets in his doctor-prison penthouse, back in Cleveland.

I've been thinking a lot about what I want. And *god*, I want a romance. A man who is ready to sweep me off my feet, and who sweeps his own damn self off his feet in the process. I want to create a magical life with this man.

And the part that frustrates me most?

Dominic was almost him. It's like I could peer into a crystal ball and see our combined future with startling clarity. That future could be...if only. If only any number of things that just aren't.

And if I'm being honest with myself, that was the same with Stop-With-The-Fucking-Emails-Already Carl. I could see our happily-ever-after in so many ways. But it just wasn't that way. And there's a fine line between hopefulness and delusion.

I'm not going to be deluded anymore. I want the man who shows up for me, for himself, and *for us*.

Okay, maybe I'm being too pensive with my cocktail. I've only been thinking about Dom nonstop for a couple months now, why not a little longer? The intensity of my attraction to him—on all levels—is either a signifier of a soulmate or insanity. I'm tending toward the latter.

"London!"

Hazel's voice rings clear over the hullabaloo of voices and violin chords. I seek her out, and there she is, my gorgeous best friend, her mahogany hair swept into retro waves off to one side and falling to a bright red A-line dress, matching red nails, and a red clutch.

"Hey, girl!" The smile leaps naturally to my lips, but as she glides closer, my gaze falls over her shoulder. There's someone tall, dark, and handsome across the room, half-turned away from me as he chats with someone. Broad shoulders strain a slate-gray dress shirt paired with dark slacks. Tightly trimmed dark hair gives way to delectable finger waves at the top of his head. Grayson stands at his side, an eerily similar build and height.

When the two of them turn our way, the icy-hot realization shivers through me.

I am looking at Dom.

Dominic freaking Daly.

His ice blue eyes find mine, and I am paralyzed, staring at him like a gopher trapped in fear as a…whatever hunts gophers descends on it. A hawk? Dominic is *definitely* a hawk, with the way he's looking at me. Hazel approaches me and wraps me in a hug, jostling me out of my stupor.

"What's wrong, girl?" she asks, gripping me by the arms. "You look like you just saw a ghost. Cute dress, by the way."

"Oh, uh—" How do I navigate this ridiculous NDA, on top of not falling at Dom's feet like a willing, fertile plaything? "I just realized, I might have left my curling iron plugged in."

Grayson and Dom approach, two massive walls of gorgeous man. Jesus, maybe it's better for humanity if Dom and Gray keep fighting. I'm pretty sure I just dropped an egg, along with half the ovulating population of the room. Together, their masculinity and power is somehow quadrupled. God forbid the entire Daly clan get together for a group picture. I'm sure that several women within a five-mile radius would fall dead—or pregnant—immediately, and probably there would be a worldwide extinction of some smaller prairie animal, just because.

"What up, London!" Grayson pulls me into a friendly side-hug, jostling me a little like he always does. Dom sizes me up from a safe distance away, but no distance is safe. My entire body is on electric pinpricks, wondering where to go from here.

"Hey, guys," I say, my voice withering under the intense scrutiny of Dom. Do I pretend I don't know him? Should I pull the *wow, haven't seen you since you played varsity baseball, not that I attended your games just to watch you, even though I did* line? Maybe I should reintroduce myself as if we're formally reacquainting as the adults we think we are. Instead, all I can come up with is, "Can you believe that quartet is playing Journey?"

"I thought that sounded *really* familiar," Grayson confirms.

Hazel is unfazed. "We invited Grayson's brother Dom. Remember him from school?"

Yes. I remember him from school, and from last month, when his cock was buried so deep in my mouth it touched my brain, Egyptian style. "Yes, of course. Hi, Dom."

My heart is racing now. I can barely look at the man, lest my remaining bit of cool evaporate in a defeated puff.

Dom clears his throat, burying his hands in his pockets. He hasn't stopped looking at me for even a second. "I've run into London a few times in Cleveland."

"Oh, you have?" Hazel sounds so delighted by this.

"We go to the same fancy gym," I blurt. "It's actually a little too fancy for me."

"*Too* fancy? What's the problem, you don't like imported moist towelettes soaked in the cool glacial waters of the French Alps?" Hazel cracks.

I snort. "Wow. Honestly, if they had that, I might stay."

"It's a pretentious place," Dom offers.

Grayson smirks. "That must be why you like it."

Dom's jaw flexes. Hello, brotherly love. The tension multiplies like dividing cells. Hazel grabs Gray's hand and gives it a little squeeze.

"You'd fit right in there," Dom says, giving his younger brother a friendly clap on the back. Grayson grimaces. "If you ever think about saying hi to me in Cleveland, I'll give you the grand tour."

"I don't know if you have enough space for me in that penthouse," Gray shoots back.

"I could clean out a broom closet for you, if needed," Dom says coolly.

I bite back a laugh. I shouldn't be egging this on, much less look like I'm rooting for Dom. I'm not rooting for either of them. I'm rooting for a white flag.

But I can't resist joking around a little. "That's very accommodating," I say. Hazel snickers.

"You should go stay in his broom closet," Hazel says, nudging Grayson. "You'd fit right in at the gym."

Grayson narrows his eyes at his girlfriend. "Real funny. I'll overlook the fact that you're calling me pretentious. And are you trying to say you want me out of the house?"

"No, I'll come with. Because all we need is a broom closet, baby," Hazel says, her eyes sparkling as Grayson dips down to snag a kiss from her lips.

"It's a strictly platonic broom closet," Dom clarifies, but it doesn't matter. Hazel and Gray are giggling like schoolkids while making out right in front of us. I shake my head and catch Dom's gaze over Gray's shoulder. I look away quickly, ready to move on. Away from the blatant kissing, yes, but also away from the man who makes me quiver at the memory of his kisses.

"I'm going to get a drink," I announce to my lip-locked friends, tipping the last of my dry martini into my mouth. It's my first one, so I'm still good, but I need to be careful. As much for taking care of my blood alcohol content as protecting myself from Dom's magnetic gaze.

Because the truth is, seeing him tonight has solidified something: I fucking want him. *Still*. And I'm too chickenshit to hear the truth about his dating status anymore. I don't want to know that he's finally engaged or banging Julianne on the daily. I just want that vulnerable man I knew back in the sunshine-filled penthouse, asking me to marry him like he fucking meant it.

Have I gone crazy?

"I'll take another dry martini, please." I pop the P just as a familiar vetiver tang reaches me. Dom has sidled up beside me, angling himself directly at me. Making it more than clear that he intends to occupy my attention.

I glance up at his blue gaze only briefly before deciding it's too hard.

"London," he says.

"What?" I snap, but I can't turn away from him. A little bit of that radiator-grade heat is reaching me. Sinking into me. Making me feel reckless. "Why'd you follow me?"

A little smirk toys at his lips. "I wanted a drink."

"Oh. Well, go ahead." I step away, and he watches me for a moment, running his tongue over his top teeth. The bartender takes his order and credit card while we stare awkwardly at each other from opposite ends of the bar. Another person steps up to place an order in the middle of our standoff, giving us both a polite smile and probably wondering why she suddenly feels like wilting.

Dom's jaw is flexing nonstop as he watches me. My gaze flits between our slow-as-molasses bartender and Dom, wondering which one will cause my early demise first.

Dom breaks first. He pushes away from the bar and comes to my side, leaning so close, I can feel his heat again. So close that when I close my eyes, all I can see is that shy smile he gets when he serves me breakfast in the morning.

"London," he says again, and this time I catch the urgency in his voice.

"Why are you here?" I honestly don't know if I'm disgruntled or overwhelmingly relieved. I fear it's the latter.

"I told you," he says in that infuriatingly sexy baritone. "I wanted a drink."

"No. I mean in Bayshore. I thought you were supposed to be doing open heart surgery or saving people's lives in Cleveland right now."

"I cleared my schedule." He sniffs, scanning the party over my shoulder. "I thought I could use some time off."

My brows draw together. Doesn't sound like the Dom I know. "Well, yeah. I think everyone agrees you could use some time off."

"That and..." He pauses, and it's heavy, like he's double- and triple-checking whether he should continue. "I thought I should come see my family."

My throat clamps at that, and I look away. *Do not get emotional right now, London, swear to olives you will not get emotional.*

"Oh," I manage to say. "That's nice. How are your brothers?"

"Connor's not coming home this year, since he and Kinsley started their business. Maverick's a little pissed at life, and Weston...I honestly have no idea where he is. Mom's pretty sure he's going to show up by lunch tomorrow though."

I snicker. "Sounds like a typical Daly brother report. And Grayson?"

"Well you know how he is," Dom replies.

"Yes, but do you?"

Dom wets his bottom lip, understanding creasing his face. "Not yet. But I'm getting there."

Thankfully, the bartender shows up with my drink at the exact moment the tears are threatening at the corners of my eyes. I don't know where they came from or why this is making me want to weep like a Hallmark movie, but here I am. Maybe I'm *actually* ovulating. If that's the case, then I'm fucked. Because there will be no force in the world great enough to keep me from mounting Dominic Daly.

The bartender hands over a second dry martini then, which Dom scoops up. When my brow arches, he says, "I got whatever you got." He takes a sip, then nods. "This'll do."

I glance across the room and catch Hazel smiling over at us. Panic slinks through me.

"Dom, I don't know how to do this." I force a bright smile and wave at Hazel across the room, holding up one finger so she knows to wait for me. "We signed a contract, and now they're here, and..."

"I know. I don't care." He glances over at his brother and Hazel then looks down at me, his serious features making my knees weak. "We don't have to explain anything we don't want to. In fact, here's what we'll do. You and I will drink these as fast as possible, and then we will quietly disappear and make our way to my car, where we will make out like teenagers until I convince you to come to a hotel room I'm thirty seconds away from booking."

My eyes flutter shut. Not with the sexy talk. Now I'm really doomed. "Dom—"

"I'll get us the best suite in Bayshore. Lake view and all. For the morning." He steps closer, blocking my view of the rest of the room. I tip my head back. Dominic consumes me. He is all I can see. All I can smell. All I can conceive of. In a lower voice, almost a growl, he adds, "Believe me when I say you look fucking gorgeous in this dress. It's just that I need you naked and laid out so I can give you what we've both been dying for, London."

I bite my lip. Every inch of my body is screaming *yes*. "And your status...is..."

"Single, but not ready to mingle. Just waiting for one woman."

A grin tugs at my lips. "Oh yeah? Who is she?"

"You know her. Her name sounds like a famous city."

I fake gasp. "You're waiting for Paris Hilton? I doubt she even knows where Bayshore is. You're gonna be waiting for a long time, buddy."

He grins, setting his drink down on the bar behind me. Then he cups my face in his hands, bringing his lips dangerously close to mine. "The longer we wait, the more questions they'll have."

"If she's seen you touching me like this, she already has a hundred of them," I say.

He wets his bottom lip again, his gaze dipping to my lips. "I've got a hundred of something I want to give to you."

I giggle. "Dr. Daly, don't be so naughty. We're still in public."

"A hundred laughs," he clarifies with a mischievous grin, just before dipping down to press his impossibly soft lips against mine. When he pulls away, my lipstick is on his mouth. I gasp, hurrying to wipe away the evidence.

"We can't kiss," I whisper. "This is a new lipstick, I didn't know…"

"Fine. I'll contain myself until you give me the word." He leans forward, bringing his lips to my ear. "Just know that you won't make it out of the parking lot before I make you come."

A shiver races through me. I take a big sip of my martini, the alcohol and lust streaking through my veins like it's a race. I think it's time to close my tab. I signal for the bartender's attention, and when I ask him to close my tab, he shrugs.

"He already took care of it," the bartender says, jerking his chin at Dom. Dom watches me with a shit-eating grin on his face.

I should have known from the second I laid eyes on him that it would end up like this. Quiet dirty talk at the bar of an unnecessarily fancy gala. Secretly buying my drinks. An attraction that doesn't just sizzle, it pops out of the frying pan and scalds an eyeball. There's something too wild and passionate between us to control it. The most I could have hoped for was ignoring it. But now? I'm ready to become its victim again.

"You know what you did right here?" I ask, nudging Dom with my shoulder. "You just romanced the shit out of me."

"I'll make the reservation," he says, pulling out his phone.

"Good." My gaze swings to find Hazel and Gray across the room, buried in a conversation with one of the city commissioners. "I'll go start saying bye."

Maybe they didn't see anything. For right now, that's all I can hope for. I'll figure out what to tell Hazel later.

All I know is that something has shifted inside Dom...and I'm powerless to resist the tide.

CHAPTER TWENTY-SEVEN

DOM

I stay true to my word. London comes before we even leave the parking lot.

Burying my hand in her panties is all it takes. Massaging that gorgeous, hard clit of hers until she throws herself against my leather seat and moans my name.

Once clarity returns to her eyes, I bring the back of her hand to my lips, my kiss grazing her knuckles.

"Dom," she breathes, her gaze falling to my crotch. I've been rock hard since I cornered her at the bar.

"Don't worry. You'll sit on it." I lean across the console and brush a kiss to her forehead. She laughs throatily.

"So where's our home for the night?"

"Some new boutique hotel downtown." I adjust my pants before I start the car. It hums to life as London checks herself out in the mirror and replaces her sparkly dress over her legs.

"Oh! I know what one you're talking about. They renovated an abandoned factory. Apparently the rooms are really nice." She leans over to look at me, swiping her thumb over my mouth. "You have lipstick *all* over your face."

I could care less about the rooms or the lipstick. I just care about getting London wrapped around me. "We'll be finding out...and leaving our review."

"About the rooms or about the sex?"

I can't fight the silly grin that takes over as I ease out of my parking space to join the light downtown flow of traffic. "Only one of those will be made public. I'll leave the choice to you."

It takes approximately one minute to reach our destination from the parking lot of the Bayshore Theatre. We could have walked, but they might have towed my car, and I'm not sure I should flaunt this hard-on if I don't have to. London doesn't help by fondling the crotch of my pants before undoing her seatbelt.

"I love what you're doing, but you're making it real hard to get out of this car."

She snorts. "Real hard is an understatement."

"I'm going to imagine Mrs. Krantz from senior year giving a very boring lecture on Chaucer while we slowly get out of the car," I tell her. "And in the meantime, you're going to need to avoid bending over, touching your hair, your neck, your mouth, or basically any other part of your body."

Her sharp laugh pierces the crisp air as she tugs a faux fur jacket over her shoulders. As we start a slow walk from the side lot to the main doors of the four-story, brick-front boutique hotel, I realize I overlooked one important thing.

"Oh, and you can't walk in front of me." My cock is like iron, and there's no coaxing it down while I'm staring at the luscious apples of her ass in that dress.

She snickers. "How about we toss a burlap sack over me, and you can just roll me up to the room like I'm part of your luggage?"

"Excellent idea." Contrary to all my own requirements, I wrap my arm around her waist and bring her against me. She fits like a glove, and we fall into step easily, grinning at each other like a couple of teenagers in love. I recognize the look on her face. It was the look I saw on Hazel's face tonight. The same warmth pouring out of Grayson.

If the last couple of weeks apart didn't seal the deal for me, then this evening has.

I need this woman in my life. Even though it was the last thing I wanted to do, I fell in love with her.

My throat catches as we stroll into the white-tiled foyer. Ferns and exotic knotted trees line the walls in enormous pots, and a sleek reception desk awaits us in the middle of the greenery. I give my name and soon we have our keys. The moment the elevator doors close, I have her backed up against the wall, claiming her mouth with my own, coaxing one kiss after another from that pretty pout.

When the doors open, London is laughing, and she leads me down the hallway. She can barely finish a sentence. I can only imagine what the lipstick situation is on my face.

But once the door swings open, my primal side takes over. I sweep her into my arms, kicking the door shut behind me as I cup her face in my hands and kiss her like I've been meaning to. Deep, thorough kisses, our tongues plunging and seeking, moans slipping out between the cracks. I kiss her so hard, I stop breathing.

A bed appears behind her. I ease her down onto it and hurry to undo my belt. With kiss-bitten lips and a drugged haze in her eyes, she begins shimmying out of her own clothes. Her heels come off first, then her panties. Normally I'd protest, but I can't do anything but get the fuck out of my clothes right now. The urgency is too great.

I stumble as I'm taking my pants off. I catch myself on the edge of the bed, laughing.

"Don't hurt yourself, doc," she says, finding the secret zipper on the side of her dress. She stands a moment later and steps out of the dress, then—totally naked, save her sparkling, silver and gold necklace—sinks to her knees in front of me.

"Look who wants to say hi," she purrs, nuzzling my cock through my briefs. My cockhead is poking out from beneath the waistband of my underwear. "Your dick is perpetually escaping."

I shuck my dress shirt and toss it somewhere. I don't give a fuck about any of my possessions right now.

"Don't worry, he won't go far," I murmur, raking my fingers across the top of her head. She swipes her tongue over the escapee tip, and the sensation is so glorious that I almost stumble again. London tugs my briefs down, my cock bobbing before she engulfs the length of me in her mouth.

She moans as she takes long, measured pulls at me, slobbering and sucking at my cock like it's the best thing she's ever tasted. I fist the top of her hair without realizing.

"Fuck." My chest heaves as she disconnects from my dick with a loud *pop*. "Your mouth feels so amazing, beautiful. God, I love it when you suck me off."

"I love doing it," she purrs, dragging her tongue from ball sack to cockhead. "The way you look at me when I do this..."

My eyes flutter shut. If she knew what was circulating inside me right now—not just the white-hot precursor to my orgasm, but all the *other* things—then she'd know that the look means I'm not letting her go after tonight. That I'm going to make sure we start spending our free time together. That I'm going to start *making* free time—for her.

But I can't say shit because she dives down for another pull at me, and everything inside me dissolves into a hot buzz.

I stop her when I come too close to the edge. I want my release to happen inside of her for our first time back together. While she's looking up at me like a messy-haired sex goddess, I urge her onto the bed, covering her body with my own.

"London," I say, my voice coming out gruffer than anticipated, "I'm so fucking close to the edge right now that you could *actually* blow on my dick and I'd come."

She giggles, her legs splaying open as my hips fill the space there. "I'll be sure to hold my breath."

"Mmm, that's kind of kinky. Asphyxiation stuff. I'd rather have you moaning my name."

"You always want me moaning your name," London says, grinning ear to ear. Her skin is hot silk against mine, and when our bodies form a delicious seal, I can't remember a time not being here, pressed up against her, feeling her heartbeat against mine. I scoop my hands beneath the wings of her shoulder blades, mashing her breasts to my chest.

"But it sounds best when you say it," I murmur, trailing kisses along her collarbone. My cock is throbbing at the slick entrance of her pussy, but I don't push inside yet. Even though it's killing me. "And even better if it's the only name on your lips."

Clarity creases her face, and we share an intense look, something that makes every inch of my body draw tense.

"Are you coming back with the marriage proposal again?" She says it lightheartedly, but I catch the whiff of seriousness behind her smile.

"Maybe." I flex my hips, my cockhead pushing into the slick velvet of her pussy. "But only if you'll accept. Otherwise I'll pretend it's a joke."

Her eyes flutter shut as I push myself deeper inside. A low moan escapes her. "Dooommmm."

"Yes, beautiful." My own voice wavers as I sink inside her. Electricity sparks across the tops of my shoulders, something deep and powerful churning inside me. My lips find hers for another kiss, our mouths pressed together as I bury myself inside her.

There's no other way to describe it except to say the world falls away. All that I can see, touch, taste, and smell is London. Every flinch and flex of her around me translates into intensity and feeling. I want to live here forever. With London wrapped around me, drowning in this giddy sense of *maybe you are who I've been too scared to hope for.*

I didn't want to love again, but then London happened.

The knowledge is bone deep, which is why my attempts to ignore it, ignore *her*, haven't worked. She feels right for me in a way that I thought was a red flag after getting cheated on. But being here again, at the doorstep of love, reminds me that maybe love can really have a space in my life. In my heart, of all places.

London's little moans as I work myself in and out of her are enough to push me over the edge. I've been beating back this orgasm since the second I laid eyes on her, and I hold out until the sweat is dripping off my temples. London's thighs go rock hard around my waist as I bury myself in her for the last time. We come together, her pussy a vice clamp around my pulsating cock, and I release my rounds inside of her.

She is languid and all smiles as we collapse onto the bed. Spent and sated. I can barely move myself off her, but I make sure to pull her into my arms.

Because now that London's back in my life, she's not leaving again.

CHAPTER TWENTY-EIGHT

LONDON

My walk of shame back to my parent's house the next morning is epic. Not only is my face the human representation of Fifty Shades of Bronze Eyeshadow, my dress is hilariously inappropriate for the nine a.m. return I muster.

It's not like anybody cares. I'm almost thirty; I can do what I want. At least I tell myself this as my mom lifts her brow as I slink through the kitchen, the smell of turkey already filling the air. Dad is outside doing something with the back landscaping, so luckily he doesn't notice.

Just like how nobody will notice that I spent the night with Dom Daly in the boutique hotel downtown...and that we're planning on repeating the event every night until we both drive back to Cleveland.

I smile to myself as I work on formally removing my makeup from last night's gala. What a night before Thanksgiving. Honestly the best one yet. A text message arrives while I'm moisturizing.

DOM: Miss you already.

I bite my bottom lip. This man is *too* romantic for claiming to be such a curmudgeon. I'm loving every second of it.

LONDON: Same here. Is it too early for doing joint T-giving? Just so we can play footsie under the table.

DOM: Your parents cool if all 10 of us show up?

LONDON: Ten? You have some other brothers I don't know about?

DOM: Daly relatives. You'd like them. Do you want to come over later?

I'm touched by the offer. I truly am. I'm just not sure how I want to drop this bomb on Hazel yet—or what my explanation will even sound like.

LONDON: To the hotel? Yes.

DOM: I meant to my mom & dad's.

LONDON: I don't know if I'm ready for all that. What would we say?

His silence is enough of an answer. He doesn't know. And honestly, I'm riding too much of a high to want to dive into the technicalities of it all. I just want to enjoy this, while we're vacationing in Bayshore.

Truth is, I joked about marrying his ass last night, and he joked right back with me. Which means that the offer is still technically on the table. And if that's the only way I can keep our boutique hotel vibe going, then...I think I've finally come to my decision.

I should do it. Even if it involves a pretend-wife appearance and a staged wedding and an eventual divorce when we decide we don't want to do this...

My throat clamps at that—maybe I'm not as okay with it as I claim.

It just seems inevitable. As inevitable as my continued, undeniable attraction to Dom. If I can't beat it, join it—right?

My logic doesn't seem particularly sound, but I don't have time to figure out a better workaround. It's Thanksgiving, after all. And then it's back to the hotel.

Once I've cleaned myself up, I start helping my mom in the kitchen. Johnny Cash music fills the house. It's our Thanksgiving tradition—has been since I was a little girl. Back then, Willow and I would dance around while popping the biscuit cans and giggling hysterically. Now, it's just me, quietly chopping carrots for the stuffing while Mom hums *Ring of Fire* behind a tired smile.

An enormous framed portrait of Willow hangs in the dining room. Her senior picture. I grin at her every time I pass the photo while I spread the tablecloth and set the table. My parent's house, like mine, is filled with vases of different shapes and sizes. We are constantly feeling Willow around us.

My dad comes into the dining room while I'm laying out the silverware. "Mom says you came home at nine this morning."

I struggle not to roll my eyes. My dad is a chronic worrywart. "Yes, Dad."

"On Thanksgiving morning?"

"Well, I was out late last night," I tell him, fiddling with a fork. "It was the smart thing to do. Spending the night."

He grunts in a way that only men over sixty can. Like a warthog mixed with a deeply dissatisfied grandfather. "You should have been here for the basting. You know your mother loves to do the basting with you."

I grin. Even though he's harping on me, I relish it. Because he's my dad, and it's Thanksgiving, and these are the small moments I'll look back on in ten or fifteen years and cry and laugh about. I'm living it. I'm in it *now*.

We finally eat around one and are in a turkey-induced coma by two. After zoning out to enough football, I finally drag myself into the bathroom for a long bath with a glass of chardonnay. Because fuck it, it's Thanksgiving.

Dom is ready to meet around seven. As soon as I get the text, my body is filled with pins and needles. The way it has been since laying eyes on this man. He is my bona fide man crush, even though at this point, what I feel for Dom is way beyond crush level.

I tell my mom that I'll be out with friends and probably won't be home that night. There's no drama. She just kisses my forehead thirteen times, hugs me extra tight—like it might be her last ever, because for her, once, it was—and sends me on my way.

I drive downtown feeling a lot like I'm on a secret mission. But what's the goal here? Get laid, obviously. But there's more to it than that. I need to quiet this raucous voice inside of me demanding more Dom. It's a feisty, needy presence, like a toddler demanding more snacks. Sometimes, I think I won't ever get enough. God knows how traumatic ignoring him these past weeks has been.

He's waiting in the room for me when I get there, dressed in black sweats and a red OSU hoodie. I blink a few times as he pulls me into his arms.

"Hey, beautiful." His baritone at my ear is a reassurance. But I push him away and hold him at arm's length.

"Hang on," I say. "Look at you."

He smirks. "What?"

"I've never seen you...dressed down." And somehow, it's the hottest of all. Dr. Daly, off duty. God, fuck me now. He wears a hoodie better than anyone.

"It's football Thursday," he says. "You've seen me in workout clothes before."

"Yeah, but this is like...hotter." I slip my hands into the front pocket of his hoodie. "This is the type of shit I want to steal from you."

His grin is heartbreaking, the type to nudge me into marrying him. He cups my face in his hands and presses a soft, minty kiss to my lips. And then another. We kiss slowly, thoroughly, as if this is part of a science experiment and we'll be tasked with naming every sensation afterward. *Tickles in my belly. Heat radiating outward from my heart. A clenching, ravenous sensation in the groin.*

The bed hits the back of my knees. Instead of tossing me onto it like he did yesterday, he breaks the kiss, swiping his thumb across my jawline.

"This place has a TV, you know," he says, in a sultry voice that is hilariously at odds with his words. A laugh bursts out of me.

"Are you telling me you want to watch Skin-a-max?"

He places soft kisses along my cheeks, down the bridge of my nose. "No. Well, maybe later, but just to laugh at how bad it is. But until then…I want to watch a movie."

I lift a brow as he breaks away to grab the remote and arrange pillows on the bed. The bed is *extra* comfy, a king with about fifty throw pillows. I help him form a nest before we sink back into the comfort.

"You say 'watch a movie' like it's a big deal," I tease.

"It is. I sort of only do it once a year."

The deeper meaning of his suggestion hits me. I am truly seeing Dr. Dom on his downtime. The man beneath the white coat. And he's chosen me to spend his sacred off time with.

"We don't have to, though, if you don't want to," he says. I think I catch a tinge of nervousness.

"I think it's perfect." I clasp his big hand in both of mine, bringing his knobby knuckles to my lips. "And *you* have to pick."

"Fine. But when we get hungry later, *you* have to order the delivery while I'm eating you out," he teases, pulling me into his arms while he scans the guide channel.

Warmth creeps through me, blissfully slow and sweet. "I suppose that's only fair."

I nuzzle into his soft hoodie, cozying up to him as if we've done it a thousand times before. And oh, lord—I hope it happens a thousand times more.

Tucked into my favorite small town, with the view of the lake slowly fading into darkness as the last rays of sunlight disappear beyond the horizon, buried in the arms of a man that I thought was the worst but has turned out to be the best.

I need to figure out a way to make this be the norm.

And maybe it means forfeiting my dream wedding and my dream marriage.

As long as I can make those things as meaningless as Dom believes them to be, we're golden.

I swear I can hear Willow laughing hysterically inside my head.

CHAPTER TWENTY-NINE

DOM

I'm ready to order the wedding invitations by the time we wake up on Friday. These past two nights with London have been heaven, and I'm already dreading my return to the hospital tomorrow morning.

I don't want to be away from London for even a second.

Which is why when I get a call from one of my old frat brothers from OSU, I don't hesitate to take the call in front of her. I might even call her the g-word, if the conversation goes there.

"Hey, buddy." I answer the phone easily, even though we haven't spoken in over a year. His name is Carl. He's in public relations in Columbus and was a junior to my freshman in college. I always meant to ask London if she knew him in the industry, but I hate the question that inevitably comes from patients—*Do you know my doctor friend so-and-so from Washington? He did med school there too, so clearly you probably know him.* I won't prompt the same eye roll from London if I don't have to.

"D-Day! What up!" Carl uses my frat nickname whenever possible. He sounds exactly the same as always, and in my mind's eye, he's still the bulky football scholarship frat guy I met my first year of school. In reality, though, he's balding a little and bulkier, but not because of football anymore. Mostly just beer.

"Oh, nothing much."

"Not getting ready to do some Black Friday shopping?" He cackles like this is the funniest thing ever. "I bet you could get some scalpels half off today, right?"

I smirk. "Home Depot, maybe. Definitely wouldn't get them from Wal-Mart."

Carl laughs. "No, dude, I just wanted to see if you were in town. I had some business that took me over west of Cleveland—"

"Where are you?" I push to standing, scratching at my bare chest as I look out over the sparkling lake. All the trees lining the boardwalk are bare, but the sunshine makes up for it.

"Bayshore, dude."

"No way. So am I. What are you doing here?"

He sighs. "Honestly...my girlfriend is from here, and she and I have been on the rocks for a little while, so I wanted to surprise her, take her out shopping."

"That's nice. She go to Bayshore High? Maybe I know her."

"I don't fuckin' know. So you wanna meet up? Let's get lunch, dude."

"Yeah, lunch sounds great." I twist to look at London, pointing at the cell phone and giving her a thumbs up sign. Not like she can hear Carl's side. She's brushing her hair, staring at me through the mirror from the other side of the room, giving me a quizzical look that says *What are you trying to tell me?* "I'm gonna bring my girlfriend too. That cool? I bet we all went to school together."

I catch London's private smile and the start of a blush on her cheeks. She likes it. So do I, actually.

"Yeah, dude, sounds fuckin' great." There's no limit to the number of f-bombs former frat brothers will drop when talking to each other. "I'd love to meet her. You text me the time and place, and I'll see you there, dude."

We hang up, and I'm all smiles, but as soon as I pocket the phone, a pang of doubt hits me. The last time I brought a love interest around one of my old friends, they started fucking around behind my back. *But that's not going to happen here.*

"Who was that?" London asks, nudging me with her shoulder as I sit down on the vanity bench beside her.

"An old frat brother. He's in town, and we're going to get lunch, and I'm outing you as my girlfriend whether you like it or not."

"Girlfriend? I thought I was supposed to be your fiancée."

My heart rate picks up. "Do you still want the job?"

She resumes brushing her hair, staring at herself in the mirror. "If it's the only option..."

Excitement unfolds inside me, but I hurry to squash it. I don't want to get ahead of the game. "I met with the board members earlier this month. They say I'm at the top of the list. I even told them I was engaged, not married, so it doesn't mean we have to have the ceremony right away." The words are tumbling out of me. "If we did it by January, maybe February..."

She's nodding, still staring at her reflection, but I catch a tremble in her chin.

"What?"

She shakes her head, setting the brush down. "Nothing. It's fine. I always wanted an August wedding, but I can try to figure out a new theme set around February. Maybe Valentine's Day or something. Frigid cold and ice."

My heart sinks a little. She doesn't like it, but she's going along with it. "Well, we could always do a getaway thing...quick and simple, a weekend in the Caribbean where we hire it all out..."

"I doubt half my family could go abroad on such short notice. Most of them don't even have passports." She nibbles at her bottom lip.

"Puerto Rico, then. Or, hell, south Florida."

Tension creases her face. "We'll figure it out."

But her words lack conviction. By the time we're ready, I'm feeling guiltier and guiltier. As we're walking from the hotel to the lakefront restaurant where we're meeting Carl, I try to sweeten the pot. We've been talking about it on and off between other conversations, and I feel like we'll be hashing out details nonstop over the coming weeks.

"I'll give you my credit card," I say as we're scuffing our way down the boardwalk. The lake breeze today is fresh and crisp. I take a deep breath of Lake Erie, trying to calm the distant anxiety that has been swirling inside me all day. The voice inside me whispering that I've been here before and heartbreak is lurking around the corner. "You can get any wedding dress you want. Spend whatever you want."

She smiles up at me, but it's not genuine. "That's sweet of you."

Her lack of enthusiasm settles like a boulder inside me. I can't shake it. The fact that she's not one hundred percent excited about this bothers me more than I anticipated. I repeat my logical rationale to myself: *It's a temporary solution to reach a larger goal. Everyone ends up happy.*

Everyone except maybe London.

As we're nearing the restaurant, a place called E. Lago, fronted by lake-facing floor to ceiling windows, London gets a text. She swears after she reads it.

"It's my Mom." London looks upset as she pockets the phone. "I need to go home real quick."

"What happened?"

"She's locked out of the house with all of her purchases from this morning and is freaking out. My Dad is stuck in line at Walmart for Black Friday. I have the only spare key."

"Don't they Black Friday shop together?"

She sends me a severe look. "Don't you know? Divide and conquer. At least in my family."

I look behind us. The restaurant is less than fifty feet away, and if I looked hard enough, I could probably pick out Carl's face in the long line of windows. "That's fine. Do you want me to take you?"

"No. You go meet your friend. I'll be back, just order me...I don't know. You pick. Like Zimbo's." She sends me a sweet smile and pushes up on her tiptoes to kiss me.

"Hurry back," I tell her.

"Promise." She sends me one last rosy-cheeked smile before hurrying back down the boardwalk the way we came. The loss of her at my side feels like a whoosh of cold air, and I try not to feel too disappointed as I head into E. Lago without her.

I spot Carl immediately, tucked into the corner, flanked by windows on both sides. I guessed right—he was mere feet away from us, probably shit talking me through the glass as we approached. He looks a little concerned as I walk up to him.

"Carl!" I hold out my arms for a bro hug. He claps my back forcefully.

"There's D-Day," he says, but the smile fades quickly as we sit down. He's already got a frosty glass of beer in front of him. His knee bounces as he crosses his arms over his chest. "I thought you said you were bringing your girlfriend?"

"Fiancée," I correct him with a grin. "And yes, she's coming. She just had to run home for a minute to help her mom. She'll be coming soon."

Carl's frowning as his gaze bounces back and forth across my face. "Can I be honest with you?"

"Of course." I smile up at a server as she stops by to take my drink order. "It's Black Friday. Let's start with a beer."

She snickers and heads away. I bet everyone else in the place is using the same excuse to drink early. Carl palms the top of his head. His dark blond hair has thinned to where you can see his scalp now. His mid-thirties have not been kind to him in the hair department.

He clears his throat. "I know her."

"Who? London?" Something about the way he's acting now is dropping enough red flags to make a blanket. My gut cinches, waiting for the big reveal. The surprise history. The darkest part of me is suddenly clenching and fearful.

"Oh yeah." He whistles low. "We used to work together. She's why I'm here."

It takes a minute for his words to settle in, to remember that he said he was here to visit his girlfriend. *She's his girlfriend.* That's fucking impossible.

"Seriously?"

Carl nods, fishing for his phone. "I had no idea *she* was the girl you were bringing along. Christ, I would have warned you."

"Warned me about..."

"That we've been dating for the past three years!" He shakes his head, his mouth a thin line as he swipes through screens on his phone. The server returns with my beer and offers to take our orders. Carl orders a perch sandwich; I do the same, even though I've lost my appetite.

"I thought you said you two were on the rocks..." I begin, a very unsavory knot tightening in my gut. I'm still hesitant to believe it fully, but there's a certain macabre side of me dancing in glee right now, pointing its finger at me chanting *I fucking told you so.* The majority of my body is swirling in disbelief and confusion. Because there has to be a mistake. He mistook London for someone else. *It has to be.*

"We have our issues, don't get me wrong," Carl goes on, something wry twisting at his lips. And then he turns his phone around so I can see the screen.

And there they are.

Him and London.

Plain as fucking day.

"Huh," I say, scanning the photo up and down no less than a hundred times. She's wearing a fur-lined coat. The wind is whipping through her hair. And it looks like they're standing in front of Lake Erie. I can't tell anything else. For all I know, it was taken last week.

All of my excitement, happiness, and starry-eyed hope crumble to the ground in useless shards. I shift my gaze to the lake over his shoulder. There's a really special brew of humiliation and rage burbling to life inside me. Accompanied with that gut-wrenching sense of déjà vu.

I've been here before.

And I specifically never wanted to be here again.

"I suspected she was a fucking slut," Carl mutters.

"Carl," I say, his name coming out harsher than even I expected. "Watch your mouth."

"Am I wrong?" He brays an incredulous laugh, gesturing to the space between us. "She was here just a second ago. I'm sure she had to leave because of some convenient emergency. It was just like that with her fucking client too."

"Her client?" I'm reaching for my phone, wanting to text London, but can't figure out how to unlock my phone. I type in the password three times while Carl continues—each time wrong.

"Yeah. Didn't you ever wonder why she just up and moved to Cleveland? She was blacklisted in Columbus." Carl looks really serious now, his frown bordering on a scowl. "Because she sluts around with clients."

I make a fist and press it to my mouth, unsure if I should scream or pinch my entire body, checking to make sure I'm awake. This doesn't make any sense. But I'm staring at a man I've known since I was eighteen who is telling me things that I don't want to believe, but with startling accuracy.

Why is London on his phone? Why is he in Bayshore, of all fucking places? Why does he know more about London than I do?

Bile is churning in my gut, and I'm suddenly not hungry. London texts then.

LONDON: Can we meet at the hotel room?

I stare at my phone, unable to comprehend anything.

My worst nightmare is coming true. I *am* fucking doomed to be cheated on. By everyone. But especially right when I've decided to open my heart and take the plunge to get married.

It happened in residency. And what do you know—another cheating scandal unfolds *the same day* London and I began talking seriously about our future.

I'm not just angry. I'm heartbroken. But I've got to keep it together.

"I guess what I don't understand then is why you're here," I say slowly, trying to remember how to string together sentences.

Carl narrows his eyes. "Isn't it obvious?"

"Not exactly."

"I fucking love her. She's a great fucking lay and—" He cuts off, frowning into the distance. "Whatever. I'm an idiot."

Anger sears through me. *A great fucking lay.* Has she been screwing both of us? The flashback to my ex is too painful. She was the whole fucking reason I decided that closing myself off was smarter. And here I am again—in the same boat, because I forgot the lesson. Carl might be an idiot, but I'm a bigger one.

"Maybe we both are."

Carl and I share a heavy look. Highly unpleasant silence settles between us, broken only his slurping his beer.

"Sure didn't think our reunion was gonna go like this," Carl mutters.

My phone vibrates again.

LONDON: Dom, did you see this? Will you meet me at the hotel?

I fumble with my phone to respond, finally remembering how to use my damn fingers.

DOM: Yes.

DOM: Why aren't you coming?

DOM: Do you know my friend?

As I'm about to write a fourth question, I set the phone down. I'm not in the right state of mind for this. I chug nearly my entire beer while we wait for the food. Part of me still can't trust what's coming out of his mouth, because of the way my med school buddy lied to my face for a year straight, before it came out that he'd been fucking my fiancée the whole time.

But the bizarre circumstance of him being here—in Bayshore, seemingly waiting for a woman who is also usually not in Bayshore but now suddenly is—seems too suspect. It can only be because they arranged it. It can only be because London has been lying to me.

Somehow, we manage to talk about the rest of our lives. Carl updates me on his business and his Columbus life, and I give him the executive summary of my cardiological endeavors.

The food comes then, and we eat in silence. This is, by far, the worst lunch I've ever attended, even though the perch sandwich is great.

While we're waiting for checks, I ask him, "So what now?"

"What do you mean?"

"Are you going to confront her?"

Carl shrugs. "I haven't decided yet. What about you?"

"Yes. I'm on my way to talk to her now."

Carl looks out the window toward the lake. "Sorry it came to this, man."

His words ring through my head as we say goodbye and I head back toward the hotel. I'm more than sorry it came to this.

I'm fed up and over it.

CHAPTER THIRTY

LONDON

I don't think I've spent a worse hour of my life than the one waiting for Dom to return to the hotel room.

I went back to the restaurant, as promised. But I didn't even make it past the hostess stand.

Once I saw Dom with Carl, I bolted. I didn't think or decide—I just acted. Because as soon as I saw that man, I knew why he was here.

A month and a half of unanswered emails, some of which were getting belligerent. He's not here on some peacemaking mission. The whole motive of why he "wants me back" is suspect anyway. He's a sociopath looking to dominate me, and what are the odds that he's Dom's frat brother from OSU?

I can't even imagine what they must talk about during lunch. And deep inside, I'm praying that they don't put two and two together. I know Carl will stir the pot—I just know it.

As soon as Dom returns to the room, his face betrays it all. Dread flows down around me, coating me, making me so anxious I can barely move.

"Dom," I begin, once he's shut the door behind him and hasn't looked at me once. Maybe I should try the casual route. "Did you bring back any food?"

He massages his temples. "I totally forgot."

"That's okay. I can go grab something." I wipe sweaty palms against my skinny jeans, and I watch him for a signal. An impossibly heavy silence fills the room.

"Did you—" I begin.

"You know Carl," he says at the same time.

"Yes. He's my ex." My mouth is suddenly so dry I feel like I haven't had a sip of water in three years.

Dom stands with his hands propped on his hips, studying the floor like he's trying to solve a math equation written there. "Why didn't you tell me about why you relocated to Cleveland?"

My heart is racing so fast I feel like I'm going to faint. I sink down onto the edge of the bed. "I touched on it briefly once before. I told you there was an issue with my former employer—"

"An issue? You were blacklisted."

I don't even know where to begin with this story, and already the tears are threatening my composure.

"For fraternizing," Dom goes on. "Which sounds an awful lot like what's going on here."

The outrage strikes first, but it's dominated by shock. My mouth flaps as I struggle to formulate a response. "Fraternizing?" I can only imagine the story that Carl fed him. "That's bullshit—"

"I guess I just don't understand why you'd string both of us along." Dom rubs his face. He hasn't made eye contact with me once since he set foot inside the hotel room.

"What do you mean string both of you along?" Now my voice is quivering. I'm ten seconds away from ugly crying. "Carl has been emailing me for *weeks*—no, *months*—and I haven't written him back once. He's desperate. And he's a *liar*."

"I don't know." Dom's voice is faint, distant, like he's mentally checked out. He walks toward the big bay windows facing Lake Erie and frowns out at the scene. "It's just a little too messy for me."

"Messy?" My mind is freewheeling, a top spinning out of control, and no matter how hard I try to anchor myself, I can't. "Yeah, you could call it messy. You could also call it unfortunate. Inconvenient. *Fucking terrifying* is another adjective, because this man who I halfway dated for three years has suddenly decided that he wants to hunt me down. A man who never really saw me as more than a pair of legs, even though I tried desperately to make something meaningful with him. And still, at the end of it? I don't even think he knew anything about me."

Dom says nothing, which only stokes my anger further. The longer he acts like this, the more he's drilling home his point. One hour with Carl has superseded everything we shared together. A man he sees but once a year—or less—has more credibility than I do.

And isn't that just how it fucking goes for me? My throat clamps with anger, and tears blur my vision. I move around the room, collecting my things on the bed in my sad rage.

"I don't know what he told you. But I can guarantee it wasn't the truth. I wasn't blacklisted for fraternizing. I was blacklisted because I whistle blew Carl's ass for encouraging me to sleep with a high-dollar client just to keep him on the roster. And when I outed him, he turned everyone against *me* so that he could keep his status and position. But no, I'd much rather you listen to and accept his version, without even *trying* to hear my side."

Dom is a statue at the window. For all I know, he's not even hearing me.

"Because if you do that, you're doing me a favor, actually." I have no idea what's coming out of my mouth now, just that it's propelled by exasperation and fury and powerlessness. "Better to not waste my time on someone who's just going to blindly accept the first story he hears. Apparently you have no sense of due process. Jesus, at least have a *conversation* with me before you convict me."

"He's one of my oldest friends," Dom says, turning to face me. And now I can see the anger creasing his face. The *hurt*. He finally meets my gaze, and I almost wish he hadn't. It makes all the thoughts in my head evaporate. "I have more to consider than just whether or not you make it a habit of sexing up your colleagues or behaving inappropriately with clients. This is about my life too. My reputation. And there's no way in hell I can show up in Chicago next month with you on my arm, when they're going to dig so deep they find out every last sorry detail about this fucking affair you couldn't restrain yourself from having."

His words land like a machete. It slices through the remaining wisps of composure I've been feigning. A sob launches out of me. The ugly crying has begun.

"Jesus, Dom. I was fucking groped against my will—you think that's an affair?" My voice cracks, and I realize this is it—I'm done defending myself. I came to Cleveland to escape the persecution that I and so many other women don't deserve, just for possessing a vagina and any semblance of curves. After the past few days, I thought I'd finally found my Prince Charming.

But it turns out he's actually King Asshole.

"Fuck you," I continue. "You are a 258-point asshole."

"What does that even mean?"

I can't explain to him the asshole scorecard. I can't even remember how to breathe. "It means fuck you for believing him, fuck you for not believing me, and fuck you for treating me like I'm some piece of trash."

I throw the last of my things into the overnight bag I brought along and zip it so forcefully that the tie breaks off. I toss it and scoop the bag into my arms, heading for the door. Dom doesn't try to stop me.

I struggle to open the door around the huge bag in my arms. The tears are flowing so fast, I can't even see straight.

"Never contact me again," I warn him in a low, trembling voice.

I storm down the hallway, unable to slam the door behind me the way I want to. Even if I didn't have my broken bag in my arms, I don't think I could muster it. Every inch of my body feels like Jell-O from the shock and rage. I sob into the contents of my duffel bag as I wait for the elevator. His words lash through me over and over again.

I know I should be thankful that I weeded out the bad seed before I did something as stupid as marry King Asshole. But the only thing inside me right now?

Heartbreak.

CHAPTER THIRTY-ONE

DOM

It doesn't take me long to realize I made a huge fucking mistake. No—bigger than huge. *Cosmic.* This mistake is the asteroid that murdered the dinosaurs, and I lobbed it willingly at London like the asshole sadist I am. The acid that spewed from my mouth shocked even me, and I sit with my head in my hands on the side of the bed for what feels like hours.

Once the fog of my past heartbreak stops choking me, I realize that I should have taken a walk after that lunch. Should have spent some time at my Mom's house before coming back to the hotel room, angry and bewildered and ready to pounce.

So I call Carl. He picks up on the third ring.

"D-Day! You get everything sorted out?"

"I forgot to ask you one thing," I say, something hot and lurid pumping through my veins. I squeeze my hand into a fist over and over again, wishing that Carl were in front of me instead of wherever he is. *I got fucking groped.* London's words won't stop ringing in my head. "You remember London's sister, right?"

A pause on the other end. "Uh, yeah, why?"

"Willow?" I prompt.

"Yeah, of course. I met her a few times. Nice enough. Why?"

I nod, pinching the bridge of my nose as the realization sweeps through me in choking waves. *Dom, you fucked up. Big time.* "She just always talks about her sister. I wondered if you'd met her. Hey, you still in town?"

"Yeah, actually, I'm at E. Lago still."

"Let's meet up on the beach." I swallow a thick knot of emotion. I want to hug London for the next three days straight, or I need to beat Carl to a pulp. Only one of those will satisfy me. And since London very well might never speak to me again...well, the choice makes itself. "Maybe we can talk over this a little bit more. I have some questions."

Truth is, I have no questions. London's reaction alone was enough to dissolve the carefully-seeded doubts that Carl planted. But still, I chose the reaction I always do. Snark. Acid. Asshole.

Maybe Grayson was right. There is something wrong with me.

A tear escapes as I hurry to leave the hotel room. I refuse to entertain the notion that I've ruined things forever with London, but I can't think about my next steps with her until I meet Carl. I'm methodical, even in revenge and reconciliation.

He's just stepping onto the boardwalk when I reach the lakefront. He waves, smiling over at me like he didn't just drop a huge bomb in both of our lives. In fact, he seems completely unfazed that the woman he's supposedly winning back has been seeing someone else.

If Carl were normal, he'd be dipping out too. But no. He told me he's sticking around so he can meet with London later. It doesn't make sense. None of it makes sense.

The confusion piles up, egging on the rage, outlined by the distant sense of loss I refuse to accept. Carl's smile slowly fades the closer I get. He stumbles backward, apparently realizing the fire in my eyes means I've come for him. But I'm faster. I catch him by the dumb collar of his ugly windbreaker and haul him up onto the grassy knoll in front of E. Lago.

"You're a fucking liar!" When he falls, I pin him to the ground. He's got poundage on me, but I've got muscle mass.

"Jesus, Dom, what the hell is wrong with you?"

I cut him off with a punch to the mouth. That one is for telling London she should sleep with someone who assaulted her. And then another punch—that one's for him lying about literally everything.

My knuckles are bleeding. He might be missing a tooth—or two. He struggles beneath me, swinging haphazardly at me. I pin his left arm with my knee—I know it's his dominant side from being the victim of his hazing back in college—and I punch him as much as I can stand. It's not as much as the theatrical side of me likes—I am a medical professional, after all, and not an MMA god.

But my medical knowledge helps me here. I know where to punch him to steal his breath the worst. I know which rib to break so that he'll be fucked up just enough, but not bad enough to puncture a lung.

"Fuck you," I wheeze before hauling myself off him. He immediately rolls over onto his side into the fetal position, moaning and groaning and whisper-screaming curse words at me. "And stay away from London."

Fuck him for lying. Fuck him for trying to ruin what I have. What I *had.*

I leave the scene quickly, avoiding the bewildered looks of passers-by as I hurry down the boardwalk and back to the hotel. I get in my car, and while I'm heaving in the driver's seat, I write London a text.

DOM: I fucked up I fucked up I fucked up I fucked up I fucked up

DOM: I'm so fucking sorry I cannot even begin to convey

I toss the phone. I doubt she'll write back. Definitely not today, and probably not ever. I peel out of the hotel parking lot, heading for Mom and Dad's house. My heart is throbbing, and I don't know why I'm going home. I just know I need them. My family. Something to ground me and stabilize me.

I pass Gray's house first. He and Hazel are standing at the front door, tons of bags in their hands.

I slam on the brakes and roll down the passenger-side window. "Grayson!"

He squints over at me, confusion creasing his face. "Dom? What's up?"

"Hey, Dom!" Hazel waves with her index finger through the labyrinth of bag handles.

I ease closer to the curb and park. I head over to them, my sneakers scuffing along the uneven brick pathway just as Hazel manages to unlock the door. "Ha! Black Friday won't keep me from getting all the bags in one trip."

Grayson's confusion turns to horror as his gaze washes over me. "Dude, what happened to you? You've got blood everywhere."

I look down, noticing for the first time that I do, in fact, have blood everywhere. Spatters have created a red artistic rainbow across my gray T-shirt. I hold my hand out—it's shaking—and my knuckles are blood caked.

"Dom. Is everything okay?" Grayson sounds serious now. He guides me by the shoulders into the house. Hazel drops all the bags inside the front door and heads to the kitchen. Water runs in the sink as Grayson leads me to the sofa near the front door.

"I guess I wanted to talk," I say, the words sticking to my throat. Why *did* I stop? But right now, I can't think of anywhere else I should be. "Gray, I think you're right."

"About what?"

Hazel shows up then with a damp washcloth. She hands it to me and then says she's going to grab the first aid kit. While her steps thunder up the staircase, I say, "I'm an asshole."

He laughs a little, but the smile fades fast. "I know. We all are."

"No, I mean...I fucked up." My head drops to my hands. Hazel returns a moment later and sits in front of me, opening the first aid kit. "Hazel, you don't have to do this."

"You're shaking. I've got it," she insists.

I swallow hard, watching as she puts peroxide on a cotton ball. "I have a secret. London and I have been dating."

Hazel pauses mid-cotton ball application, her eyes as wide as saucers. "Excuse me?"

"You serious?" Grayson laughs incredulously.

"*Were* dating. I ruined everything today. It's why I look like this."

Hazel drops my hand defiantly, her brows drawing together. "You don't mean—"

"I would never hurt London. No, I fucked up her ex. Carl."

This time, Hazel gasps so hard that it damn near echoes through the house. She stares at me in disbelief. "Is he here? In Bayshore?"

"Yes. Though he won't be getting very far. I sort of...well..." I lift my hands as proof. "But it didn't happen until after I said some really fucking horrible things to London that I'm pretty sure she'll never forgive me for."

"He's been emailing her," she confirms in a low, shaky voice. "Like a sociopath. It worried me, but I didn't think he'd show up."

Disgust ripples through me, threatening to drown me. If I'd known...if London had felt safe enough to tell me...if I'd fought harder to keep her at my side...maybe all of this could have been avoided. I squeeze my eyes shut while my throat turns into a vice.

Hazel begins quietly tending my wounds. Grayson clears his throat, shifting on the couch beside me.

"You want a beer?" he suddenly asks.

"No. I want a time machine. And I want a new life."

Silence thuds between us. I catch Hazel and Gray exchanging a look. The rawness of the moment prompts me to speak. "You're an inspiration, Gray, you know that? Both of you are. I want what you guys have. I thought I had it, for a minute."

Grayson's face looks softer than I've ever seen it. He squeezes my shoulder. "Brother, you can do anything you want to. You'll get that new life if you want it bad enough. And I think you'll get London back too."

Hazel tuts. "I can't believe you're Mr. NDA."

"That's why you both had convenient excuses to leave the other night," Gray says, nudging me. "You sly dog."

"I'm not that sly," I say, sadness crashing through me again. The adrenaline of the beatdown is wearing off, and all that's replacing it is self-pity and despair. "I'm just an idiot."

Hazel tuts again before she reaches for the Band-Aids. I can't help the doctor in me. "No, grab the gauze first." She course corrects, and I guide her through how to properly bandage my fingers. Once I'm all set, she offers a small smile.

"You should spend tonight here," she says softly, glancing at Gray. He nods.

"I need to be at the hospital tomorrow," I say glumly. "I should drive back tonight."

"What time?" she presses.

"Eight."

"Just spend the night here. It's better if you're not alone," she says, patting my knee before standing up and carrying off the first-aid kit.

"She's right," Gray says finally, squeezing my shoulder again. "After all, that's what family's for."

Gray's words ring through me the whole evening. Hazel tries to call London but now her phone is off, which makes me feel worse. Hazel eventually goes to check out one last Black Friday sale for a house she's staging, leaving Gray and me alone.

And we just...talk. About everything. About the situation with London, of course, but about our jobs. Our futures. Our pasts. Why we're so fucking competitive. Why it's all sort of Dad's fault.

I don't think Gray and I have shared more than a hundred words over the past six years, and tonight, we talk enough to fill a damn book. Gray orders pizza for dinner from our local favorite, Cameo Pizza. While we're enjoying the long, greasy strips of pepperoni pizza, downing each bite with more beer, someone knocks at the door. Hazel answers it—Maverick's there.

"You guys got Cameo?" he asks in lieu of a greeting, immediately sitting at the coffee table where the huge boxes are spread open. "And you didn't even fucking tell me."

Grayson and I share a smile. I smack the back of Mav's head.

"Hello to you too," I say.

He waves me off. "We'll talk after Cameo."

Our pleasant dinner turns into a fight over which movie we should all watch. All in all, it's the most relaxing family night I've ever had. Spending time with Gray and Mav is more fulfilling than I expected. Plus, I feel like Gray and I have cleared the air somehow. Maybe it was because we finally address that time he almost drowned in Lake Erie. I was fourteen. I tried to laugh it off on the way to the hospital—once again, asshole reflex striking at a young age—which he took as subtext that I'd rather him dead. But actually, I confess, I was so terrified and so at a loss that I couldn't do anything but try to make light of it.

Mav finally goes back to Mom and Dad's house, and Hazel heads to bed.

Gray and I, though, we stay up talking. Scheming, more like. With more beer and eventually the pizza leftovers, our conversation turns to goals and dreams. I confess to him my Bayshore clinic plan, relating the situation with the building.

By midnight, he's convinced me to quit my job and go after the clinic dream.

By one a.m., he's drawn up a makeshift contract on a piece of paper pledging GrayWork's support on the renovation project.

At two a.m., we clink our last beers and hug it out.

To the future.

CHAPTER THIRTY-TWO

LONDON

I take Friday night to myself. To sulk and stew and replay all Dom's hurtful words a million times in my head each time I think the tears might finally stop. It feels like torture, honestly. Like self-flagellation. *Oh, you think you might have a shot at breathing through your sadness-congested nose again? Think again, London! Here's a replay of the time Dom insinuated you were an untrustworthy wench!*

Once Saturday rolls around, I stay burrowed in my bed until curiosity forces me to finally check my phone. I scroll past the new messages from Dom, double back, read them all, and then delete his number from my phone, and *then* I block it. Next, I find approximately five missed calls from Hazel, as well as a few text messages asking me to call whenever I feel ready.

Which is weird, since she technically doesn't know that I *wasn't* ready.

"Hi, Londonnn," Hazel coos once I call her. "How are you, babe?"

"I don't know," I sigh.

"Listen, I know everything," she says in a low voice. "Dom came over last night and spilled his heart out. He ran Carl out of town. Dom's back in Cleveland now, so you don't have to worry about seeing him, since I'm sure you're mad—"

"Wait, what?" I sit up in bed, my tear-clogged head suddenly spinning.

I can hear Grayson in the background. "Oh my *GOD*, did you see this?"

"What is it?" Hazel asks Gray.

"Dom made the fucking paper!"

Curiosity is killing my cat now. "Guys, what are you talking about?"

"Here, I'll put you on speaker." The phone rustles, and then I can hear both of them more clearly. Hazel explains the *Bayshore Herald* just posted an article headlined "Black Friday Brawl." And the star? Dominic Daly himself.

"It says charges are pending!" Hazel gasps.

"Read the damn thing!" I shout.

"A Bayshore native and a Columbus man were filmed in a brutal beatdown on the Bayshore boardwalk on Friday afternoon, on the property of E. Lago restaurant." Hazel goes on to read, including the statement from the police officer who speculates that the brawl might have been Black Friday-related, according to the testimony provided by Columbus man, Carl Mack. "Oh my god, do you think Dom's going to go to jail?"

"It doesn't matter," Gray asserts, "It was for London's honor. He'll gladly accept a jail sentence."

I can't even think, much less formulate a response, with all this news circulating in my brain. The man who claimed I would be a stain on his perfect doctor record for the foundation now is getting charged with assault? "What the *fuck* is going on?"

"Changes are afoot," Gray says wistfully. "My brother is a good man."

I press a hand to my forehead. Maybe this is a fever dream. "I'm sorry, what? I thought you two hated each other."

"We're brothers," Grayson says. "We have our issues; then we figure them out. It's whatever."

I look around my room, trying to locate some evidence that I woke up in an alternate universe. There has to be something. I need a talisman, like in *Inception*. Just one look at it, and I'd know I was still dreaming. I've had thirty years to get my reality grips in place, but there's nothing.

"I need to fall asleep and wake up again so things start making more sense," I say slowly.

Hazel takes the phone off speaker and pries for information. Despite feeling exhausted, I give her the executive summary of what Dom said to me at the hotel room.

"I can't tell you what to decide, babe," she says softly. "And I hate that he said those things to you. But I'll say one thing—I've never seen Dom like the man who showed up at my house last night."

It doesn't matter. Even though Hazel's words haunt me for the rest of the day, none of it matters. Because I'm decided on the issue. Dom is an incorrigible asshole who does not deserve my time, space, or love. I will eventually fall out of love with him—I just might need to hang his hurtful words on poster board around my apartment to remind myself how much of an asshole he is.

Hazel takes me out for coffee later, and then on Sunday we grab lunch before I drive back to Cleveland. Monday is business as usual, even though I swear my cheeks are still residually puffy from all the tears I spilled Friday through Sunday.

Luckily, my client load is big enough to distract me, at least until five p.m. But Monday evening is when the first piece of mail rolls in. It's a postcard of the rooftop restaurant where Dom and I first met. On the back, in a doctor's scrawl, it reads, "This is where I fell for you. You were smiling into the sun, and I knew I was in trouble."

Tears immediately creep to my eyes, and I toss the postcard in the trash. It stays there overnight. On Tuesday morning, I quietly rescue it and put it into the back of my bottom desk drawer.

On Wednesday, another postcard. This time, it's a picture of Cleveland nightlife. Zimbo's is in the background. On the back, Dom has written, "I would die a happy man if I could ever take you to Zimbo's again."

By Friday, with three postcards tucked into my bottom drawer, I get an email from Nancy at Dom's office. She is unable to contain the full extent of her bewilderment.

London:

I don't entirely understand what's going on anymore, but I feel confident that somebody around here has an idea, even if it's only God himself. And no, I'm not talking about Dr. Daly.

I'm hoping Dr. Daly has given you the heads up, but in case he hasn't, he's asked me to contact you strictly via email to inform you that your contract with him has ended, effective immediately.

What I don't understand is why he pulled out of the board position. He got his confirmation letter Monday, but who am I but his lowly servant?

He's been uncharacteristically happy, too. We went out to lunch this week, just him and me! Can you believe it? He ordered a cheeseburger with sparkling water.

The weirdest part of it all is that Dr. Daly showed up from vacation with a broken hand, which means that he can't perform surgeries for the next two months. Not sure if that's relevant, but while we're talking about all the strange developments, I thought you might like to know.

I'm so sad this means we won't be seeing each other anymore. Can we please plan a girls' night here and there?

Best,

Nance

I reread the email enough times that I break into tears over my keyboard. I don't know what makes me happier—the fact that Dom pulled out of the board or that Nancy wants to have a girls' night. Probably the Dom thing. Maybe.

Even though I should still hate him for how horribly he treated me, he is slowly mending our fence. Even from afar, with his number and email blocked on all possible devices. He doesn't quite deserve an award, but he deserves a mention.

I see him. I notice. But it doesn't mean all is well.

My heart might pine for his shy breakfast smiles and his impossibly dirty mouth, but my head is finally prevailing for once. I shouldn't—and I *won't*—forget the fact that once again, another man didn't believe me. He might have beaten Carl up—which, yes, let's be real, that's amazing—but it doesn't negate the fact that Dom was so ready and willing to lap up any sordid story about me.

He was a 258-point asshole before Thanksgiving weekend, but he managed to snag the highest-scoring entry of the entire scorecard. The entry that wasn't even on there. *Blindly listen to made-up stories and question the content of London's character: 1,000,000 points.*

How can I ever trust him again?

I try to cling to this train of thought as the days while on. One week goes by without Dom, and then another. It's almost mid-December by the time I realize I've amassed fifteen postcards from this man. One of the postcards simply says, "I was afraid to love again after my ex cheated on me. I should have told you sooner. I never imagined that you would be the one to heal me."

Oh, and I can't forget the small vase with a note that says, "I bought this for you in Chicago."

Will this continue forever? At least Carl's emails have stopped. Their Black Friday brawl was good for one thing, I suppose. Though trading emails for postcards makes me worry what might be next in the pipeline: smoke signals from my next lover after a fallout?

I've gone back to fantasizing about Dom, sometimes touching myself nightly, just wishing I could have one last night with his solid heat at my side.

In the middle of week three post-Dom, I get a call from Hazel. We talk about holiday plans, and she encourages me to come to Bayshore for the weekend.

"I guess I could," I say, looking out my office window at the snow-covered Larchmere sidewalks. "If we don't get that snowstorm they're predicting."

"Leave early on Friday if you can," she says. "Please, Hazel, you *need* to come to this party! There's a soft opening downtown, and you know how much we loooove fancy openings!"

I sigh, darkening the square I've been drawing obsessively on a post-it note during our call. "You're right. It would be nice to get out again. I've been sorta cooped up."

"See? Exactly. Just re-arrange your schedule a little and head over to Bayshore after lunch on Friday. You can even stay with me, and we'll go together on Friday night."

Once our plan is set, I work on conjuring excitement for the outing. Part of me is disappointed that I won't run into Dom in the magical way it happened the night before Thanksgiving, but I quickly rebuke that side of me. I should be *grateful* I won't run into Dom.

But the truth is, I'm pining for him. Between Nancy's email and Grayson's suddenly-glowing review, it's hard not to notice there are some real changes happening. I'm curious. I make it a plan to pry for information once Hazel and I are alone together.

Friday comes, and Hazel and I are drinking the first glass of chardonnay by five p.m. Grayson is getting ready too, and with how dressed up they are, I'm glad I brought my A-game.

At one point during our makeup session at Hazel's vanity, Gray pops his head in and says, "Hey, something came up so I..." He glances at me briefly. "Gotta go take care of it."

"Sure," Hazel says.

"You'll take Mav?" he asks her.

"Oh, the whole family is going?" I murmur as I press a bobby pin into the side of my head.

"Mm-hmm," Hazel says, finishing the front curl of her updo. Gray gives her a kiss on the forehead before he hurries out of the house. Odd, though, that *all* of the Dalys are coming.

"Why the big family affair?" I ask, reaching for my blush.

Hazel laughs, maybe nervously. "Family friend, I guess. I don't know, I didn't ask too many questions. I'm just going for the cheese tray."

"And wine," I add.

"And photo ops," she says with a laugh.

"And the chance to wear our amazing dresses." I brush on a little blush and then sit back, admiring my makeup. "Can't ever forget that."

"I wish Connor and Kinsley were here," Hazel says, on the verge of gushing.

"Why?"

"I think it'd be fun to hang out with Kinsley more." She shrugs. "Wouldn't you like to get to know her better?"

"I guess," I say slowly, but in my head I'm thinking it sounds a lot like she wants us to form a trio of Daly significant others. Which, maybe in an alternate reality. But not this one. "There's a lot of people I'd like to get to know better though."

Once we finish our hair and makeup, we're ready to go. Hazel drives. Our first stop is the Daly household four doors down, where Maverick is waiting outside, bundled up in a puffy black coat. He slides into the backseat, smelling like weed and cologne.

"Why didn't you go with your mom and dad?" Hazel asks.

"Fuck my dad," Maverick mumbles, immediately staring out the window. It's quiet for a minute, and then Maverick finally seems to notice us. "You both look nice."

"Thanks, we try," I remark wryly. "Where's Weston?"

"He's there already," he says, and then sinks back into his own world.

Hazel drives us to the eastern edge of downtown. She pulls into the street parking of the backside of a building I've never noticed before and definitely never visited.

"We'll go in the back," she says, and leads the way up a rickety staircase to a door labeled 331 E. Water Street. I'm not sure why she's so intimately familiar with this event and its inner workings, but I'm just eager to get out of the biting December wind and into a warm place with wine.

We're welcomed into an empty back office of sorts with a stunning view of the lake. The space looks half-finished, at best, and Hazel sweeps toward a doorway heading to a brightly lit room. Conversation and jazz music drift our way.

We step into the main room, and everything hits me all at once. Everyone turns to me like it's my surprise birthday party, the air pulled taut with all the waiting gasps, but instead of everyone saying *SURPRISE!* and throwing penis-shaped confetti (is that only at my birthday parties?), Dom steps into view.

He's wearing a perfectly pressed black dress shirt with black pants and black shoes. His hair is longer, a little unruly, and he's tamed it in a way that looks almost retro. The sight of him steals my breath, my energy, my everything. Hazel is tugging my coat off, then, urging me to give it to her, while Mrs. Daly sweeps up to me and presses a glass of wine into my hands.

"Welcome to the party, darlings," she says. "You both look *so* lovely."

Maverick has wandered off to join Weston across the room. The other people in attendance—probably family friends or who knows what—resume conversation. There's no penis confetti to be seen, even though this counts as one of the bigger surprises of my life.

I turn to Hazel. "What, exactly, are we attending?"

Her grin turns sheepish. "A clinic opening?"

The details begin to sink in. A poster hung on the wall with the blueprint of the future clinic, which is springing to life around us. I see the sign in the front window that says "COMING SOON: BAYSHORE'S FIRST CARDIAC CLINIC."

Dom doesn't come near me. He just watches me, rubbing at the back of his neck, looking more vulnerable than I've ever seen him.

"Why am I here?" I ask Hazel, but I'm looking at Dom.

"Because he wanted you to be," Hazel says sweetly, squeezing my hand.

Tears are pressing to my eyes, and I don't quite understand why. I need some cool air, *stat.* I finally jerk my eyes off Dom and turn back the way we came. Hazel doesn't stop me, but footsteps thunder behind me. Just as I reach the back door, Dom's bass pierces the air.

"London, please don't go."

I steel myself before I turn to face him. He's a wall of man before me, somehow more handsome and domineering than I remember.

Or maybe it just seems that way because the pieces are clicking together; he's becoming that man we both know he's always wanted to be. This honest version of himself is far sexier than I've ever seen him before, which just intensifies my need for a breather.

"I'm not leaving," I whisper. "I'm just hot."

Dom pushes open the door then, inviting in a gust of cold air. I sigh with relief, and the door clangs shut a moment later. We watch each other for a moment, everything bloated and unsaid in the air between us.

"I wouldn't blame you if you left," he says, his voice uncharacteristically raw. "I'm a 258-point asshole."

"You earned every single one of those points." I cross my arms defiantly—it might help prop me up against the pending onslaught of tenderness that he is poised to send my way. I can tell by the way he's looking at me. The way he's got regret slashed across his features, combined with the sweetest, softest look in the world. He's preparing himself to melt at my feet. Beg for forgiveness.

Yes, he turned me into melted horny butter. But I might have made him melted repentant butter.

"I'd like to see the scorecard," he says. "As a learning tool."

I sniff. "I don't know. You'll probably just dispute the entries. Doesn't seem like you trust much of what I say." And suddenly, all the emotions are bubbling back up to the surface. Everything, from the very beginning. From when he called my methods pointless, all the way to when he said I couldn't restrain myself from having an affair with Carl. My throat clamps shut, and I turn away from him so he won't catch the sheen of tears in my eyes.

He reaches for my hand, pulling me closer to him. I crumple against him like a willing rag doll, unable to resist palming the hard planes of his chest.

"I've never regretted anything more than how I treated you the day after Thanksgiving. I don't regret much in life, but that will haunt me until the day I die. Along with a few other choice words I've said to you since we met."

More tears well up. I can't speak at all now.

"You are the most amazing, talented, gorgeous, vivacious piece of glitter I have ever met."

A laugh tumbles out of me, even though I'm supposed to be angry. "Did you just call me glitter?"

A smile tugs at his lips. "I'm an asshole with a scorecard. It only makes sense that you're the most sparkly thing out there."

"Dom, I don't know—"

"London, I love you," he says at the same time.

The tears that were threatening finally make good on their threat. They begin dripping down my cheeks. His arms go around me, pulling me into a deep, warm hug.

His heat isn't oppressive though. His heat provides balance. It provides clarity. It provides a lightning strike of truth that makes the tears flow faster.

I cling to him, and his grip goes tighter around me.

"I love you, too," I wail into his chest. "Fuck, I do."

"Please forgive me, London," he murmurs into the side of my head. "You don't have to now. I know I hurt you so bad, and you didn't deserve any of it. But believe me, I will spend the rest of my life trying to make it up to you."

"Does that mean weekly postcards for the rest of our lives?"

"I have a few other ideas, if the postcards aren't effective."

"They've been effective. But I want to see what else you have planned."

"It wouldn't be very smart of me to reveal all my romantic ideas all at once," he whispers, his blue gaze searching my face.

"Ah. So you finally accept that you're romantic?"

"Accepted. Absorbed. Inscribed on my tombstone already."

I roll my lips inward to squash the giggle threatening to spill out. "What else will be etched on that? You better not miss your chance to immortalize your Black Friday beatdown."

"Fine. Here's what it'll say." He wets his bottom lip, his palms sliding to the swell of my hips. "Dr. Romantic, Black Friday Legend, Swallowed by the London Fog."

This time, the laugh rockets out of me. "You make me sound like a plague. Or at the very least, something you'll need to clear up with medication."

"It's fine. If you're an illness, I want to be under the weather for the rest of my life."

My cheeks are straining from how hard I'm smiling. "Okay, you're dangerously close to losing the romantic title."

He presses his forehead to mine, drowning me in his mahogany musk. "Let me rephrase. I want you in my life, beautiful. For now and for always."

Everything inside me is melting under his sweet words, including my balance. When I stumble, he grips me by the elbows, a sexy smile waiting for me.

"Where did you find this building?" I whisper.

"My Grammy Ethel left it to me when she passed," he says quietly, his gaze stuck on my lips. "It was what she left behind so that I could find my soul mate."

It doesn't make a ton of sense, but now's not the time to question it. Our lips are getting closer.

"Why aren't you in Cleveland?" I ask, barely able to concentrate on anything that isn't this pending kiss. "How did you have time to...you know...start a clinic?"

"I took some personal time. Breaking my hand helped. But I plan to go part time in Cleveland, so I can do this clinic part time too."

A maniacal giggle escapes me. "And what about Nancy?"

"Coming with. She already agreed to work part-time in Bayshore."

This news sounds too good to be true. But I somehow don't think he's asked this group of thirty people to show up just so he could pull my leg. "Dr. Daly, be careful. It sounds like you're edging closer to a work-life balance."

"Mm-hmm. It'll pair nicely with the woman I love and all the free time I plan to spend with her."

"Doesn't sound much like the personality-free Barbie you were looking for three months ago," I tease.

"No. I only want you. The matchmaker of my dreams."

His words push something hot and delirious through my veins. I am so in love with this man I could faint, and I would only want to be revived by his beautiful yet arrogant hands. "You know, they say you're not supposed to fall for the matchmaker."

"Fuck what they say," he growls, and then he dips down for the kiss that has been teasing us for the past few minutes. Our lips connect with passion and hunger, all the restrained emotions of the past few weeks brimming and spilling over. We kiss until he backs me up against the door, his hardness making itself known against my lower belly.

"We should wait," he finally says breathlessly, "even though I am so hard for you right now I could use my cock as a baseball bat."

I giggle, nuzzling into his neck, relishing the vetiver scent there. The scent I'll be relishing for so many days and weeks and years to come. "Just think about Chaucer again from senior year."

He grunts, tapping his balled fist against the wall. "Not helping this time."

He snags one last kiss and then puts a safe distance between us. "I have an announcement to make, London. But I won't make it until you give me your blessing."

Already I'm thinking of the staged wedding he wanted to plan, until I remember—he pulled out of the board. We don't need to get married.

"I want this to be *our* space. I'm not asking you to run it with me, since I know you have your own business. But I left this back room for you, so that you could have your own Bayshore outpost. Maybe you won't want to take clients here, I don't know. We could find a house near Hazel and Gray, that way we could all have like, I don't know, date nights." His normally assured, clipped statements are giving way to nervousness, and it's melting my heart more than he knows. "You wouldn't even need to come back, I guess, if you didn't want, but I mean—"

"Oh my god, *yes!*" I shriek, jumping up and down. This is the proposal I've been waiting for without knowing it. "Dom that is *amazing*! I love the idea. I love it so much. Everything about it." I swallow a knot of emotion. "I love everything about the idea. I love everything about *you*, because I am so freaking wildly in love with you."

Relief washes over his face and then he cups my face in his hands, showering kisses on me. "I love you so much, London." He murmurs it over and over again as we kiss.

I'm definitely crying by the time we break apart, and he squeezes my hand in his. "Should we go tell them all?"

"Yes. Absolutely." I laugh, dabbing at the corners of my eyes.

"And, don't worry—we'll save the August wedding announcement for another year," he says, his eyes sparkling.

He leads me into the bright and clamorous room. All the Dalys are smiling at us, and from the way Hazel has clapped her hands together, I know she knows.

Once Dom commands everyone's attention, my hand clasped firmly in his, my gaze washes over the friends and family gathered.

I've never felt prouder to be at Dom's side. This is the first time it's happened in the open, in front of all his loved ones, but it sure won't be the last.

Because moving forward together, toward a new joint future, is the only thing that feels right. And doesn't it just make sense? We both started in Bayshore. Spent our twenties—and found heartbreak—in different parts of the country. Found each other in Cleveland, trying to reach new, great heights. And then came tumbling down back to our small hometown, where it all began.

But Bayshore doesn't only mark the beginning of our individual stories. The future home of the Bayshore Clinic will be blessed by our love story, because this is the place where our futures finally aligned.

EPILOGUE

LONDON

Six months later

"London, I've got good news!"

Hazel pushes in through the back door of the clinic, as she does every Friday at noon. It's our scheduled weekly lunch date, and the excitement in her voice makes me sit up.

"What is it? Tell me immediately!"

Her lips pinch together like she's trying not to burst at the seams. "Where's Dom? He should hear this too!"

I call for Dom, who has just walked out the last patient of the morning. This clinic has been formally open and seeing patients for the past month, and there's been a pretty intense learning curve to our new lifestyle. Most of it centers around the fact that Dom's bleeding heart has him close to quitting the clinic in Cleveland altogether.

The demand is so great here, and he finds this work way more fulfilling. I just think he should wait to make the leap until a little bit more time goes by. Plus, we still need his Cleveland salary for other things...like buying a house in Bayshore.

"What's the news?" His voice thunders through the clinic, his footsteps echoing as he approaches my back office. He grins at me first, then jerks his chin toward Hazel. "What's up?"

"Big news. Had to tell you in person." She squeals. "The Warrens accepted the offer you made on their cottage. We are going to be *neighbors* soon!"

Dom pumps his fists into the air, and I leap from my chair, hugging Hazel first. Then Dom scoops me up and twirls me in a circle. I tasked Hazel with finding us the first available house on her street, ASAP. As Bayshore grows, that real estate is getting more coveted, so we had to offer a pretty high number to compete with the other people eyeing the house. It's a good thing Dom sold the penthouse—that has been a big help as we prepare to buy a house together *and* adjust to his new lower salary.

"This is the best day ever!" I cry out.

"Back to Bayshore, baby," Dom murmurs, pressing a kiss to my lips.

"And finally moving out of your childhood bedroom," I tease. Though really, we've been mixing it up. Some weekends, we stay at my parents' house. Others, we crash with Hazel and Gray. It's been so fun to get to know the Daly family better. To become a *part* of the Daly family.

Because I'm here to stay. That's for certain. The fact that Hazel and Mrs. Daly have included me in their biweekly brow sessions is proof enough.

"They like having us there," Dom responds. "Hell, I'm sure my mom wishes Hazel and Gray would move back in."

The doorknob jiggles, and Weston's mussed chestnut hair appears. We all greet him exuberantly. Weston, too, has made it a point to visit me most Fridays. Sometimes he sits with me and sketches, though he never shares what he's working on.

"What's up, family?" He fist bumps all of us. "Just thought I'd come say hi. Did I miss something?"

"Just the fact that you will now be able to come crash at London's and my house in the near future, as well as Hazel and Gray's."

Weston gives us all high fives. Hazel excuses herself, telling me she'll meet me at our lunch spot in a half hour. Dom retreats to his office through the doorway, leaving Weston and I smiling at each other in the sunny office.

"How's the writing coming?" he asks. I've been working on a memoir-style book titled *The Algorithm of Love*. It's about my (mis)adventures as a matchmaker, and after everything that happened with Dom, the words have been leaping from my fingers.

"I just hit chapter ten today," I tell him with a smile.

"Can I read it sometime?"

"Of course. You'll be one of the early readers."

Dom bursts back into the room then, hands on his hips. "You know what? I want to make this day even better."

"Oh yeah?" I say wryly. "What, you gonna get down on one knee now?"

A shit-eating grin takes over his face as he reaches into his pocket and produces a small, glinting ring. He walks up to me, and, keeping eye contact, slowly sinks down onto one knee.

"Oh my god, I thought I was kidding," I gasp out.

"London Marie Hayes, I've been imagining this proposal a million different ways since last year. But the truth is, it doesn't matter whether or not we have a ring, because what we have goes way beyond the title and the piece of paper. Still, I want us to celebrate our love, because we deserve it. I don't care when we do it, I just care that we spend the rest of our waking days together. And I'm going to show you as much as I can, as often as I can, that I am worthy of your love. I almost lost it once, and I don't plan on losing it again. Because against all odds, you helped the cardiologist find his heart." His throat bobs and he swipes at his right eye quickly. "London, you *are* my heart. Will you marry me?"

My mouth parts, and all I can do is stare in shock for a moment. Then, "OF COURSE I'll marry you! I've been ready to marry you since the second I met your fine ass!"

Dom is grinning ear to ear as he stands and pulls me into a warm, steady hug. When my toes touch the ground again, he slips the ring onto my finger. I coo over the sparkly diamonds and the fact that it fits perfectly.

"I secretly sized one of your other rings," Dom says.

"How long have you been planning this?" I ask between kisses.

"Since the night you came to my secret soft opening in December. I bought the ring the next week."

"You guys, I got *all* of that on video," Weston announces, waving his phone in the air.

I squeal, clasping a hand over my mouth. "Are you serious? Was this planned?"

Dom laughs, shaking his head. "Not at all. But Weston's got a knack for that sort of thing."

Weston's easy grin is the same as all his brothers'. It's like looking at an unnerving mix of Grayson and Dom sometimes.

"You should be a wedding photographer," I say, holding my hand out to admire my engagement ring. "Or a videographer for the proposals."

"I'm going to a Caribbean wedding this month," Weston says, scratching at the back of his neck. "I could try it out there."

"Do it, and let me know how it pans out. That has all the makings of a beautiful love story, you know."

"Yeah, but if it doesn't involve his inheritance, it won't lead him to true love," Dom says with that mysterious tone people use when they talk about urban legends.

I swing my gaze to Weston. "What was your inheritance?"

He laughs a little, like he's embarrassed. "It's a necklace. It's made with some crazy fucking gems. I've never seen anything like it before."

"So, you're saying the necklace will lead him to true love," I tell Dom.

"I'm just saying be careful," Dom warns him, clasping his arms around my waist from behind me. "So far, our inheritances have led to each of us finding the love of our lives."

I snicker, tipping my head back to look up at Dom. "But really?"

"Grayson inherited the house, which led him to Hazel. Connor inherited the wedding rings, which he plans to use to propose to Kinsley. And me...?" He jerks his chin at the space around us. "We're standing in my inheritance and look at what just happened."

"It's a good story and all," Weston says, raking a hand through his hair, "but trust me. I'm not settling down anytime soon. Besides, I think the necklace was just an accessory for the fat stack of cash that came with it."

Dom shrugs, looking doubtful. "Whatever you say, bro."

Weston laughs, pushing through the back door. "I'll see you love-birds later."

Once it's just us in the back office again, I face Dom, sinking into him, burying my face in his chest.

"I love you, beautiful," he murmurs into the top of my head.

"I love you more."

"Impossible," he whispers. "Because I loved you first."

"Unverified claim," I shoot back.

"Couldn't you tell, with all my attempts to get you out on a date before you were ready?" he asks, his grin stretching ear to ear. "I didn't stop at anything."

"You knew what you wanted," I whisper, tears coming to my eyes. And god, I know what I want. And it's this man. "You just wanted to make me yours."

"As long as we both shall live," he adds quietly, and captures my lips in a tender kiss. One that inspires and fulfills as much as it excites.

Which is exactly what Dom does in my life. That's exactly how I envisioned it should be.

Except there's one big difference with my reality now.

It's even better than I could have imagined.

THE END

Ready for more? Hang tight for Weston's story, Make Me Choose: an enemies-to-lovers island romance (http://books2read.com/make-me-choose)

Do you love a good series about brothers? The Daly brothers aren't the only ones I've written about! Check out the Fairchild brothers and their dramatic, controversial rise to wealth in *The Bad Boys of Wall Street* series. The Price of Revenge (http://books2read. com/price-of-revenge), starts it off with a bang in a sizzling enemies-to-lovers/second chance romance.

Needing more small-town romance vibes? Check out my co-written series with Whitley Cox, which is set in a quirky and quaint small town in coastal Oregon named Winter Harbor. Book #1, The Bastard Heir (http://books2read.com/the-bastard-heir), kicks off this steamy and angsty series about the estranged Winters brothers, their mysterious inheritance, and their second chances at love.

READ 'MAKE ME CHOOSE'

CHAPTER ONE of Make Me Choose

Bayshore #4

NOVA

Is this farts or is this joy?

Inside my head, I sing this line to the tune of The Clash's "Should I Stay or Should I Go?" The plane I'm on is just now cresting the northern ridge of Aruba, offering me a pristine view of the island below. My stomach lurches again—this is definitely joy. Because, motherfuckers, *I'm about to be on Aruba!*

It's the same every time I travel. Nervous belly in advance of a new locale. Possibly a foreign tongue awaiting me, though according to my research, I may be hearing plenty of English. This constituent country of the Netherlands (thanks Wikipedia) was not exactly on my Top Ten Next Destinations list, but when my bestie from another chestie told me she was getting married on this twenty mile long hunk of Caribbean goodness (thanks again Wikipedia), you know I put in my vacation request to my supervisor before we'd even ended the Skype call.

My knee is bouncing as I look out the plane window. All I can see is the turquoise water of the sea and the frayed edges of the island giving way to white sand beaches, which is the mathematical equivalent to *one week of paradise.*

And holy crap, I need the getaway. Travel is in my blood, but I can only afford to donate said blood on strictly scheduled vacations and long weekends crammed around the edges of an uninspiring full-time job. Besides, if I ever tried to do something wild like *travel for more than two weeks at a time,* I'm pretty sure my family would have a collective heart attack and stage an intervention.

That's how my family is. They don't travel. Hell, they don't even leave New York State. The wildest thing they've done so far is name me Nova, which came from my father's brief obsession with the movie *Planet of the Apes.* There's the one fun factoid about my life.

The plane banks as it aligns with the runway. One week. Seven full days of Aruba magic. I'm only assuming it will be magic, of course, since I've never been here before. This is my first destination wedding, which either means it will win the best week of my life until I die at age ninety, or some sort of disaster fit for a decently performing rom-com.

I peer out the window, trying to spot which beach my best friend and her fiancée are getting married on. Amelia and I met our sophomore year at Purchase College in southeastern New York. She was a free-spirited art major who loved to travel, which is how she met Rhys Henry Bradford III, her British other half. They figured they'd bridge the distances between their respective countries by heading to an island that felt energetically equidistant from both their home-towns.

I definitely can't complain once the plane touches down and I catch that first whiff of sea breeze. The plane unloads in the middle of the runway, because island life, and the humid air feels like a salve to all the stressors and dissatisfaction I left behind in upstate New York, which I have categorized into three main areas:

1.   I am a 25-year-old drowning in debt

2.   Who lives with her grandmother in a small shack behind her parents' house

3.   And uses her high-falutin' fine arts degree to…take senior high school portraits.

Of all the items on that list, my grandmother bothers me the least. Because my grandma is the fucking best.

But if it seems like things couldn't be more pathetic for a woman my age, I assure you, they get worse. I also haven't had sex in so long, I technically qualify as a virgin again. Yep, that's a thing that can happen.

I don't expect Aruba to change any of these things about me. No, I just expect a most-expenses-paid *escape*. Because that's the American Dream, isn't it? Quietly pay your bills your entire life and be happy with your one-to-two week getaway to a beach.

After I step onto the tarmac, an ocean breeze blows every last bit of my thick, red hair across my face. As I struggle to see the blue sky again, a familiar, feminine voice cuts through the air.

"NOVA!"

My best friend Amelia is jogging toward me, her arms open, pure joy written on her tanned face. Before I know it she's wrapped me in an oxygen-stealing hug, shrieking with laughter in my ear as she says "You made it, you made it," over and over again.

"Amelia! I can't believe they let you this close to the plane without a boarding pass!" We're laughing and hugging, and I'm already full of so many #vacayvibes I can hardly stand it.

"Yeah, well, I sweet-talked the luggage handler, and he said I could find you if I moved quick," she says with one last squeeze around my waist before we pull back to look at each other. If the sculpting world had a Hollywood, she would be the It Girl. She's even dressed like an incognito celeb, with a baseball cap pulled down over a low white-blonde ponytail.

"You should be an international spy," I remark as she grabs my hand, leading me toward the lone terminal. "Sculpting is the perfect cover for your next career of espionage."

She tosses her head back and laughs. "What makes you think I'm not already a spy?"

This is how it is with us: easy, fun, a little ridiculous. Exactly the sort of interaction I've never been able to strike up with the opposite sex. And trust me, I *wish* I could just be into women and call it a day. If only I didn't love the D so much. And the rolling hills of a nice pair of biceps. And the gruff bass of an unexpected "hey, babe." And, you know, about a million other things that go into the butterflies and frustrations of dating a man.

With any luck, I'll find that elusive man before I die.

We whoosh through the baggage claim, and she talks with the luggage handler on the way back in as if she's known him for years, not minutes. That is one of Amelia's superpowers: she can become anybody's best friend in minutes. My lime green luggage wobbles past us on the rickety conveyor belt a moment later.

"Let's go find our *driver*," Amelia says with a mischievous giggle once I've got all my things. This destination wedding is off to a great start. Ocean breeze: check. Private escort to the resort: check. I can't keep the silly smile off my face as I follow Amelia onto the sidewalk of the airport arrivals lane. There's a sleek black van waiting for us that looks like it could double as a party bus or an FBI vehicle. The side door slides open, and Rhys hops out, shooting me a smile fit for the British rag-mags. This is pure party.

"Nover! You made it!" His British lilt on my name never fails to delight. I laugh into his solar plexus (he's like seven feet tall) as we embrace. "Can I help with your bag?"

"I'd love that," I say. "Not gonna lie, I packed eighteen times more clothes than I'll need, so it weighs as much as an iceberg."

From inside the party van, there's a little snort. Rhys goes to the back of the van to load my bag.

Amelia says, "So, I forgot to mention…" but I can't hear her after a certain point because the person who snorted at me has now revealed himself.

First thing I notice is the hair—longish, chestnut brown tresses that are caught between stylishly windswept and bedhead. And then I notice the broad shoulders, dark tee pulled tight over the afore-mentioned hills of biceps. And once he comes to standing on the sidewalk, I barely notice that two others are following, because I can no longer focus on anything that isn't *this man.*

Because the man who stepped out of the van isn't just a casual hottie.

He's none other than Weston Daly.

The man who's made my heart flutter since I first met him four years ago. The living definition of tall, tan, and handsome. A vagabond who has never noticed me even a tenth as much as I have noticed him.

And this marks the third time *around the world* that he has come to haunt my vacation.

"…and Weston, Elliot, and Keko came along, too!" Amelia is fin-ishing up. My gaze is hopelessly riveted on Weston, and I can't tell if my face looks like petrified shock—something you'd find on one of those mummies accidentally preserved by the eruption of Mount Vesuvius, no doubt—or blatant chagrin. His icy blue eyes return my surprise-volcano-eruption stare, and the smirk that curls at his lips says volumes without him uttering a word.

"Good to see you again, Nover," Elliot, the other Brit, says. Keko, the final member of their groomsmen bro squad, waves at me. I met both of them during a trip last year to Portugal, which marked the second time I spent too many consecutive days with the gorgeous—I mean, *completely irritating*—Weston Daly.

Weston hasn't greeted me, and I won't be the first one to budge on that front.

"This is great," I manage to say, smiling brightly at Amelia. I hope she can read the strain in my eyes as *Oh, you didn't fucking tell me that Weston Daly was coming*, because that's exactly what those near-burst blood vessels are trying to convey.

It's been a year since I saw him last. Each time we've met up has been an accident—a misfortune, really—and I should have expected he'd be here too.

Because when I say he haunts my trips, I mean it. He's like a ghost I just can't get to cross over to the next dimension. It doesn't matter how many times I chant "You're free." Weston continues to appear at all my international getaways.

Rhys comes from around the back of the van. "I bet they charged you triple for that beastly thing."

It's only beastly because I need to justify all my last-minute thrift store purchases by wearing outfits outside my comfort zone at least *once*. But I'm not high maintenance, no matter what the bulging weight of my luggage suggests. Really, all I need to travel is a few days' worth of clothes, my cameras, and my travel talisman.

The talisman is important. It's my good luck charm whenever I leave the country. I've never been robbed as a result. I know this doesn't stand up to the scientific process, but I don't care. It's a gorgeous necklace that protects me and has mystical powers, surely. Even if it can't convince Weston to stop tagging along on my itineraries.

The boys are all clambering into the car, leaving the middle bench seat for Amelia and me. Once the van lurches into motion, the driver nodding his greeting to me through the rearview mirror, I feel vulnerable. Weston is sitting directly behind me, and the fact that we haven't technically exchanged a greeting but *have* stared each other down is weighing on me.

He's holding out, but so am I. And I feel like he knows that I know that.

Reggae music floats through the van while Weston's existence sizzles behind me. Amelia and Rhys start recounting a funny story about a passenger on their plane from England who insisted on gherkins to the point of requiring an emergency landing in Boston, and I'm trying to listen while also spying on Weston without actually turning to look at him. This is a hopeless task.

"So...no hello?"

The bass rumble of Weston's voice near my ear sends goosepimples flaring up and down my spine. I catch a waft of his scent—sandalwood and spice. If he were anyone else, and we were *anywhere* else, I'd be taking my panties off by now. But no. Despite how intolerably *good* it feels to have his hot breath graze the back of my neck, I will not give in to him.

"Sorry?" I turn slightly, feigning confusion.

"Just was wondering if you'd ignore me for the rest of the day or the entire week."

I suppress an annoyed sigh. "There was no ignoring. I greeted you with my eyes."

"Oh. Did you *smize*?" he asks, which makes me laugh. *Almost.* "I must have missed it."

"Don't let it keep you up at night," I say, heat and curiosity curling through me.

Because Weston is *exactly* the type of guy that I have dreamt about for a lifetime and never once considered a possibility. Confident, attractive, impossibly put together men? They never go for someone like me. If I had a warning label, it'd say "Fat and Sassy". And then in much smaller font, right below, it would say "And incredibly unsure of herself; please tell me I'm funny".

But Weston can do whatever he wants in this life, without reassurance. He's *that* attractive. I've watched with my own two eyes as he sought out and dominated cute backpacker girls in our shared hostel in Amsterdam, like they were doltish gophers and he was an incredibly dapper coyote. He floats around the world unperturbed and totally at ease. He eats confidence for breakfast.

And if he weren't so annoying, I'd sort of look up to him. Because that confidence breakfast is what I've been missing since college graduation. Except this guy is the *last* person on Earth I'd ever ask for advice.

"...and then we can go surfing!" Amelia wraps up, clapping her hands together.

"Surfing," I repeat, pretending I've been listening.

"The lessons will be free," Rhys insists. "If you've never learned, now's the time."

Bless his accented optimism. "I'm not a big...swimmer."

Though I am big and I know how to swim, I don't make a habit of flinging myself into waves that could drown me. Rhys doesn't need to know the details, though.

"Well you could at least sit on the beach with us," Amelia suggests, just as the van runs over a jagged pothole. I slide out of my seat—that's what I get for not buckling—and crumple into a pile against the front passenger seat. I catch the annoying twinkle in Weston's eye as he tosses his head back and laughs.

What a confident and sexy way to start off my trip. If Weston eats confidence for breakfast, then I must eat puffed embarrassment. I grimace, collecting myself onto the bench seat of the van. It's not like I came down here to bang random hotties—it's not my MO—but Weston reminds me of how not his type I am. And yes, part of me would pawn a lung to be his type.

I stare out the window while the van merges onto the highway outside the airport. Palm trees buttress the road, and cotton candy clouds dot the pristine blue sky. We make a few turns, pass an astonishing number of deep purple flowering bushes that I can only gawk at, and then we pull onto a one-way street that immediately bleeds into white sand beaches and resorts.

My heart stutters as the asphalt turns into a neat cobblestone driveway. My fingers twitch, wanting my camera, but I'll have plenty of time for that. It's what I came here to do, after all. Take pictures of everything as my best friend's *official* wedding photographer. But for right now, I want to simply absorb these perfect early moments.

The driver pulls the van under the palm-frond-bedazzled overhang of a sandstone resort while Rhys and the rest of the group bicker about what time they should start drinking.

Sometimes, when I'm feeling itchy for a trip but don't have the money or time off (which is often, with how much debt I have), I scour the internet for reviews of faraway resorts and destinations. I've noticed that some resorts aren't truly *resorts* like you might expect. You could slap a cow barn onto a Motel 6, label it a wedding venue, and register the whole thing as a resort, technically, as a certain establishment in Florida attempted, according to Google Maps.

But this place?

This is a resort with a capital *Ritzy.* There is a swimming pool in the foyer *just because,* which also doubles as a glass-topped atrium. I stare at the clouds through the ceiling as Amelia leads me toward the front desk, which looks to be carved from volcanic rock. I can't tell if I'm in a fantasy, the future, or a Salvador Dalí painting come to life. Hopefully it turns out to be all three.

"I can't believe you're getting married in Aruba," I tell her as we wait for my room key. The guys disappeared as soon as we crossed into the foyer, and I'm reminding myself I don't care where Weston is.

"It sounds ridiculous," she admits.

"You're going to be Rhys's *old lady*," I remind her, craning my neck to take in the ever-changing wonders of the resort once we're checked in and she whooshes me down a wide hallway bedecked with Grecian columns. I'm on the lookout for melting clocks, Dalí-style.

"That means I'd have to join a motorcycle club," she corrects me.

"No, *he'd* have to be in the club. Unless you've been hiding your loyalty to the Viper Sculptors MC all these years."

"Viper Sculptors MC. Where we sculpt a bitch, *and* cut a bitch!" She snort laughs, which only makes me laugh harder in return.

Suddenly the hallway we're in opens up to a sprawling patio, leading out to so many things that yank at my attention I don't know what to absorb first. There's a pool shaped like a skinny kidney. A gazebo draped in vining orange flowers. Signs point to a spa area, promising even more treasures I can't quite fathom.

And then there's the boardwalk. Amelia leads me, her flip-flops a'floppin', along the wooden walkway that crisscrosses the resort. My wheeled luggage goes *clack-clack-clack* behind me. Everything is lush and fragrant and oh-so-beautiful.

We pass a fountain with teal water. A statue dripping with pearls. An honest-to-god tiki bar. And then the boardwalk gives way to white sand, the type of sand you only see in commercials, with palm trees towering above us and the most fascinating series of thatched-roof huts sprawling out along the border of the beach.

"This is where the bridal party is staying," Amelia says in a reverent whisper. I'm considered the bridal party, even though I'm technically the photographer and not a bridesmaid. She wanted me to be both, but I wanted to give her the gift of eternal photos more. Besides, how can the photographer include herself in all the bridal party pictures? Selfie sticks aren't exactly a beacon of professionalism in the photography world.

She gestures toward the huts, and I drift toward them at her side. Each one is a different tropical color. Bright orange. Vibrant yellow. Relaxed green, if that's even a color. My wheels get stuck in the sand, but I don't care. I abandon my luggage. Who needs changes of clothes anyway? Not me. Not when I'm here, in Aruba, about to behold my own personal *Crayola hut.*

Laughter and low voices register with me, but I'm too laser focused on the prize to notice who else is out here in this dreamy transition between resort and full-fledged ocean beach. The waves create a mesmerizing soundtrack as I pass Amelia in our sandy trek to the huts. I'm pretty sure she told me which one was mine, but I don't need to confirm. I can hear it calling to me in the salt-tinged breeze. *My fated teal vacation home.*

More laughter, and then the vinyl *thud* of a ball.

"Nova—" Amelia begins, just as I swing around to look at her.

A ball whizzes past my face. Something white and high velocity. My breath evaporates, and I freeze.

And that's when I find out where Rhys and the guys went. They headed straight for sand volleyball. Except now they're all shirtless, and I feel like I just stumbled onto the set of an Abercrombie & Fitch shoot.

And then I spot him. Again.

Weston Daly.

Except this time, he's shirtless and his body might as well be sent from God himself as a little care package he wanted to bestow upon humanity.

"Did you have to get in the way of our game?" He saunters toward me, the lines of his abs practically yanking me by the earlobes to make sure I notice them. Dark swim trunks cling to sculpted thighs in the same way a koala hugs a bamboo tree. His chestnut hair pairs too well with the dimple in his left cheek, and the outrageous glint of his ice-blue eyes.

My breath disappears. I can't stand this man. Yet I have never *not* wanted to jump his bones.

"Oh, Jesus," I spit, annoyance flooding me.

"First you barely acknowledge me, then you get in the way of my game?" Every step closer feels like a threat, and I can't explain why. He's too beautiful. He's too virile. He's too much of everything I've ever wanted.

And I hate him for it. Because he's never wanted *me*.

"Your *ball* got in the way of my *path*," I explain to him.

"Excuse me, Princess Nova." Weston bows exaggeratedly. "Continue on your way. I'd hate to have to cross your path while I get my volleyball."

"You don't need to be ridiculous." To Amelia, I say, "He's gotten more ridiculous since last time, hasn't he?" And he has. Our tense stand-off in the van should have been my warning. He was only gearing up to unleash the full brunt of his attack: shirtless, using all his muscles, looking like *this*.

Weston has an intolerable smirk on his face, hands propped on his hips. And it only makes his biceps pop even more. And when he speaks again, I can *feel* the scrape of his bass voice inside me.

"Even though you're the more ridiculous one, I'll overlook it this once," he says. "Because we're about to spend the next week together, *neighbor*."

There's something about the word *together* that excites me. Ignites me, even. But I squash it. Tamp it down, because I learned everything I need to know about this man the first day I met him. He might be hot enough to send my ovaries into shock, but luckily I can see right through his sexy, sandy smirk.

Weston Daly isn't just out of my league—he's in a league I don't want any part of.

One populated by beautiful drifters and callous playboys.

And I learned long ago just how far away I need to keep men like him.

KEEP READING 'MAKE ME CHOOSE' (http://books2read.co m/make-me-choose)

AUTHOR'S NOTE

The choppy waters of Lake Erie in the summertime are a special sort of haven, shrieking sea gulls and all. This series is set in a fictionalized mixture of my hometown and a neighboring town in northern Ohio. Writing this series has become a love song to my homeland.

Even though I grew up mostly critical of my little slice of the world (like most moody, dissatisfied teens—HA!), I now recognize it for what it is: a gorgeous spot in the Midwestern landscape, one that is capable of producing all the love and emotion and depth that a romance author could hope for.

I sincerely hope you enjoyed this visit to Bayshore...and I hope you'll continue this journey with the brothers of the Daly family!

LET'S STAY CONNECTED!

Stay connected with me via my newsletter (http://bit.ly/EL-news letter), where I share teasers, sales, and other exciting news. (Plus, if you haven't heard, I have an MMA romance series available, and **you'll get the prequel novella FOR FREE** when you sign up to my newsletter).

Or join my reader group, EMBER'S BLOSSOMS, to hang out up-close and personal! Early looks at new covers, exclusive access to ARC sign-ups, and more.

FACEBOOK
INSTAGRAM
GOODREADS
BOOKBUB
http://www.emberleighromance.com/

And before you go...
Please consider leaving an honest review about this book! Even just
a few words or a line mean so much to us authors.

ALSO BY EMBER LEIGH

THE BAD BOYS OF WALL STREET
The Price of Revenge
The Price of Passion
The Price of Infamy
The Price of Forever

WINTER HARBOR
(co-written with Whitley Cox)
The Bastard Heir
The Asshole Heir
The Rebel Heir
The Matchmaking Heirs

THE BAYSHORE SERIES
Make Me Lose
Make Me Fall
Make Me Yours
Make Me Choose
Make Me Hot

Make Me Smile

THE BREAKING SERIES
Breaking the Rules
Changing the Game
Breaking the Sinner
Breaking the Habit
Breaking the Fall